WAITING FOR MORNING

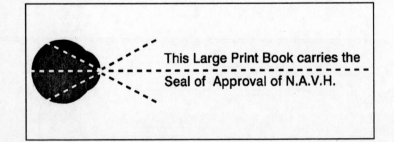

This Large Print Book carries the
Seal of Approval of N.A.V.H.

WAITING FOR MORNING

MARGARET BROWNLEY

THORNDIKE PRESS
A part of Gale, Cengage Learning

GALE
CENGAGE Learning·

Detroit • New York • San Francisco • New Haven, Conn • Waterville, Maine • London

GALE
CENGAGE Learning

LIBRARY OF CONGRESS CATALOGING-IN-PUBLICATION DATA

Brownley, Margaret.
    Waiting for morning : / by Margaret Brownley.
        pages ; cm. — (Thorndike Press large print Christian historical fiction) (A
    brides of Last Chance Ranch novel)
    ISBN-13: 978-1-4104-5612-0 (hardcover)
    ISBN-10: 1-4104-5612-9 (hardcover)
    1. Large type books. I. Title.
PS3602.R745W35 2013b
813'.6—dc23   2012048727

Published in 2013 by arrangement with Thomas Nelson, Inc.

Printed in Mexico
1 2 3 4 5 6 7 17 16 15 14 13

To my husband, partner, and best friend, George, for your love, patience, and willingness to eat out. God gave me the world when He gave me you!

HEIRESS WANTED

Looking for hard-working, professional woman of good character and pleasant disposition willing to learn the ranching business in Arizona Territory. Must be single and prepared to remain so now and forevermore.

CHAPTER 1

Dobson Creek, Colorado
April 1896

Something was wrong. Molly Hatfield felt it in her bones. She cast an anxious glance around Big Jim's Saloon. A couple of regulars were already passed out; others sat staring into amber drinks. It was one o'clock in the afternoon, a time when most men were at the mines.

On this cold April day, icy wind blew off the snow-covered peaks and the batwing doors squeaked in protest. Sawdust raced across the tobacco-stained floor, clinging to wooden chair legs and the soles of dusty boots.

Shaking away her uneasiness, Molly turned back to the burly owner standing behind the bar. If he detected anything out of the ordinary, he kept it to himself. He didn't even seem to notice the lace tucked in her bodice for modesty. He insisted his "girls" dress in costume at all times, including face paint, even when not working.

A stogie clamped between his yellow teeth, he squinted down his bulbous nose and counted out each pitiful coin as if doing her a favor.

Her lips puckered with irritation. What pleasure could he get from making her beg for her weekly wage? Or did he simply enjoy the power he held over his dance hall girls? The truth was Molly needed him more than he needed her.

"Please hurry." Why the sudden need for haste she didn't know, but she was anxious to get back to her fourteen-year-old wheelchair-bound brother. Not wanting to bring one so young to the saloon, she'd left him waiting in the lobby of the King Hotel, out of the cold. She'd done it before and he'd always been safe there. Still . . .

Big Jim's bushy black eyebrows met in an upside-down V, but any effort to pick up speed was negligible.

From outside came the dreaded sound of pistol shots — six loud blasts in rapid succession, snapping through the air like an angry whip.

Molly sucked in her breath and Jim's head jerked back, hands frozen over the till. Six gunshots meant fire and fire meant trouble.

Thinking fast, she scooped the money from the bar without waiting for the full count and darted out of the saloon.

People screamed and raced by, practically knocking her over. While pocketing her precious coins she dropped one, but to dive for it would be sheer folly. She would be trampled to death.

"Fire, fire!" someone shouted as if the gunshots hadn't already sounded the alarm.

"Where's the fire?" she cried. *Please, God, don't let it be the hotel. Not the hotel.*

"The King!" someone yelled.

Dear God!

Heart pounding, Molly swam against the stream of people. Swallowing the metallic taste filling her mouth, she lashed out, "Let me through. Let me through!"

She plowed headlong into the oncoming crowd with wind-milling arms. She'd failed to save her brother once but — *please, God* — not this time. *Don't let me fail him this time.*

Horses whinnied and pulled at traces. Dogs barked. A steer barreled down the street followed by several frenzied goats. A man shoved bills into the hands of a wagon owner and signaled for several children to pile inside.

Billows of dark smoke loomed over the

red light district, turning gray skies almost black. Pushed by biting, raw winds, the fire quickly leaped jackrabbit-style along Benson Avenue with a fierce roar, gobbling up the wood-framed buildings that made up the heart of town. The clanging of bells and pounding of horses' hooves signaled the arrival of the shiny new fire engine, the mayor's pride and joy. Several men dragged an old pumper up the street, its heavy iron wheels skidding on the icy road.

Mine whistles shrieked in the distance and already miners poured into the street with buckets and shovels.

"Let me through," Molly cried. Smoke burned her eyes. Her vision blurred. "My brother is at the hotel. Will somebody please help?"

"Good luck, lady," a man yelled out.

A drunk stood in the doorway of the drugstore laughing his fool head off.

The closer she got to the hotel, the thicker the smoke. Molly pulled a handkerchief from her sleeve and covered her mouth. A man dressed in a canvas coat waved her back with a stick of dynamite.

"Ya better run, lassie."

Already, the dynamiters were getting ready to blow up houses and businesses around the hotel in an attempt to stop the fire.

Her way blocked by vehicles, Molly nearly panicked until the pumper truck moved just enough to let her squeeze by. Crunching her skirt in sweaty palms, she darted past the dynamiter. A wagon shot out of an alley in front of her and she leaped aside. It missed her by an inch, splashing her blue taffeta skirt with mud.

Farther down the road a large pox-scarred man stopped her. "If you don't plan on meetin' your Maker today, you better get a move on, ma'am."

Mr. Wright, the owner of the hardware store, fired a shotgun into the air. "You're not blowing up my place," he yelled, seemingly oblivious to the flames already devouring the roof of his establishment.

While the two men argued, Molly dodged around them. Fire equipment blocked the street in front of the hotel. Flames shot from second-floor windows and long, fiery tongues licked the sky.

Icy fingers of fear gripped her but she pressed on, dodging falling timbers and bright sparks. A fireman with a blackened face squirted a thin stream of water onto the burning building. A stream of spit would have been more useful.

A dynamite blast from across the street sent a faro table crashing to the ground mere inches away, splintering into pieces.

She grabbed the fireman's arm with trembling hands. "My brother! Have you seen him?" She shouted to be heard above the explosions, screams, and roar of angry flames. "He's in a wheelchair."

"Sorry, ma'am. Ain't seen no wheelchair."

"Please, he may still be in there," she cried.

The fireman shook his head. "I've got me a wife and seven kids. I ain't goin' in there. The roof's about to cave in."

She spun around and stopped Mr. and Mrs. Merrick, who were pulling a wooden trunk. The man was one of Big Jim's regulars, his wife a staunch church member. "Help me — my brother is in that building."

The woman shoved Molly away from her husband, a spiteful look on her face. "Get out of the way, you harlot."

Molly stumbled back to catch her footing. Staring at the flames in horror, she screamed, "No, no, no!" Something welled up inside, something bigger, stronger, and more urgent than fear. *He can't die. He mustn't die.* She wouldn't let him die.

Shooting past the startled fireman, she ran so fast she hardly knew what she was doing.

"Hey, you can't go in there!" he shouted.

14

She dashed beneath the overhang and darted through the door of the hotel. The ceiling and walls were ablaze, the smoke so thick it blinded her. Dropping on hands and knees, she held her head close to the floor. Throat closed in protest, she gasped for air, eyes burning.

"Donnnnnnnnnnny!"

The roar of the fire and crackling wood drowned out her voice and she yelled again and again. Where had she left him? *Think.* The fireplace.

She reached the stairs. She'd gone too far. Panicked, she spun around on all fours.

Where was it? Where was the fireplace? She scrambled around the floor spider-like until spotting the wheels of her brother's chair. "Donny!"

A massive wooden beam plunged from the ceiling, missing the wheelchair by inches. Sparks flew onto her skirt. She brushed them off and scooted forward, mindless of the hot embers beneath her palms. Above the roar of flames came the explosive sound of dynamite.

"I'm here!" she gasped.

Her brother was slumped over, head on his chest. Scrambling to her feet, she grabbed the push handle and steered the wheelchair blindly through the smoke-filled inferno. It was by sheer determination that she found the door. She exited the hotel, coughing. They barely made it out in time before a thunderous roar announced the collapse of the second floor.

She barreled forward. The wheels wobbled, the chair shook. It was like pushing a mule uphill, but she didn't dare pause until they were a safe distance from the burning buildings. Forced to catch her breath, she sank to her knees in front of her brother and grabbed his hands.

"Donny," she rasped. She stroked his ash-covered face, her blistered hands leaving a trail of blood.

He looked at her with watery eyes. "I . . . I was so scared."

"You're safe now," she managed, her voice ragged.

"I didn't think you'd come —" He coughed so hard she feared he would hack up his insides. "I thought —"

She grabbed the canteen from his chair and forced water down his throat. "I'm here now. It would take a whole lot more than a fire to keep me away." A blast of dynamite made her jump to her feet.

"You're gonna have to move, ma'am," a fireman shouted.

"We're going, we're going." She pushed

the chair a few inches when the front wheel sank into the mud. Grunting, she yanked at the chair, muscles straining, but it wouldn't budge.

Wiping sweat from her forehead with the back of her hand, she picked up a smoking timber, stuck the heated end in the mud, and shoved it under the front wheel. She gave it a mighty shove and the wheel broke free.

Dodging wagons, fire equipment, frantic horses, people, and dogs, she kept going until at last they reached their canvas home, one of dozens that dotted the area outside of town where most of the miners lived. She filled a glass from the bucket of well water and handed it to her brother, then poured a glass for herself.

A cracked marble-top washstand, two cots, and a table and chairs were pushed to the side to make a space for walking. A cookstove filled a corner. Their prized possession was the spinet piano carted around Cape Horn by their mother all the way from Ireland. A tightly strung rope served a dual purpose, providing a place to hang clothes and a small measure of privacy.

The tent was patched and the canvas badly stained, but unlike the expensive homes on Strathern Avenue, their humble dwelling remained intact. At least for now. But if the wind changed . . .

No, no, mustn't think about what might happen or could happen. Donny was safe. That's all that mattered, though she feared for his lungs.

Dynamite blasts in the distance kept her on edge but she tried not to show it.

Donny wiped his mouth with the back of his hand. "They're g-g-getting closer."

"It just sounds that way," she said, hoping he didn't notice her shaking hands. No sense them both worrying. "Let's get you cleaned up."

It was just the two of them. Their papa had died three years earlier from miner's consumption, but never before had she felt as alone as she did at that moment. Even God seemed a distance away, though she prayed.

Trembling, she stoked up the fire in the oven with more vigor than it required and put water on to boil. Donny's chest rose and fell with each wheezing breath and she hoped the steam would help him.

She reached for his medicine. Careful to pour only three drops on a handkerchief, she held it to his nose. Within seconds his breathing improved. She covered him with a blanket and wrapped her blistered hands in a wet cloth.

If Donny so much as suspected how very close she was to panicking, it would frighten him even more and make his asthma worse. For him, she had to be brave.

She shivered. It was cold — so cold — and the flapping of the canvas walls indicated a worrisome wind change.

The thunderous sound of hooves followed by shouts made her mouth go dry. She ripped open the canvas flap and froze; a wall of orange flames was heading straight for the tent they called home.

CHAPTER 2

Arizona Territory — three weeks later

Never could Molly imagine a more sorrowful excuse for a horse. No amount of whip cracking made the swayback dapple go one whit faster. Patience spent, she swiped a wayward strand of hair from her face.

"He walks like he's wearing hobbles," she muttered.

Her brother sat on the wagon seat next to her in stony-faced silence. No surprises there. Donny had hardly spoken a word since they'd left Colorado. Punishing her, no doubt, for dragging him to this godforsaken desert. Well, she had news for him; she didn't want to be here either.

Certainly she didn't want to be on this lonely dirt road fighting with a belly-dragging horse in eighty-degree heat. But with Dobson Creek in ashes, it wasn't like she had a lot of choices.

Her brother depended on her to be strong

and she hadn't let him down. She had done such a good job of convincing Donny that things would work out, he didn't know how scared she had been. How scared she still was.

She wasn't about to let a dumb-fool horse get the best of her now. "Gid-up!"

The weathered old buckboard lumbered along, creaking and groaning as if each turn of the wheel would be its last. At that rate it would take a month of Sundays before they reached the Last Chance Ranch — if there was such a thing. There better be because it certainly was *her* last chance.

She was tired and hot and hungry and probably lost. Definitely lost. "Do you see anything?" she asked with considerably less hope than when she'd last asked the question. "A ranch or sign?" Anything but cacti, sand, endless blue skies, and the tail end of a stubborn mule-horse. Nothing seemed to move, not even the occasional lizard sunbathing on a rock.

"Nope."

She shot a glance at her brother's rigid profile showing beneath the stiff brim of his flat cap. They shared similar raven hair, upturned noses, and emerald-green eyes — all inherited from their Dublin-born mama. Donny's stubborn expression was entirely

21

his own.

"I hope your disposition improves before we reach the ranch. No one's going to hire me if you're rude or unpleasant."

God knew she needed the work, if you could call what Miss Walker offered a job. Heiress to a cattle ranch? She still couldn't get over the absurdity of it or the desperation that brought her here.

Even if the strange offer was legitimate, what chance did she have of proving to the owner she was capable of learning the cattle business? Especially with a wheelchair-bound brother in tow, a boy with weak lungs to boot. Why, oh why, hadn't she been more forthright in her telegram and told the ranch owner that she had an invalid brother? It wasn't her intention to be secretive, but experience had taught her to tread with care.

Her anxiety increased with every cactus they passed. The desert might be good for bad lungs, but it didn't look good for anything else.

The livery stable owner had said to follow the road. So where was the ranch? Where, for that matter, was anything?

"Whoa." The horse went from barely moving to completely stopped. She reached for her canteen and offered it to her brother.

"Here. Be careful. That's all the water we have left."

He took the canteen without so much as a glance her way. After a quick swallow, he handed it back, wiping his lips with his shirtsleeve.

She took a sip before recapping the top, a drop of precious water falling upon her purple frock — one of the few she'd been able to save before escaping the fire. The heat and dust had taken their toll, but there was little she could do about it. She straightened her leg o'mutton sleeves and checked the hatpin holding her fancy plumed hat that matched her dress. She debated the wisdom of applying more complexion powder to her heated face and decided against it, though she couldn't resist dabbing more rouge onto her parched lips.

The smell of smoke seemed to cling to her body and no amount of scrubbing had dissipated the acrid stench. She sprayed toilet water behind her ear — a temporary solution at best. The stench of burning wood and even burning flesh would soon come back to haunt her.

A strange rumbling in the distance broke the silence. She dropped her mirror into her drawstring purse and glanced around. "What is that odd noise?"

Her brother shifted the best he could in his seat and looked over his shoulder. "Sounds like a mining trolley."

"There are no mines out here." In the mountains maybe, but certainly not in this flat, barren land.

The noise grew louder, followed by a loud blast. Startled, Molly ducked. "Quick. Put your head down. Someone's shooting at us!"

She reached behind the seat for the double barrel shotgun and haversack and slid down to the floorboards. Her brother, unable to move his legs, slid his torso sideways until his head was hidden by the back of the seat.

"They want to rob us," he said, his eyes wide. "Arizona is full of highwaymen. Horrible men who rob you and leave you in the desert to die. I read about them."

"Now's a fine time to tell me." Dropping to her knees, she slid two cartridges into the weapon. "Stay down — and pray!"

Her father's shotgun was the only thing of his she'd been able to save from the fire. Fortunately, he'd taught her how to use it. The air exploded with more gunfire and she hunkered even lower. Pushing the barrel of her weapon along the top of the seat, she took aim, the long plume of her hat bobbing up and down.

Something roared straight at them. Since

it was stirring up so much dust, she couldn't make out what it might be. Why hadn't someone in town warned her of road thieves?

Another shot rang out, this one loud enough to pass as cannon fire. Something shiny emerged from the cloud of dust. The sun bounced off the barrels of two weapons, practically blinding her. What kind of an outlaw was this? Panicking, she pulled the trigger.

Her warning shot worked; the strange rumbling noise stopped. She fired again to let the road agents know she meant business and quickly reloaded. A long, uneasy silence followed. The sulfurous odor of gunpowder slowly faded away, along with the blue haze.

Heart thumping, she held her breath. Had . . . had she shot someone?

"Do you see them?" Donny whispered at last. "Do you see the bandits?"

"N-No," she stammered, her voice barely audible. "I can't see anything."

"Hello there," a man called and she jumped.

Gulping, Molly straightened to peer around the seat at the man waving a white handkerchief. Was it a trick?

Slowly she stood, knees shaking. The seri-

25

ous end of her weapon pointed at the stranger's chest, she kept her finger on the trigger. "Don't move."

The man jammed his handkerchief in his pocket and glared at her. "What in blazes do you think you're doing? You could have killed me." His Texas drawl did nothing to hide his anger.

Ignoring her warning, he bent next to a high-wheeled carriage and ran his hand along the front like someone might check for a wound. What appeared to be "weapons" at first were in reality two shiny carriage lanterns. There was no sign of a horse or mule and she couldn't imagine how he got there — or what had caused that ungodly blast and rumbling sound.

He turned to face her, hands on his hips. "Now look what you've done." He indicated the front of his rig where she assumed her bullet hit. "Why did you shoot at me?"

"Why did *you* shoot at us?" she stormed.

He looked momentarily baffled. "I wasn't shooting at you." He pulled off his hat and ran the back of his arm over his forehead. A tall man, six feet or more, he wore dark pants and a white shirt, the sleeves rolled to his elbows. "My motor backfired."

Motor? She cast a puzzled glance at the

dusty black phaeton parked half off the road.

Next to her, Donny sat upright. "He's driving a horseless carriage," he whispered, his eyes rounded. "I read about those in my science magazine."

Horseless . . . ? She'd never thought such a thing possible. "What . . . what do you want?" she called.

"I want you to put your weapon down," he replied. He sauntered to the side of her buckboard, holding his arms out as if to prove he had no intention of harming her. "I'm a doctor and I'm heading to the LC Ranch. One of the cowhands has taken ill."

LC. *Last Chance.* "I'm heading there too," she said. He certainly didn't look like any doctor she'd ever met. For one thing he couldn't be a day over thirty. Up close he was even more handsome than he looked from a distance, but that didn't give him any right to go around scaring people.

The man pushed his hat back. A swath of dark brown hair with reddish highlights fell across his forehead. He gave her a once-over — a very thorough once-over with the bluest eyes imaginable, and also the boldest.

As a dance hall girl she had grown accustomed to men's leering gazes. It was part

27

of the job and, for the most part, she'd learned to disregard them. Indeed, she'd developed a hard shell for protection.

It was hard to ignore the doctor, though. Not only was he handsome, his sharp assessing gaze seemed to go beyond the surface. She feared her carefully constructed façade was in terrible danger of melting away like face paint in the sun.

"Doctor Caleb Fairbanks at your service." He gave a slight bow. He'd dropped his angry tone, but it was his crooked grin that made her lower her weapon. "I guess we had ourselves what you might call a misunderstanding."

"I'm Molly Hatfield and this is my brother, Donny." She moistened her lips — a mistake as it only drew his gaze to her mouth. She lifted her chin, hoping he wouldn't notice her blush. "You nearly scared the life out of us."

"I have to say, ma'am, the feeling was mutual." He sounded sincere and not at all threatening.

"I — I apologize for what I did to your . . ." Her gaze drifted to his vehicle. Horseless? She swung her gaze back to the man's square face. "But if you go around making loud popping sounds, you can expect to be shot at."

"I'll keep that in mind. Apology accepted, but I'm afraid you'll find Bertha less forgiving."

She glanced around but didn't see anyone else. "Bertha?"

"My motor buggy."

She stared at the vehicle, not sure what to make of it *or* its tall owner. "You mentioned the LC Ranch. How far is it?" she asked.

He tossed a nod westward. "Just a couple miles up the road. Keep going. You'll see a sign." He glanced at her brother before leveling his gaze back to her with a tip of his hat. "I'd best get a move on." He gave her a broad wink before walking away.

Her mouth dropped open. Of all the nerve! Even the miners of Dobson Creek with all their rough talk and leering looks were never so outrageous as to wink.

Her brother stared at her burning face with reproach. As if the doctor's blatant gesture was her fault.

"What?" she snapped.

"Nothing."

Sighing, she stored the rifle and grabbed the reins.

The doctor wound his buggy like a mechanical toy, mounted the seat, and drove by them, the motor huffing and puffing. A previously unnoticed dog sat on the seat next to the driver, barking. The horn made a loud *Ah-ooh-ga* sound and the brazen doctor lifted his hat as he passed.

The strange vehicle took off with astonishing speed, spitting and sputtering like an arthritic man about to take his last breath, and vanished down the road in a cloud of dust.

CHAPTER 3

Dr. Caleb Fairbanks was still smiling when he reached the LC Ranch. Never could he have imagined meeting up with the likes of Miss Hatfield practically in the middle of nowhere. She fairly dazzled in that bright purple frock and ridiculous feathered hat, but it was her sparkling green eyes that left the biggest impression. Those and her pretty round face and nicely shaped mouth.

He only wished she hadn't shot two holes in his prized automobile. Perhaps the smithy in town could fix it. Anyone driving these machines spent a great deal of time on repairs, and the sooner he got on friendly terms with the owner of the blacksmith shop, the better.

Miss Hatfield was right. If he didn't get the problem fixed, an unfriendly bullet might very well hit him next time instead of Bertha.

Just as he pulled up in front of the adobe

ranch house, his motor backfired again. He switched off the engine. The auto shuddered and gave a final gasp before altogether dying.

"I guess this is it," he said. His little dog, Magic, tilted his head, one pendent ear cocked, and gazed at him with dark brown eyes, his fluffy tail curled over his back.

The two-story adobe house with its red tile roof, courtyard, and wraparound verandah was the largest building Caleb had seen since arriving in Cactus Patch. The outbuildings, barn, corrals, and twenty-foot windmill were as well maintained as the house.

A horseman galloped up to Caleb's vehicle and dismounted. "Who are you and what is this . . . this . . . what gives you the right to bring this rattletrap on my property?"

Much to Caleb's surprise, it wasn't a man but a woman dressed in a split riding skirt, masculine shirt, Stetson, and boots. He'd been warned about Miss Walker, owner of the ranch, but nothing had prepared him for her militant demeanor.

"It's a horseless carriage, ma'am, and I'm Dr. Fairbanks." He pointed at his dog. "Stay."

The woman quickly wrapped the reins onto the hitching post and turned. She regarded him from a well-worn face, hands planted firmly on her hips. Wisps of gray hair showed beneath her hat. "What happened to Doc Masterson?"

"He's retired, ma'am. I'm taking his place."

Her eyebrows shot up. "Retired? That's ridiculous. The man can't be more than sixty years old. What's he going to do with himself?" The way she carried on, one might think the man was but a babe-in-arms.

"He never told me. Just said he wanted to go back home to Kansas."

Despite her advanced age, which he guessed to be somewhere in the midsixties, she stood perfectly tall and straight, easily reaching his shoulders in height. She displayed none of the round shoulders or stiff joints he'd observed in many women her age.

"You don't look old enough to be a doctor," she said, her voice sharp as a snapping whip.

It was a comment he'd heard countless times before. A doctor's ability was often judged on the basis of a gray or balding head. So far neither his medical degree nor experience had resulted in a single strand of silver, and his chestnut hair remained as full as ever.

"I'll be thirty-one come November," he said.

Miss Walker glared at him like a schoolmarm scolding a pupil. "Have you ever had arthritis or gout? Or even a pain in your sacroiliac?"

"No, ma'am, can't say that I have."

Her lip curled. "Then how do you expect to treat such conditions?"

"The same way a person like yourself knows how to deliver a calf without giving birth to one," he drawled. He meant no disrespect but he didn't know how else to answer her.

"I see." She looked him up and down. Was that reluctant approval in her gaze or wishful thinking on his part? "Do yourself a favor, young man. Get a horse."

Caleb slapped Bertha's shiny side. "This is like having two horses, ma'am."

"It's noisy and smelly and I won't have such a thing on my property." She whirled around and walked away. "What are you waiting for? We're wasting time. Show me what you can do."

Caleb grabbed his leather bag from the seat of his vehicle, gave his dog another order to stay, and ran to catch up with the ranch owner. Not only did she dress and talk like a man, she walked as quickly as one too.

She led him into the barn. The smell of fresh hay offered a pleasant contrast to Bertha's odor of oil and burning rubber.

She stopped in front of a stall that held a red roan. "This is Baxter."

Caleb was momentarily speechless. Obviously the woman meant it when she said to get a horse.

"I'm afraid purchasing a horse at this time is out of the question, but —"

"Purchasing!" She narrowed her eyes. "This is *my* horse and there's something wrong with him. I summoned Dr. Masterson to tell me what it is."

Caleb rubbed his chin. It seemed like a day for misunderstandings. "I . . . I fear there's been a mistake. I'm a *medical* doctor. I treat humans."

"If you are indeed what you say you are, then you treat infections and disease. This animal is suffering from one, if not both."

Caleb could see that. The horse looked at them with dull eyes, nostrils flared. He also appeared to be trembling.

"He's not eating and he's been lying down," she added.

Just then one of the cowhands joined them. Miss Walker introduced Caleb in a no-nonsense voice. "Fairchild, meet

Ruckus."

"That's Fairbanks," Caleb said, shaking the man's hand. "*Doctor* Fairbanks."

"This man claims to be a doctor, though he's only thirty," Miss Walker added.

"The same age as the Lord was when he started ministering," Caleb said.

Ruckus grinned. Obviously, he was used to the cantankerous ranch owner. Caleb guessed from the man's strong grip that he was somewhere in his midforties, though his craggy face and leathery skin made him look older. He had a horseshoe mustache and a crooked nose, most likely the result of someone's misplaced fist.

"What happened to Doc Masterson?" Ruckus asked.

"Retired," Miss Walker said. "Can you imagine anything more ridiculous?"

Ruckus shrugged. "I reckon more people would retire if they lived long enough, but out here if a bullet don't get you the weather likely will."

Caleb hoped the ranch hand talked in jest, though nothing in his demeanor suggested it.

Miss Walker ran her hand along her horse's neck. "Well? Don't just stand there. Do something."

Caleb set his bag on the ground away

36

from the horse and opened it. Dr. Masterson had warned him about the old lady and told him to get on her good side. He wondered if such a thing existed. Out of habit he reached for his stethoscope, then thought better of it.

"Let's have a look."

He ran his hands along the roan's sweaty flanks. A horse's pulse is normally slower than a human's, but Baxter's pulse was elevated.

Ruckus hooked his thumbs onto his gun belt. "You won't find anything. No founder, no nothin'."

That's what Caleb was afraid of. Carpeted with a thick layer of fresh straw, the stall was spotless with plenty of hay and water. This was a well-cared-for horse and his caretakers weren't likely to let a common disorder slip by without notice. Whatever ailed the gelding was probably something uncommon.

He'd doctored many animals in his youth and once considered going into veterinary medicine. He soon learned, however, that working with animals took a great deal of guesswork. He much preferred working with patients able to voice complaints and describe symptoms.

He flexed each leg and examined each

hoof, watching Baxter's reaction. Nothing.

He checked the horse from one end to the other. None of the animals he worked with in the past had anything seriously wrong with them, and he hoped the same was true for Baxter. It wouldn't look good if the first patient he treated upon arriving in Cactus Patch should die.

Miss Walker watched him with observant gray eyes, measuring his every move and no doubt comparing him to Dr. Masterson.

One by one Caleb dismissed the possible diseases that came to mind. The best he could do was make an educated guess based on a slight, almost imperceptible swelling of the lymph nodes around the neck and a watery discharge from the nose.

"I think your horse has the early stages of strangles," he said.

"That's not possible," Miss Walker exclaimed. "None of the other horses are infected."

"What about the new horses?" Caleb asked. He'd passed a corral of wild mustangs.

"We keep the new horses isolated from our regular ones," Ruckus said.

"Then I don't know what to tell you." Caleb snapped the lid of his black case shut and straightened. "We'll know for sure in a couple of days." If he was right, abscesses would probably form and rupture, after which the horse would feel immeasurably better.

"Meanwhile, I suggest you keep him away from the others. Keep buckets and any equipment isolated. The bacteria can be carried from one stall to another on boots or clothing. I suggest you assign one person as his caretaker until we know for sure what we're dealing with."

"If indeed it is strangles, how serious is it?" Miss Walker asked, her voice edged with skepticism.

"With care, most horses recover. As long as he doesn't develop a secondary infection like pneumonia, he should be fine. Meanwhile, watch your other horses for early signs of infection. The sooner you isolate them, the better your chances of keeping the disease from spreading."

Ruckus pushed his hat to the back of his head. "Well, I'll be. Never considered strangles."

Caleb picked up his black case. "It's not the first thing that comes to mind."

Miss Walker ran her hand along her horse's side. "We're still not sure that's the correct diagnosis."

"We'll know soon enough. I'll stop by in a

day or two and check on him," Caleb said.

"That's good of you," Miss Walker said. It was the first thawing Caleb had heard in the woman's voice, but her suspicious regard of him was still evident in her gray eyes.

Caleb recalled the shotgun-bearing woman he'd met en route. He was used to dealing with strong and opinionated women like his sister, Lucy, back in Texas, but these Arizona ladies were a whole different breed.

"We're mighty obliged to you, Doctor," Ruckus said.

"Glad to be of service. Is there somewhere I can wash my hands?"

"There's a barrel outside," Ruckus said. He closed the stall door and led Caleb to a barrel of water outside.

Caleb scrubbed his hands, bid the man good-bye, and strolled to his car. He glanced around but didn't see any sign of Miss Hatfield's buckboard. That meant she was still on the way to the ranch and he was bound to pass her on the way back to town. He smiled at the thought.

He just hoped the fetching woman in purple wouldn't come at him with that confounded shotgun again.

He gave the L-shaped crank on the front bumper a good turn. Bertha coughed and wheezed and snorted like an angry bull before finally spluttering to life. Caleb then mounted the high leather seat behind the steering column. Magic greeted him with wagging tail and Caleb scratched him behind an ear before pulling away from the ranch house.

The blare of his brass bulb horn sent chickens scattering to the sides of the road. A cattle dog barked and ran the length of the fence that contained him. Magic barked back.

"It's all right, boy."

To the right a mustang circled a corral, mane flying and tail held high.

Caleb steered the chugging car around a rough patch in the road. So that was Miss Walker. Her message had urged the doctor to drop everything and hurry to the ranch. No wonder Doc Masterson was so eager for Caleb to respond. He should have suspected something was amiss. If she was an example of the type of patient to expect in Cactus Patch, who could blame the old doctor for retiring?

Still, Caleb liked the area, liked the mountains and canyons and ever-changing colors of the desert. He even liked the weather. It was every bit as hot as Texas but without the humidity, though he heard that would change during the monsoon rains.

A herd of broad-beamed Herefords blocked the road ahead and Caleb pulled out the clutch and applied the brake, stopping in plenty of time. The cattle mooed as they ambled along, guided by mounted cowboys. A steer gave the auto an anxious glance and one calf stopped to stare but his mother pushed him along.

It took several moments before the last straggler cleared the road to join the large milling herd that seemed to stretch for miles. Resisting the urge to honk his horn, Caleb thanked the men with a wave of his hand.

Caleb drove slowly so as not to startle the cattle. Bertha gurgled, then backfired, not once but twice.

Magic gave a playful bark and Caleb glanced over his shoulder. The cattle that moments ago appeared so placid now stomped around in confusion, heads thrown back, mouths open, their loud bellows heard even over the rumbling motor.

Drat! Heart thumping, Caleb slammed his foot against the gas pedal and took off ahead of the stampeding cattle.

CHAPTER 4

Molly stopped the wagon and set the brake, more out of habit than need. The horse didn't go fast enough to need a brake. She pulled a handkerchief out of her sleeve and mopped her face before handing the near-empty canteen to Donny.

The sign clearly read Last Chance, but where was the ranch? The desolate, inhospitable terrain hadn't changed one iota since she'd left the town.

She moistened her parched lips. Even the plume on her stylish hat drooped and she batted it away from her face. She wished she'd been able to save a more practical hat from the fire, but her panicky state at the time had not allowed for discernment. It seemed more important to grab Donny's medicine and belongings. She'd only managed to save a couple of her own frocks, none appropriate for ranch work or, for that matter, even street wear.

She shaded her eyes against the glaring white sun and surveyed the road ahead. Who in their right mind would live in such a desolate area?

"How much farther?" Donny asked in a thin voice.

God only knows — but she didn't want to worry him. "I'm sure we're almost there."

She pulled a pocket watch out of her purse. It was a little after three o'clock. She wished she'd gotten an earlier start. The train had rolled into town that morning, but by the time she'd hired a driver to help her transport Donny and her few belongings from the station, had a bite to eat, and rented a rig, it was nearly two before she got started.

Something caught her attention.

"Oh, look. Straight ahead." She narrowed her eyes on the distant horizon. A dust cloud. "Do you suppose the doctor's coming back this way?" The thought wasn't altogether unpleasant. "Maybe he can tell us how much farther we have to go."

A low rumbling sound like thunder seemed to rise up from the very earth. The horse lifted his ears and stomped the ground. It was the most energy the animal had shown since leaving town. The mare hadn't seemed that anxious when the doctor's vehicle made those ghastly blasts or even when she'd fired her shotgun.

Donny craned his neck. "I don't think that's the doctor," he said with a worried frown.

She batted a drooping plume from her face and craned her neck. "What do you think it is?"

The dust rose like a wall, spreading out on both sides of the road as far as the eyes could see. The rumbling sound grew louder and the buckboard began to shake.

"Oh no!" Hands on her chest, she stared in horror. A long line of running cattle turned like a school of fish and headed straight for them.

"Get down!" she screamed, as if safety was simply a matter of ducking. She released the brake and grabbed the reins. "Gid-up!"

Donny scooted down the best he could, the last bit of color draining from his face. "Cattle can run twenty miles an hour. We can't outrun them."

"I know that!" The old mare couldn't even outrun a tortoise. She forced the horse into a U-turn until the back of the wagon faced the stampeding cattle. The wagon offered little protection, but it was the best she could do.

Shotgun and haversack in hand, she

climbed over the seat and hunkered behind the valise and wheelchair. No bullet could halt the thunderous hooves, but maybe she could make them veer off course. Loading and aiming her shotgun, she fired two shots.

"Look. There's the doctor!" Donny shouted.

She quickly reloaded. "I told you to stay down!"

Through the churning dust, she could barely make out the horseless carriage leading the stampede. The vehicle weaved from one side of the road to the other, the frenzied cattle practically on its tail.

Fairbanks drove straight at the buckboard. Molly froze and Donny cried out.

Just when she thought the doctor would plow into them, he stopped just a hair short, wheels screeching. He then spun his vehicle sideways across the road. Gears grinding, he drove the horseless carriage back and forth, shielding the buckboard and honking his horn. The vehicle rammed from one edge of the road to the other, backfiring. Smoke poured from its wheels.

Molly watched in horror, unable to move.

The doctor's tactic worked, for at the last possible moment the herd split in two. Half of the cloven-hoofed beasts ran to the right of them, the other half to the left. The heated hides and clashing horns stampeded past on either side, rocking the buckboard like a boat in choppy seas.

The churning, choking dust cut visibility to zero and the deafening roar of pounding hooves seemed to go on forever. The horse whinnied and tried to pull free of its traces, but the brake held and the wagon moved only a few inches forward.

Finally the last of the cattle ran by and the rumble of frantic hooves gradually faded in the distance with only a few stragglers and men on horseback bringing up the rear.

Molly lowered her weapon and let out a long, harrowing breath. "Th-They're gone," she said, wetting her dry lips. She stood her weapon on the butt end and made her way back to the driver's seat.

"Donny, are you all right?"

Donny lifted his head. Wheezing, he gasped for air and nodded.

"Everything okay?" a male voice called. The doctor stood next to the buckboard, his previously white shirt now gray, sweat streaking his dust-covered face. His eyes looked even bluer, peering at her with grave concern.

"I — I think so." She brushed off her dress and coughed. Nothing could be done for the dangling plume of her lopsided hat.

"Thank you."

Dr. Fairbanks slapped his own hat against his thigh, a futile effort in the dust-filled air. "Sorry about that," he said. "You aren't the only ones spooked by Bertha."

"*You* did that?" she choked out. "You caused the cattle to stampede?" Not waiting for him to answer she ranted, "You could have gotten us all killed!"

The doctor had the good grace to look remorseful. "The lady definitely needs work."

Her mouth dropped open before she realized he was referring to his horseless carriage.

He placed his hat on his head. "And now that you've shot more bullets into Bertha, so do the front and sides."

She folded her arms and glared at him. For the trouble he and his ridiculous vehicle caused, he deserved considerably more than a few bullet holes.

He shifted his gaze to Donny and frowned. "Is your brother all right?"

"Other than being scared half out of his wits, he's fine," she said, her voice cool. She had no intention of discussing her brother's condition with this annoying, incompetent man. If his unfortunate choice of a vehicle was any indication of his medical skill, she'd best keep Donny away from him. She'd dealt with enough snake-oil doctors back in Colorado to last a lifetime.

"You'd better give him a drink," he said.

Donny held his canteen upside down. "We're out of water."

Molly gave herself a mental kick for not preparing better. "I had no idea it would take so long to drive to the ranch."

The doctor's gaze sharpened. "I have extra." After fetching a canteen from the front seat of his vehicle, he handed it to Donny. "Drink this. It'll help."

Donny took several gulps before handing the canteen back. He still wheezed.

"How much farther?" she asked. If she didn't get to the Last Chance soon, she would scream.

"Just a mile up the road," Dr. Fairbanks replied. He tossed a nod toward Donny. "I have some medicine in my bag that might help his bellows."

Bellows! He made it sound like Donny was some sort of a machine. "Thank you for your concern, but what my brother needs is rest. If you would kindly move your . . . vehicle, we'll be on our way."

She didn't mean to sound ungrateful, but she had spent a good portion of her wages on doctors. None offered any hope of his ever walking, but all promised to cure asthma. One doctor had advised Donny to take up smoking as a way to build up the lungs. Another suggested Donny wear a muskrat pelt with the fur next to his chest. Oh yes, she had every reason not to trust a member of the medical profession.

"Very well," he said. This time he didn't wink. He simply turned and walked with long strides to his horseless carriage.

He took hold of the handle in front and cranked, jumping out of the way when the vehicle roared to life. He then climbed into the driver's seat next to his barking dog and backed away until the road was clear, allowing her room to turn the wagon around. The doctor honked his horn as she drove by, but she didn't bother to wave.

He had caused her quite enough problems, thank you very much, and she was happy to see the last of him. Right now her main concern was for Donny.

"Let's sing," she said. It was the last thing she wanted to do. Her mouth was dry, her throat parched, and she was bone-tired, but singing never failed to relax Donny and calm his breathing. "Hush, little baby, don't you cry . . ."

Donny made a face. "Ah, gee. That's for infants." He brightened. "Let's sing 'Old

Man Harrington.' "

"No, absolutely not."

"Ah, come on, Molly. That's your best song. You know everyone laughs when you sing it."

She tossed him a stern look. "It's not a proper song for a young man to sing and I never want to hear you mention it again."

"How about this one, then?" Donny could barely get the words out between his ragged breaths. "This one makes people laugh too. O-O-Old man Bill Whit-ey, f-f-fell in a beer keg. What so —"

"Donald Thomas Hatfield!"

Donny tried to laugh but instead he coughed. She nonetheless gave him her best "motherly" look, but she couldn't remain annoyed at him for long. He was right — it did make people laugh. The song was set to the same English drinking tune as the popular "Star Spangled Banner." Once, during a saloon fight, angry fists gave way to loud guffaws when she stood on a table and sang it. Even so, she didn't want her brother singing about drinking.

Donny could be irritating at times, but she loved him dearly. It was her fault he couldn't walk. Somehow, some way she had to make it up to him — if it took the rest of her life.

Spotting a windmill ahead, she snapped the reins, but the horse lumbered forward at the same slow speed. Never had she seen such an enormous windmill; its slow-turning blades spanned a good twenty feet. She pulled up alongside it, letting the horse drink from the trough while she dipped her empty canteen into the wooden tank out of the animal's reach. While Donny drank his fill, she spotted a red-roofed ranch house a short distance away.

"There it is," she said with false cheerfulness. Everything looked so . . . big. The sky, the size of the ranch, the house. She only wished she didn't have the feeling that her troubles had also grown in size.

CHAPTER 5

No sooner had Molly pulled up in front of the two-story adobe ranch house than a tall thin man with a skinny moustache walked up to her buckboard to greet her.

"Name's Stretch," he said, tipping his hat and revealing a mass of black curly hair. "Kin I help you?"

"I'm here to see Miss Walker," Molly replied, trying to look as dignified as a droopy plumed hat and dusty purple dance hall gown would allow.

"Miss Walker ain't here right now. We had ourselves some cattle trouble." His gaze followed the swinging plume of her hat. "You ain't one a those women lookin' to be the boss lady's heiress, are you?"

His skeptical look did nothing for her self-confidence. "I should wait and discuss my business with Miss Walker."

He shrugged. "Suit yourself."

"Would you mind helping me with my

brother's wheelchair?" The chair was awkward and heavy and she would never manage to lift it out of the back of the buckboard by herself. "Also, if you would be kind enough to help my brother out of the wagon, I'd be ever so grateful." She also needed help with her valise, but she didn't want to overwhelm the man with her demands.

Stretch glanced at Donny, then stuck his fingers in his mouth and whistled. He waved to the cowpoke sitting on a wooden fence. "Feedbag! Come here a minute."

The man called Feedbag hurried over. He had a black square beard that did indeed look like it belonged on the muzzle of a horse. The spurs on his boots made a strange noise when he walked and he wore bat-winged chaps.

"Grab that side," Stretch said, pointing to the wheelchair. Feedbag cast a curious look at Molly before walking to the back of the wagon. Together he and Stretch grabbed the wheelchair, heaved it over the side of the buckboard, and set it on the ground.

Just then a horseman galloped toward them at full speed. It wasn't until the rider dismounted that Molly realized it was a woman dressed in a divided brown skirt and man's plaid shirt. Her gray hair in a bun, she wore a wide-brimmed Stetson and red kerchief.

Stretch whispered, "That's Miss Walker."

Molly withered inside. The woman looked even more intimidating than she sounded in her telegram. Molly swallowed hard and forced herself to meet the woman's steady gaze without flinching. "I'm Molly Hatfield and —"

"I know who you are, but who is that?" She indicated Donny, still seated in the buckboard.

"My brother and —"

"I don't recall any mention of a brother in your telegram. Furthermore, you are three days late. Anyone without regard for time has no business on a ranch."

Stretch bobbed his head and the two men lifted the wheelchair back into the wagon with a thud.

Molly hadn't expected to be dismissed so abruptly and without so much as an interview. After all she'd been through these last few weeks, she wasn't about to go without a fight.

"Our train was late and that made us miss our connection. I explained all that in my latest telegram."

The two men reached for the wheelchair and heaved it over the side of the wagon and back onto the ground.

"If you sent a second telegram, it's probably in town waiting for one of my boys to pick it up. The telegram I *did* receive said nothing about your brother. Had it done so, I would have saved you the trouble of a trip."

Warmth crept up Molly's face. She regretted withholding information, but at the time she hadn't known what else to do. "I apologize, but I had to bring him with me. I'm the only family he has and I'm responsible for his care."

"And I'm responsible for two thousand head of cattle."

"Yes, and my brother and I had occasion to meet some of them on the way here. We were almost trampled to death."

Miss Walker cocked an eyebrow but offered no apology for her cattle's poor behavior. "That is precisely why I need someone reliable and trustworthy. If your appearance is any indication, you not only lack those necessary virtues, you also lack judgment and good sense."

Molly was used to being judged solely on appearances. The so-called Christian women in Dobson Creek wouldn't even talk to her or her brother. A woman's virtue was not only determined by behavior but also by the color of her dress. Since Molly wore bright colors *and* worked at a saloon, her reputation suffered on both accounts.

"I assure you I *am* reliable and trust-worthy. I've supported myself and my brother for the last four years and there aren't many women who can make such a claim." She was only seventeen when her father died, leaving her with no visible means of support. Her looks and voice were her only assets and she used both to good advantage. "That alone should prove I'm reliable. As for my clothes, there wasn't time to save but a few of our belongings. You probably heard about the terrible fire in Dobson Creek."

Miss Walker gave no indication of having heard the news. "I'm sorry that you traveled all this distance for nothing. If you hurry, you can reach town before dark and catch the morning train." She turned and stalked away and the wheelchair was promptly returned to the wagon.

Molly held her arms by her sides, fists tight. And go where? She and Donny had no family, no home, no money — nothing. Still, she'd rather live in a cave than deal with such a coldhearted woman.

She turned back to the wagon, her mind racing. Surely she could get a job at one of the saloons in town. Judging by the wailing sounds she heard while passing through Cactus Patch, they could use a singer like her. Not only did she have no intention of working for the ranch owner, she'd had her fill of cattle, thank you very much!

One look at her brother stopped her in her tracks. His face was gray and his lips blue and he didn't breathe as much as gasp for air.

A protective surge shot through her. It was no time to think of her wounded pride. She swung around and called after the ranch owner, "That's it? You're sending me away just like that?"

Miss Walker turned, her cold gray eyes leveled on Molly. It was obvious she was not used to being challenged.

"Have you the slightest idea what it takes to be a rancher? It takes tenacity and hard work. This land will demand everything you have to give and then some. It means sleepless nights and endless days. It means fighting droughts, flash floods, cattle rustlers, and unstable markets. It means doing the impossible on a regular basis. What have you ever done to make me think you can succeed against such odds?"

What had she done? What had she done! "I ran into a burning building to save my brother when no one else would," she replied.

"I commend you, but that hardly qualifies you to run a ranch."

Molly's heart squeezed and she thought fast. Her brother's welfare depended on her. "I was a dance hall girl in Dobson Creek," she said with a resolute nod.

A look of disbelief suffused Miss Walker's face. "A *dance hall* girl? You mean you sang and —"

"Danced," Molly said. That was all she did, which was why she got so little pay.

Miss Walker heaved herself to her full height. "And how does singing and . . . dancing prove that you have the tenacity for ranching?"

Molly forced herself to breathe. "I worked at the saloon for four years and" — she glanced at the two men listening, their expressions eager with interest — "and I still managed to keep my virtue." It was true, no matter what those old gossips said.

Miss Walker stared at her for a moment before laughing, her head thrown back like the lid of a coffeepot. Even Stretch and Feedbag joined in.

"That's a good one," Feedbag said, punctuating his guffaws by slapping his thigh.

Molly couldn't tell by Miss Walker's

amusement if she'd scored any points. The two men, however, must have thought things had turned in her favor, for they reached into the wagon for the wheelchair.

Miss Walker stopped laughing, but her dubious expression didn't give Molly much hope. "How old are you?" she asked, her voice abrupt.

"Twenty-one."

"You do know from my telegram that I would require you to sign a document forbidding marriage."

Stretch and Feedbag held the wheelchair between them, waiting for Molly's reply.

"I do."

Miss Walker arched a brow. "You strike me as a woman who is" — she raked her gaze up and down the length of Molly's form — "appealing to men, virtue or no virtue. You certainly dress provocatively enough. So why would you agree to sign a document forbidding you to marry?"

Molly had no trouble answering that question. "A woman caring for a crippled brother has no chance of landing a husband. The moment a man finds out about Donny, he runs the other way."

"I see." Miss Walker glanced at Donny before turning her gaze back to Molly. "And I assume you know this for a fact?"

60

"Yes, ma'am. I've had twenty-two marriage proposals in all. Soon as I told them about Donny, every last man took off like a mule with his tail on fire. Didn't matter if they were young or old, none of them wanted the added responsibility."

Miss Walker pursed her lips and thought for a moment. "Your loyalty to your brother is commendable."

"I'll be equally loyal to you and the ranch. All I ask is that you give me a chance."

Miss Walker scrutinized her. "How do you propose to take care of your brother *and* keep up your duties?"

"Donny only needs help getting in and out of bed. He's quite capable of taking care of himself throughout the day." That wasn't true — God forgive her — but she didn't dare reveal the full extent of Donny's needed care. At least not yet.

Donny nodded in agreement and Molly felt a tug of her heartstrings. Though he was very much against coming to the ranch, no one would ever guess it by his beseeching expression.

Miss Walker studied Donny for a moment and brushed a wayward strand of hair away from her face. "I'll probably regret this, but I'll let you stay."

"Thank you, I —"

"I don't want thanks — I want blood and sweat." The ranch owner's gaze slid the length of Molly like a dressmaker measuring for clothes. "I generally give candidates a set time period to prove themselves. I'll give you till mid-September to show me you're as capable of learning the ranching business as you are at protecting your virtue."

One of the men laughed but Miss Walker ignored him. "If by some . . . miracle . . . you succeed, we'll discuss the terms of our agreement. Until that time you'll be paid less than the normal salary to make up for your brother's room and board."

The wheelchair landed on the ground with a thud and both men brushed their hands together. Stretch grabbed the valise and set it next to the chair.

Miss Walker hadn't seemed to notice the wheelchair rising up and down like a barometer in changing weather. "I feel it fair to warn you that only one previous candidate lasted for more than a week. Most barely made it through the first couple of days."

Molly refused to be discouraged. She knew nothing about cattle, but life on a ranch couldn't be any harder than living in a mining town.

Miss Walker's gaze settled on Molly's

62

velvet slippers, now covered in dust. "Do you have anything remotely similar to ranch attire?"

Molly glanced down at her gown. It was the most fashionable one she owned, but next to the ranch owner's practical garb it looked downright dowdy. "I'm afraid most of my clothes were lost in the fire."

"I'll see what I can rustle up. Meanwhile, your room is waiting. I'll have my housekeeper prepare a room for your brother." She glanced at Stretch. "See that the horse and wagon are returned to the livery stable." With that Miss Walker strode toward the ranch house, her jingling spurs sounding like a death knell.

Molly waited for the two ranch hands to lift Donny into his wheelchair. The man named Stretch pushed the wheelchair through the courtyard and he and Feedbag hauled it onto the shaded verandah and into the house. A young Mexican woman greeted them, eyeing Molly up and down.

"My name is Molly." She pronounced each word precisely. She guessed the housekeeper was somewhere in her teens.

"Rosita," the woman replied, pointing to herself.

Relieved that the woman seemed to understand English, a dozen questions leaped to mind, but they could wait till later. She turned to the two men.

"Thank you."

"Glad to help," Stretch said. He and Feedbag left and Molly took in her surroundings. The entry hall opened to a large spacious room.

Compared to their tent home, the house was quite grand with its red tile floor, stone fireplace, and floor-to-ceiling bookcases. A stuffed steer head hung over the mantel and Indian rugs adorned the adobe walls.

Donny gazed longingly at the overstuffed bookshelves.

"This way," Rosita said. She started down a small hallway and then waited for Molly to follow with the wheelchair. Though the doorway was wider than average, the chair caught on the jamb, leaving a dent in the wood. Molly wiggled the chair back and forth until she was able to push it through.

Donny's room was in the same wing as the kitchen. It was a small room, obviously meant to be used by a cook or housekeeper. A single window faced the front of the house, shaded by the roof overhang. There were no stairs to worry about and for that Molly was grateful.

After settling Donny in his room and giving him his medicine, Molly followed the Mexican housekeeper upstairs to the second floor. The woman led the way to the end of the hall. Molly's room was considerably larger than Donny's and opened onto a lovely balcony that stretched the length of the house.

The cheerful room was furnished with a single bed, chest of drawers, washstand, and desk. Molly ran her hand across the bed, absorbing the smooth softness of the quilt. She couldn't imagine sleeping in such luxury.

Molly's spirits rose for the first time since the fire. Suddenly aware that the housekeeper stood staring at her, Molly smiled.

"Have you worked here long?"

Rosita gave a curt nod. "Long enough." Her formal manner and stiff voice seemed designed to discourage unnecessary conversation. She pointed to the garments on the bed. "Miss Walker sent clothes. I'll fetch hot bath."

A *hot* bath? That was a luxury Molly hadn't counted on. Back home she managed to heat water for a bath with hot rocks, but if she was in a hurry, she settled for the cold stream that ran outside their tent.

Even more amazing were the indoor privies, one near Donny's room and the other just down the hall from hers. She imagined this was how kings lived, not ranchers.

"A bath would be most —"

The housekeeper left the room, slamming the door shut with a bang and leaving Molly's sentence half-finished.

Molly shrugged. No matter. She glanced around, unable to believe her good luck. She touched the walls, the floor, the door leading to the balcony. She never thought to live in a house with plaster walls, wooden floors, and glass doors and windows. Strangest of all was having a room to herself. A blanket strung across the tent from a rope was the only privacy she'd ever known. She wasn't sure she liked being so far away from Donny, though. What if he needed her in the middle of the night? Or his asthma grew worse?

Pushing her worries away, she opened her valise and lifted out a scarlet frock.

Even as a child she insisted upon wearing bright clothes and refused to wear the sedate hues her mother favored. Her father flinched whenever he saw her coming, raising his hands in front of his face as if to ward off a bright light.

"You look like a peacock," he'd say fondly. Or "Put a star on top and you'd pass as a Christmas tree." But he always sided with her whenever her mother complained, calling her his little sunshine.

"When a man spends his days in a mine, he welcomes a bit of color," he'd say.

"I can understand a bit of color," her mother would reply, "but does she have to wear all the colors at once?"

What neither parent had known, had no way of knowing, was that her flashy clothes, and later her makeup and hearty voice, had all been cultivated to protect her brother. No one stared at him with pitying eyes when she was around. No one stared at him at all. People were too busy staring at her.

It had been hard at first. By nature she was reserved — shy. But she'd soon found out that if you pretended to be someone else long enough, you eventually forgot who you were. It was for the best, really. As Donny's protector and caretaker, she didn't have time to be anything else.

CHAPTER 6

Cactus Patch buzzed with news of Miss Walker's newest "heiress," and that infuriated Bessie Adams. She'd practically knocked herself out these past few weeks planning her nephew's wedding and not a single person she'd encountered in town mentioned it — not one. Not even the customers gathered in Mr. Green's mercantile early that Wednesday morning.

Incensed, Bessie strolled down an aisle checking out the produce, basket on her arm. Now that the nice new doctor was boarding with her and Sam, the list of needed groceries had almost doubled, but her mind was on her nephew's upcoming nuptials.

The wedding of Luke Adams to Kate Tenney would be the event of the decade. The town had never known anything like it. Every lamppost, every wooden sign, every door on Main Street had been decorated with large white ribbon bows. Bessie spent hours writing invitations, planning the food, overseeing the bride's dress, and explaining to her thickheaded nephew and groom-to-be why all this fuss was necessary.

It wasn't every day that a man got married. Seeing Luke properly wed fulfilled the promise made on her sister's deathbed to care for her two orphaned boys.

Bessie picked up a head of lettuce and gave it an expert squeeze. Mr. Green called over to her.

"What do you say, Bessie? Wanna bet?" He shook a cardboard box of money. "How long do you think Miz Walker's latest *heiress* will last this time?"

"I'll give her forty-eight hours," Harvey Trotter said. A farmer by trade, he wore overalls and a large straw hat the same color as his sun-streaked hair. Puffing on his stogie, he plopped a coin on the counter and Mr. Green wrote down the amount.

Bessie grimaced in disapproval. Trotter had a wife and six children and could ill afford such folly.

Saloon owner Randy Sprocket made a face. Thumbs hooked around his suspenders, he shook his head. "Nah. She's got a brother in a wheelchair. She ain't gonna last a day."

"Did you say wheelchair?" Hargrove was the owner of the local ice plant and Bessie never saw him when he wasn't dressed for winter. Today he wore a heavy flannel shirt. In this heat!

"Saw him with my own two eyes," Sprocket said. "She paid the Miller twins money to lift him and his wheelchair into a wagon at the livery."

"In that case, I change my mind," the ice man said. "I'm only giving her till noon."

Mr. Green noted the change on his tally and called over to Bessie. "Come on, Bess. Winner takes all. What do you bet?"

Bessie sniffed and placed a firm head of lettuce in her basket, which brought a nod of approval from farmer Trotter. "I'm not a gambler." The nerve of him suggesting such a thing to a fine Christian woman like herself.

"Anyone who's married is a gambler," Hargrove said. "Since you're the town matchmaker, that not only makes you a gambler but a dealer as well."

This brought a frown to Bessie's face and a round of laughter from the others. Bessie's temper snapped and she squeezed a tomato until it practically turned to ketchup. In all her sixty-something years she had not so much as touched a deck of cards.

"The whole idea of advertising for an heiress is ridiculous," she scoffed, shaking her head. "Even Mr. Vanderbilt with all his money didn't have such an abundance of heirs." Before his death Cornelius Vanderbilt was considered the richest man in America.

She'd lost count of how many women had traveled to Cactus Patch in answer to Miss Walker's advertisement. The way some of them carried on, you'd think they'd been offered husbands instead of cattle.

One by one those women had left — all except Kate Tenney, but that was only because Bessie made Luke chase the girl all the way to Boston. Had she not put her foot down and talked some sense into him, her nephew would have let a perfectly good woman slip away.

"It's a crying shame that none of you have anything better to do with yourselves than throw away your money," she said, reaching for a box of her favorite chocolate bonbons. The problem with the men in this town was that they drank and gambled too much.

"Ah, come on, Bessie. What could it hurt?" Green urged.

Bessie was tempted, God forgive her. "What if you're all wrong and no one wins?"

"Then we'll donate the money to the

church."

Bessie hesitated. No one had been right in the past about how long a girl would last at the ranch. Why, even she was convinced Kate wouldn't survive twenty-four hours and the poor girl lasted a full four months. But if this current "heiress" had a brother in a wheelchair . . . hmm. The church could use the money and . . . She caught herself in the nick of time.

"Gambling is wrong, no matter what," she said with a toss of her head. At least someone in this town knew how to resist temptation.

Trotter chomped down on his stogie and hooked his thumbs around his overall straps. "Are you telling us that you have no opinion?" He looked incredulous.

"She has an opinion on everything else," Green said.

All four men stared at her and Bessie cleared her throat. "Of course I have an opinion. I think the woman will surprise us all and last . . . two months." Any woman traveling all this way with a brother in a wheelchair had to have some starch in her.

This brought a round of laughter from the others.

"I tell you what," Hargrove said with a magnanimous air. "I'll put in for Bessie."

He tossed a shiny coin on the counter. "Put her down for two months."

Not to be outdone, the others slapped coins onto the counter on Bessie's behalf.

Smiling to herself, Bessie continued her shopping. Even if by some miracle she won what was now a healthy pot of dough, no one could accuse *her* of gambling.

Molly grabbed the pot of coffee and yawned. She couldn't help it. She'd hardly slept from worrying about Donny. Several times during the night she'd lit the oil lantern and tiptoed through the quiet house to his room. Only upon hearing his steady breathing could she relax enough to creep back to her own bed.

Donny wasn't the only reason she couldn't sleep. A night cough that started during the fire kept her awake and none of the usual remedies worked. Her throat still felt parched.

It was more than just lack of sleep that had her yawning. It was getting up at four in the morning and having to be ready to work at five.

She lifted the lids off the covered metal pans arranged on the buffet in the formal dining room. No one else was around and the long table for twelve looked anything but inviting.

The flapjacks, scrambled eggs, and bacon smelled good, but who could eat at such an ungodly hour? It was all she could do to force the strong bitter brew down her throat before she headed out the door.

To make matters worse, outside it was cold as a well-digger's knees. Her baggy shirt offered little protection from the chill, even with its long sleeves.

The sun had yet to rise and the sky was dull as tarnished silver. Following the sound of male voices, she turned the corner of the barn and a group of men turned to gape at her. One man gave a low whistle. Another's eyebrows disappeared beneath the brim of his high-crown hat.

One cowpoke's eyes practically bulged out of his weathered face. He scratched his temple, frowned, and cleared his throat. "They call me Ruckus."

"Pleased to meet you. My name is Molly Hatfield and I'm Miss —"

"I know who you are." He turned to the other men, all still gaping at her. "This here is Miss Walker's new heiress. Name's Miss Hatfield. Same rules apply as before. No cussing in the lady's presence."

The men whistled, clapped, and whooped until a man pointed his pistol at the sky and fired. A hawk took off from atop the barn, horses whinnied, and a cattle dog barked in the distance, but the men all fell silent.

Ruckus walked around the circle saying each man's name out loud. The man who'd shot the pistol was O.T. "That there is Stretch," he said, indicating the man she'd met the day before. He was the tallest of the bunch. "I reckon you won't disremember him."

Stretch tipped his hat. "And I ain't likely to disremember her."

Wishbone swept off his hat when he was introduced, his legs so bowed he looked like he was sitting on an invisible horse. Mexican Pete kicked Wishbone in the behind, sending him sprawling to the ground. It was a jovial group and reminded Molly of Saturday night at Big Jim's Saloon when everyone was in a festive mood and ready to have a good time after a week's hard labor.

Ruckus then surprised Molly by leading the group in prayer. Molly followed Ruckus's lead and lowered her head respectfully. The last time she'd prayed in a group was three years ago when that awful cave-in trapped several miners. The entire town had turned out to hold vigil and pray — for all the good it did them. The fact that these cowhands thought to start the day with prayer was unsettling to say the least. Was ranch work so dangerous that they needed to pray every day?

After the others walked away, Ruckus explained her duties. "Me and the boys have some branding to do, but you ain't up to that yet."

He sent her to the horse corral to meet with a man named Brodie, who barely bothered looking up when she introduced herself. Instead, he kept his gaze on a large black horse bucking around in a circle, kicking up its hind legs.

The horse trainer was a compact man, his long sandy hair tied at the base of his neck with a piece of rawhide. A scraggly beard covered the lower half of his face while sharp, observant brown eyes commanded the upper. She guessed him to be in his late twenties or early thirties.

"What do you know about horses?" he asked in a voice made gravelly by tobacco.

"I know how to ride." She tossed a nod at the mustang. "What's the matter with him?"

"Not a thing." Brodie spit out a stream of brown juice. "That's the first time he's been saddled. His name's Lightning."

Lightning raced toward the fence and Brodie snapped his whip. That stopped the horse from jumping but not from running.

A Mexican cowhand walked by. *"Muy mala,"* he called out. Very bad.

"Not bad," Brodie called back. "Just spirited." The Mexican shrugged and kept going.

Lightning slowed as he made the turn and headed toward them. Brodie slapped his whip against the ground and the horse gave a double hock kick and picked up speed.

Brodie nodded toward the animal. "His nature is to run when confronted with something new. He's gotta learn that runnin' will do him no good. I'm his last chance. He don't make it with me, he don't make it with no one."

He tossed her a pair of buckskin gauntlets and handed her a second whip. "Stand over there by that gate and make sure he don't escape."

Slipping her hands into the leathery softness, Molly crossed to the gate. The horse stopped running, pawed the ground, and turned in a circle as if chasing his tail. The saddle remained secure.

"Yee-ow," Brodie yelled. Lightning ran by him and Brodie responded by cracking the whip against the horse's heels. He then chased after the horse, popping his whip each time Lightning tried to climb a fence with his powerful legs.

The horse ran to the far end of the corral and jumped. Smashing into the corral fence he fell, landing on his side with a thump and stirring up a cloud of dust.

Molly stared in wide-eyed horror over gloved fingertips. The man with his yelling and cracking whip obviously didn't know what he was doing.

Lightning stretched his front legs, pushed out his head, and struggled upright. The horse looked groggy and uncertain.

Brodie grabbed the halter rope and tied Lightning to the fence outside the corral.

"You're lucky he didn't break his neck," she charged, not bothering to hide her anger.

"Or break the neck of a rider," Brodie said, his demeanor calm. "Let's hope he learned his lesson."

Lesson? She frowned. "What would have happened had he jumped over the fence without falling?"

"I would have made him fall," Brodie said simply. "What he doesn't learn on his own I've got to teach him. That's my job. A ranch can't run without well-trained horses." He tossed a nod toward the open desert. "You never know what you might encounter out there. Could be a rattler. Could be a raging bull, a wolf, or a bandit. A cowboy's life

78

depends on how his horse reacts to adversity." He snapped the ground with his whip. "Let's get to work."

Molly spent the rest of the morning learning how to turn a wild horse into a tame one. Brodie was a patient teacher, his movements efficient but never hurried. Now that she understood the reason behind his methods, she realized he was firm but never harsh or cruel.

"I learned to train horses in Mexico," he explained as they took a midmorning break in the shade of the windmill. He dipped a metal cup into the water tank and drank it down in one gulp. Wiping his whiskered chin with the back of his hand, he continued.

"Mexicans are the best riders. They don't treat horses like pets. A horse is a cowboy's partner and it's all serious."

"Would it be okay if I ride one of those?" she asked, pointing to a row of saddled horses tied outside the corral. She was a good rider and anxious to check out the ranch.

"Not unless you got yourself a hole ready. I ain't got time to dig no grave." He laughed at her expression before explaining, "Ain't none of them ever been ridden. They're gettin' used to saddles and learning how to stand quietly. What you see is a bunch of horses learning patience." He gave her a cockeyed glance. "I reckon that's a virtue you know nothing about."

"I know about patience," she said. "And what I know, I don't much like."

She stared at the next corral over. A black colt held his head to the ground. Keeping his forelegs in place, he moved his back legs sideways in a circle. He then lifted his head and bounded to the other side. What a strange horse.

Brodie followed her gaze. "He's blind," he said simply.

Molly frowned. The horse looked so carefree, so vibrant and full of life, it was hard to imagine that anything was wrong with him. "But he looks so . . . happy."

"Reckon he don't know any better. Soon as he weans, we're gonna have to let him go. He won't be any good around here."

A surge of protectiveness shot through her. "Let him go? You mean set him free? But he won't survive."

Brodie shrugged. "Not my problem. Not yours either. Our job is to train horses to work. If they can't do the job, they're no good to us."

Molly continued to watch the young horse. How she envied the little fellow's

80

exuberance. Or maybe it was his ignorance she envied, for he had yet to learn that physical handicaps were often met with cruelty and disdain.

Sensing Brodie watching her, she pulled her gaze away from the colt. "How long have you been training horses?"

"Since I was knee-high to a jackrabbit," he said.

"They respect you," she said. "They watch you like a teacher."

"They're watching me like a prisoner watches a guard. I'm keeping them from freedom. They figured out my weaknesses long before I figured out theirs. They've already figured out yours."

"What weak —" But already he'd turned his back and walked away.

The morning passed quickly and a distant bell sounded.

"Lunch," Brodie called from a distance.

She gaped at him. Already? It wasn't possible. Her heart thudded. *Donny.* She raced to the ranch house as quickly as her unfamiliar peg-heeled boots would allow.

How could she have forgotten to get her brother out of bed?

CHAPTER 7

He ran through the grass, the wind in his hair, the sun in his face. He kept running and running as if never to stop. He didn't know what he was running to or even from, but he had to keep running because . . .

Donny woke with a start. Fighting to hold on to the dream as long as possible, he didn't dare move. But the sweet smell of grass and the wind in his hair soon faded away like popping bubbles, along with the rest of his dream. Only the memory of running remained.

Every night it was the same dream. Every morning he woke to the reality of his life. He couldn't walk, let alone run. He could barely manage to put on his own shirt.

A clanging sound in the distance made him glance at the mechanical clock next to his bed. *Noon.* He couldn't believe it. No wonder his stomach growled.

Where was Molly? It wasn't like her to

keep him waiting so long. Had something happened to her? The thought sent cold chills down his spine. The Dobson Creek fire made him realize like never before how much he depended on his sister. Without her he couldn't survive.

Had Molly been injured? Was that why she was so late? What if she never returned? Heart thumping, he hung his head over the side of his bed and dangled his arms, his fingertips barely reaching the floor. Slowly he eased his shoulders over the edge of the mattress. He placed the palms of his hands on the floor. Tears of frustration sprang to his eyes and sweat trickled down his fore-head.

Blinking away the moisture, he measured the distance to his wheelchair. It looked like a mile away, though the room was only a few feet wide. He tried pulling himself forward using his arms, but it was no good. He wasn't strong enough. Feeling helpless as a slug, he gasped for breath.

He'd die rather than let Molly know how much he hated his life, hated being crippled, hated having to depend on her to get him out of bed in the morning and put him there at night. He hated the pitying looks from others — if they bothered looking at him at all.

If only he could escape that dream. Dreaming about running only made his reality that much worse. Sometimes, like today, he wished he were dead.

He was still half on, half off the bed when Molly burst through the door.

"Drat!" Eleanor Walker rested her hands on the pommel of her saddle and stared at the barbed wire fence that someone had cut. The problem was worse than she thought.

Robert Stackman rode his gelding beside her roan. He was both her banker and friend, but he would be more if she would let him. Each year on her birthday he proposed marriage; each year she turned him down.

The ranch couldn't survive such a partnership. Robert was too practical, too money-oriented. He understood finances, not cattle. To him, profits were much more important than legacies. He never sat up all night nursing a horse or delivering a calf. He knew nothing about the soul of a ranch or its heart.

She knew from painful experience that such differences would ruin a marriage and for this reason she chose to settle for friendship — nothing more. But it was a friendship she deeply valued.

"What did I tell you?" she said.

The grazing cattle by her windmill were not her own. She dug the wells and other cattlemen reaped the benefits. The sheer number of beeves from neighboring ranches worried her. An even greater concern was the eastern investor who wanted to finance a cattle company in the area. The man knew nothing about cattle and even less about conserving land.

Robert's horse whickered and pawed the ground. "Whoa, boy." A firm square jaw, crinkly blue eyes, and proud turn of head hinted at the good-looking man he must have been in his youth. At age sixty-two he was now more distinguished than handsome and his lush black hair had long since turned silver.

"I agree, it's a problem," he said.

"And it's about to get worse."

She thought she'd seen and done it all, but this latest onslaught of ranch companies and overgrazed ranges was something new. Three and four times the number of cattle than an acre could sustain had flooded the area in recent months. So far there had been no problems because of the record amount of rain in the past year, but sure as the day was long, another drought was around the corner. Less rain meant less vegetation, resulting in thinner cattle and lower market prices.

She narrowed her eyes. "If Mr. Hamshank has his way, the land won't be good for anything." For two cents she would gladly tell the man what he could do with his cattle company.

"I believe his name is Mr. Hampshire," Robert said.

"Hamshank, Hampshire, what difference does it make? The man's an idiot." Eleanor tried not to let her anger get the best of her, but how could she not?

It wasn't just a ranch, it was her life — had been for more than forty years ever since her family's wagon broke down on this very spot on the way to the California gold mines.

"Did I ever tell you about the Englishman?" she asked.

"The one your mother nursed back to health and who returned the favor with a heifer?"

She nodded. Her mother had considered that young cow her *last chance* to save her family from poverty's door. From those humble beginnings grew one of the largest and most successful cattle ranches in all of Arizona Territory.

"That same Englishman also gave us a

book of Shakespeare. I never met an Englishman who didn't carry the bard with him, did you?"

Robert shrugged. "What a pity your mother didn't start a library rather than a cattle ranch. It would have saved you a lot of heartache."

She laughed. Only Robert would think books preferable to cattle. She grew serious again. "Something has to be done to stop Hampshire," she said. The question was what?

"You can't stop progress, Eleanor."

"Progress? You call this progress? The railroad was progress." Before the rails arrived, she had been forced to drive her cattle all the way to Kansas. "The telegram was progress. This . . . this is madness."

"I told you what I think, Eleanor. I think you should sell."

"You know I can't do that, Robert." If only her daughter had lived. It had been more than thirty years since little Rebecca died at the age of five, but the least memory of her still hurt. If anything, it hurt even more with each passing year. Not only had she buried a daughter but very possibly the future of her ranch and certainly her family's legacy.

"I could get you a fair price. That is, if we

act now," Robert said. "I know someone who might be interested in the ranch house."

"And for good reason," she snapped. The ranch house was fairly new, built after the, '87 earthquake and subsequent fire destroyed the old ranch house and most of the outbuildings.

"We can subdivide the rest of the land," he added.

"I'm not selling and I'm certainly not dividing the land."

Robert was too much of a gentleman to show impatience or exasperation, but she sensed his disapproval. "You said it yourself," he reminded her. "Something must be done. I'm offering you the most practical solutions."

"You're offering no solutions at all." What she needed was fresh blood and new ideas to meet the challenges the ranch now faced. She had good men working for her, but day-to-day chores consumed their time and energy. What she lacked was someone with vision and foresight, someone who could help her take the ranch into the twentieth century. So far none of the women who'd answered her advertisement had worked out and it was too soon to know if Molly would.

"So what do you plan to do?" he asked.

"Fight them," she said. "I asked my lawyer to arrange a meeting with Mr. Hampshire. I hope you'll be there."

He arched an eyebrow. "What do you expect to accomplish? To talk him out of it, just like that?"

"I know it won't be easy."

"An understatement if I ever heard one." He stroked his goatee. "You can't keep running this ranch forever," he said. "Even Doc Masterson had the good sense to retire."

Eleanor gripped the bridle reins tighter. Nothing irritated her more than a reminder of her advancing years. "You know I'm trying to find someone to take over."

No doubt this latest woman, Molly, would soon go the way of the others. Eleanor sighed. She had to be out of her mind to let a dance hall girl and her brother hang around even for a short while. She should have sent them back to town the day they arrived. If only the boy didn't have so much trouble breathing.

"Each one who has applied has been progressively worse," he said.

"I had high hopes for Kate Tenney." Had indeed been ready to sign papers making her the official heiress. If only the girl hadn't fallen for the town smithy. Eleanor shook her head just thinking about it. Hard to believe that a woman as smart as Kate would settle for something as dull as marriage.

Eleanor shifted in her saddle. It would take years to train her replacement. As Robert liked to remind her, at age sixty-six she no longer had time on her side.

Could this latest girl with her ill-conceived clothing, brassy demeanor, and sickly brother be her last chance to save the ranch? The very thought made her head spin.

As if to concur with her doubts, a steer let out a bellow followed by a loud mournful moo that sounded like an emphatic *no*.

My thoughts exactly.

CHAPTER 8

Molly was breathless with excitement and even finding Donny half off the bed earlier had failed to quell her enthusiasm.

Now he sat wolfing down his midday meal, his plate piled high with meat, potatoes, and gravy. It wasn't a meal — it was a feast.

He preferred to take his meals in his room rather than the formal dining room. Molly suspected he felt intimidated by Miss Walker, but learning to live with the brusque ranch owner was a small price to pay for a chance to live in such a wondrous place.

"Oh, Donny, I just know this is going to work out." She loved working with the horses and couldn't believe how quickly the morning had flown by. "Did you ever imagine a finer home?"

Donny's fork stilled. "Does this mean I'll never have to go to an insane asylum?" Such institutions housed not only mental patients but the crippled and deformed.

Molly sat on the bed and stared him straight in the eye. "We've already discussed this."

"But Dr. Weinberg said —"

"I don't care what that bag of wind said. As long as I have a breath left in me, you will never have to live in that horrid place." She squeezed his hand. "I mean that, Donny."

He studied her with eyes far too old for his years. "What if you get married and your husband hates me and —"

"Donny, if I stay here I can't get married."

He frowned. "Why not?"

"I'll have to sign a document forbidding it. It's one of Miss Walker's stipulations. So you see? You have nothing to worry about. It's you and me together, forever. Now eat up." She glanced at the mechanical clock. "Oh no!" She was already ten minutes late getting back to work. "I've got to go. I'll be back in two hours. I promise!"

With that she dashed from the room, hoping Brodie hadn't noticed the time.

Whenever Caleb drove through town, curious bystanders gawked at him. Today was no different. The moment he rumbled down Main Street in his horseless buggy, men,

92

women, and children poured out of stores and businesses to get a better look at his amazing gasoline machine. Indeed, they almost seemed to crawl out from under the boardwalk.

As if enjoying the attention, Bertha back-fired — not once but twice. The loud booms echoed through the town like cannon fire.

The doctor's office was situated on Main between the Silver Moon Saloon and the Cactus Patch Gazette, directly across from the hotel. The only sign left of its former tenant was the neatly printed wording on the door that read *Dr. Masterson.*

The patient room was furnished with a leather examination table, sink, water pump, and a cabinet filled with carefully marked vials. Saws, knives, scalpels, scissors, clamps, and other surgical tools were arranged neatly on a tray. The W. Watson and Sons compound microscope occupied a metal table.

The room had two doors, one leading to the waiting room and one leading to a small office in back. The office had a desk and two chairs and an impressive library filled with medical books and periodicals.

Caleb sat at the desk, the swivel chair squeaking under his weight, and glanced at his newly hung diploma on the wall. He couldn't remember when he didn't want to be a doctor, and what better time than now? The medical profession was just beginning to emerge from the dark ages.

Most people called the West the new frontier, but medicine was the *true* frontier. With the discovery that germs caused disease, and the subsequent development of vaccinations for cholera and diphtheria, Caleb envisioned the day that disease would be a thing of the past.

But that wasn't all. Recently he'd read an article about a new form of photography that could penetrate flesh and expose bones to the human eye. It was hard to imagine anything so amazing.

It wasn't that long ago that a medical diploma could be obtained with only three months' schooling and no clinical experience. It was only six years ago that the National Association of Medical Colleges officially established a three-year curriculum and clinical training requirements. Unfortunately, poor schools still existed and it was almost impossible for a patient to know if a doctor had received proper training. The field was still filled with quacks and charlatans who continued to spread their ignorance and harm people's lives.

Caleb had attended Harvard Medical

School, one of the best schools of medicine in the country. Even so, he felt ill-equipped to take on the responsibility of providing medical care for an entire town. Medical knowledge had doubled since the War Between the States, but the human body, for the most part, remained a mystery. Some things, like blood transfusions, were still hit and miss. Caleb was convinced there were more elements in blood not yet discovered or understood.

The bells on the front door jingled, disturbing his reverie. Magic woke from his nap and looked up as if to say, *Well, what are you waiting for?*

Caleb rose, smoothed his hair down, and stepped into the waiting room. A woman and a boy of about five or six sat waiting for him.

"Good morning," he said. "I'm Dr. Fairbanks."

"I'm Mrs. Trotter and this is my son Jimmy. You must be the new doctor."

"Yes, I am."

She was a thin, bird-like woman with work-hardened hands. The bags under her hazel eyes made her look older than her years, which he guessed was somewhere in the mid- to late thirties.

"How can I help you today?"

"There's something not right with Jimmy and I don't know what it is," Mrs. Trotter explained. Jimmy was a rail-thin child with skinny legs and arms and a gaunt face that seemed too small to support his mop of unruly brown hair. A good wind could blow him away.

"Come in and we'll take a look." He held the door open for mother and child and led them into the examination room. Magic took one look at them before flopping down to resume his nap.

"You can sit on my special bench," Caleb said, pointing to the leather-covered table.

Jimmy stepped on the footstool and seated himself on the edge of the table, his skinny legs dangling over the side. His mother sat on a ladder-back chair and Caleb lowered himself onto a stool. "You said something's not right," he probed.

Mrs. Trotter nodded. Her salt-and-pepper hair was swept into an untidy bun beneath her bonnet as if she had pinned it up in haste. She was dressed in a no-nonsense gray skirt and plain white shirtwaist that had seen better days.

"He complains of stomachaches and hardly eats. He can't even get through his daily chores."

"How long has he been this way?" Caleb asked.

"Since the first of the year."

Caleb arched an eyebrow. "So he's been like this for several months?"

She nodded. "His father says he's just lazy."

It was the kind of response Caleb had come to expect from paternal parents. An illness was often viewed as an indictment against a man's ability to care for his family and consequently discounted or ignored. "Do you have other children?"

"Six altogether, including Jimmy."

"Do any of your other children show similar symptoms?"

She shook her head. "No, they're healthy as horses."

Caleb turned to the boy. "Take off your shirt and we'll have a look." The boy glanced at his mother for permission before stuffing a silver foil ball between his legs and reaching for his buttons.

"How old are you, Jimmy?"

"Eight."

Caleb had guessed wrong. The boy was clearly undersized for his age. "You said he doesn't eat."

"Not when his stomach hurts," Mrs. Trotter replied.

Jimmy slid his suspenders down his arms and took off his shirt. Caleb noted several bruises on the boy's chest. "How often does your stomach hurt, Jimmy?"

"Most every day," Jimmy said. He stared down at the floor as if admitting to some misdeed.

Caleb reached for his stethoscope, slipped the ivory ear bits in place, and lifted the bell-shaped chest piece to Jimmy's bone-thin torso. Jimmy pulled back, eyes wide.

"It won't hurt you," Caleb said. "It's called a stethoscope and it helps me hear what's going on inside." Dr. Masterson, like many older doctors, still used the percussion method of examination, which involved tapping the chest and listening for sounds.

Jimmy relaxed but kept his eyes on the chest piece. His lungs sounded fine but his heartbeat was weak. The boy's skin was pale but clear except for the bruises. His temperature was normal.

"Any fever?"

Mrs. Trotter shook her head. "No."

"Make two fists for me." Caleb held out his hands to demonstrate.

Jimmy followed Caleb's lead.

Caleb checked the boy's reflexes and looked in his ears and throat. "Did you know that your heart is a muscle and it's the same size as both your fists?"

Jimmy's eyes widened as he looked down at his hands.

Caleb smiled at the boy's expression. "I bet you don't know the strongest muscle in the body."

Jimmy looked up. He had his mother's hazel eyes, only his were ringed with fatigue instead of worry. "The heart?"

"It's the tongue. But I wouldn't try picking up a rock with it."

Jimmy fingered his tongue.

"Say red leather, yellow leather," Caleb said.

"Red leather, yellow leather."

"Now say it fast."

"Red leather, lellow feather." Jimmy laughed. "Red flether, bellow —

Even Mrs. Trotter laughed at her son's attempt to say the tongue-twister. Caleb was willing to bet the woman hadn't laughed much in recent months.

While Jimmy was occupied with trying to get the words right, Caleb pricked the boy's finger, took a blood sample, and reached for a bandage. Jimmy hardly seemed to notice.

"You can put your shirt back on." Caleb pulled off his stethoscope.

All kinds of possibilities ran through Caleb's head. Some, like cancer, were serious, others not so much. It wasn't the first time he'd seen a child with similar complaints. One of his instructors at medical school gave a lecture on the "mystery" illness that seemed to run rampant in city slums. So what was this illness and why was it suddenly affecting so many children?

Jimmy's lack of dental or skeletal problems ruled out the possibility of rickets. Nonetheless, he questioned Mrs. Trotter on her family's diet.

"I have a vegetable garden," she said. "We raise chickens and goats, so our children also get plenty of meat and milk."

"What does he do in his spare time?" Caleb asked.

"He doesn't have much spare time." She smiled fondly at her son. "I make him practice readin' and writin' every day. And he still has chores. Mostly he sleeps. He seems tired all the time."

Caleb tapped his chin and considered other possibilities. A number of diseases could cause exhaustion and swollen lymph nodes. Could be a low-grade infection or allergy. Mrs. Trotter said her other children were healthy, but as Lucretius pointed out in the first century BC, what was food to one might be poison to another.

"What do you think, Doctor?" Mrs. Trotter's voice and demeanor pleaded for good news.

"The bruises and pale skin suggest anemia. That means his white blood count is probably high. Anemia can be a symptom of many things."

She knitted her brow. "Like what, exactly?"

"Uh . . . allergies. Infections." He cited other possibilities. "I'd like to run some tests."

Mrs. Trotter looked him square in the face. "Dr. Fairbanks, I may not be what you call an educated woman, but I know when someone's beating around the bush. I reckon there's not much ground left around that bush about now." As if to brace herself for the bad news to come, she straightened her shoulders and raised her chin. "Doctor?"

He glanced at Jimmy playing with his foil ball. "Why don't you wait in the other room while I talk to your mother?" He glanced at Magic asleep in the corner. "You can take my dog with you."

Jimmy slid off the examining table, clapped his hands to get Magic's attention, and left the room with the dog at his heels.

Caleb blew out his breath and sat forward,

hands folded on the desk. Would he ever get used to delivering bad news? "There is a . . . condition called leukemia. I'm not saying that's what your son has, but we have to consider it."

"Is this . . ."

"Leukemia."

"Is this . . . leukemia serious?"

He sat back, as if distancing himself from her would make what he said any easier. "I'm afraid it is."

She took a sharp intake of air but otherwise remained motionless. After giving her a moment to gather her thoughts, he continued, "Leukemia is a cancer of the blood cells. I'm not fully convinced that's what we're dealing with, but like I said we have to consider it."

Her shoulders sagged and her lips trembled. His words had sunk in. "How . . . how contagious is it?"

"It's not. Or at least not that we know of."

She studied him from beneath tightly drawn brows. "If it's not contagious, how would he have gotten such a thing?"

"It's hard to say," he said. "We know a lot more about diseases than we did even a few years ago, but we still have a lot to learn."

"In other words, you don't know."

"I'm afraid not. Like I said, it's just one

possibility. Meanwhile, I'll give you a tonic to help replace any nutrients he might be missing. Just to make certain, we don't want to overlook the possibility of an allergy. It would help if you keep a diary of everything he eats and drinks. Also, list any of his symptoms and the time of day he experiences them."

A doctor was only as good as his detective skills. He stood and reached into the cabinet for a bottle of cod liver oil and handed it to her as a measure against scurvy and rickets. No one knew why cod liver oil worked, but it did.

She sat perfectly still for a moment, as if she needed time to brace herself before moving. Finally she stood. "I'll bring him back next week."

"Tomorrow," he said. "I want to see him tomorrow."

She hesitated. "My husband and I . . . we can't afford any luxuries."

"This is not a luxury." The Trotters weren't alone in their thinking. Shelter, food, and clothing were all many families could afford. "We'll work something out," he assured her. "The most important thing right now is that Jimmy gets all the care we can give him."

She stared at him for a moment before

turning to leave. She walked to the door as if in a trance. "Tomorrow."

Moments later Caleb stood at the window facing the street and watched Mrs. Trotter and her son drive away in a horse and wagon. It wasn't even noon and already he felt inadequate. He'd been warned at medical school not to get emotionally involved with his patients, but how could he not?

With a heavy sigh he lifted his gaze to the expanse of blue sky. *Heavenly Father, Jimmy needs help — bad. We both do.*

CHAPTER 9

Molly stood, whip in hand, and tried to focus. She had been at the ranch for only a week and already she was exhausted.

"Watch it!" Brodie yelled. "Don't let him jump."

Despite her best efforts the horse headed for the fence, but Brodie managed to turn him at the very last minute. Brodie threw down his whip.

"What's the matter with you, girl? I told you not to let him jump."

Molly bit back tears. She was like a butterfly afraid to light. She was forever racing between the horse corrals, barn, range, and house. Her days had no form or structure and time was but a blur.

It was muck out the stables and check on Donny; exercise the horses and check on Donny; track down a stray steer and check on Donny. Every bone in her body ached, and today she was late taking Donny his lunch, yet again.

Later that afternoon while the other ranch hands took a much-needed respite from the hot sun, she searched for Rosita. She found the Mexican housekeeper at last in the washhouse in back. The girl moved about like a shadow, hardly making a sound. Today she stood ironing sheets, a dreamy expression on her face and her mind clearly miles away.

Noticing Molly, she jumped and looked momentarily confused, like one awakened from a deep sleep. "You want something, señorita?"

"Yes, I need a favor," Molly said. "Do you mind?"

Rosita shook her head, though the brown eyes regarding Molly from beneath a starched white cap clearly said otherwise.

"I wonder if you would be so kind as to check on my brother during the day while I'm working?" Molly hadn't wanted to ask anyone for help but she didn't know what else to do. How ridiculous to think she could manage both taking care of Donny and ranch chores by herself.

Rosita set one iron down and reached for another on the iron stove. "I work for Señorita Walker. Big house."

"Yes, I realize you have much to do, but

what I ask won't take long. I'll pay you for your services."

Rosita shook her head. "No time."

"But I'm only asking for a few minutes a day, at most," Molly persisted. "I just want you to check on him on occasion and, if need be, to move his chair to another spot so he doesn't have to sit in the same place all day."

"No time," Rosita repeated. She sprinkled the bedsheet with lavender water and pushed the heavy iron back and forth. Wispy fingers of steam curled ghost-like from the sheet she pressed.

Molly left the washhouse close to tears, praying all the while that Brodie hadn't noticed her absence.

Caleb drove out to the ranch to check on Miss Walker's horse. The place appeared deserted save for Miss Hatfield's brother sitting on the porch in his wheelchair. He was either asleep or reading, hard to tell which.

"Come on, boy." He lifted Magic out of the vehicle and set him on the ground.

The steps leading up to the shaded verandah squeaked beneath Caleb's weight and Donny looked up with a start, his book falling off his lap. His eyes were the same green as his sister's but without the sparkle.

"Sorry to startle you. It's Donald, right?"

"Donny."

Caleb bent to retrieve the book and set it on the table by the youth's side. It was a book on celestial science.

"Do you remember me?"

"You're the doctor," Donny said, his voice flat, his face expressionless. The boy obviously suffered melancholy, which almost always translated to careless dress or poor hygiene. Neither was true for Donny. His black trousers and boiled shirt were spotlessly clean, his hair neatly trimmed — all signs of a conscientious caretaker.

"I hope you don't start another stampede."

Caleb cracked a smile. "You and me both." He'd been meaning to check into the backfiring but hadn't found the time. He'd have to talk to the smithy about fixing the flywheel and bullet holes.

Donny shifted in his chair and the wheels emitted a squeak. Magic barked playfully and pawed the rims, trying to get them to squeak again. Donny trailed his hand along Magic's back where the long hair parted and fell on either side of his body. Normally the dog's face was hidden, but Aunt Bessie had brushed his hair out of his eyes and tied it with a blue ribbon.

"What's your dog's name?"

"Magic."

"What's magical about him?" Donny asked.

"Nothing that I know of. He was named after the street he was born on."

"Good thing he wasn't born on Cemetery Street," Donny said.

Caleb laughed. The boy had a sense of humor.

Donny tossed a nod at the carriage parked in front. "Did you build it yourself?"

Caleb nodded. "With help from a friend's father. He owns a bicycle shop in Boston where I went to school."

A spark of interest flared in the youth's face. "Was it hard to build?"

"Took us five years to get it right. We built it over the shop on the second floor. It was the only space available." He had worked part time in the shop to cover medical school expenses and the cost of motor parts. "We had a hard time getting Bertha to the ground floor to test it."

"How did you manage?" Donny asked.

"We finally stood her on her tail end and lowered her down in the elevator."

Donny flashed a grin. "That must have been something to see."

"Yes, it was." Caleb's gaze shifted to the corrals and barn in the distance. "Where is everyone?" By everyone he meant Donny's sister, but he didn't want to ask about her outright.

"Dunno. They took off a couple of hours ago. Haven't seen them since. Wish they'd get back. I'm tired of sitting out here."

Caleb glanced at the front door, which couldn't have been more than ten or fifteen feet away. "I'll help you inside if you like."

Donny's expression grew solemn again. "My sister doesn't want me to move without her. Last time I did, I fell out of my chair and couldn't get back in."

Caleb frowned. While at the Boston School of Medicine he'd worked with paraplegic Civil War veterans. Some gave in to their affliction, replacing missing limbs with bitterness and anger. Others rose above their injuries and went on to raise families and own successful businesses. Donny wasn't missing a limb, but he was definitely missing out on life.

Something caught Donny's attention. "Look at that horse. He's at it again."

Caleb followed Donny's pointed finger. In the far corral a black colt rocked back and forth like a child's rocking horse.

"I named him Orbit," Donny explained.

"That's 'cause he has this funny habit of putting his head to the ground and circling his body around like a planet orbiting the sun."

"Sounds like a good name for him." Caleb leaned against a post, arms crossed. Magic gave up on the chair and flopped down by his side. "What's wrong with your legs?"

"They don't work," Donny mumbled, his gaze dropping to his lap.

"I can see that." Caleb waited, but when the youth offered no further explanation, he asked, "How did it happen? Were you born that way?"

Donny looked up. "I fell out of my carriage as an infant."

Caleb sucked in his breath. So the boy had been crippled nearly all his life. "Do you mind if I take a look?"

Donny's eyes narrowed. "Why would you want to do that?"

Caleb shrugged. "A funny thing about us doctors. We tend to have a fascination with the human body. I won't hurt you, I promise."

Donny studied him for a moment before giving a reluctant nod. Caleb lowered himself to one knee in front of the wheelchair. "I'm going to take off your shoes and roll up your trousers." When Donny showed no objection, Caleb reached for a foot.

He pulled off one shoe and set it aside before working on the other. "Did you know that if your blood vessels were laid end to end, they could travel around the earth twice?"

Donny stared at him as if trying to figure him out, then said, "Did you know that a quarter moon and half moon are the same?"

Encouraged that the boy chose to participate in his little game, Caleb glanced up at him. "How can that be?" Caleb wiggled Donny's shoe off.

"The quarter tells how much of the lunar month has passed and the half is how much moon is visible," Donny explained.

Caleb couldn't help but be intrigued. Obviously there was nothing wrong with the kid's mind. "Interesting."

"You can see more stars here than in Dobson Creek," Donny said, warming to his subject. "There are no trees getting in the way. You can see even more stars with a telescope."

"So I've heard." Caleb lifted a limp leg and flexed the youth's foot. "I heard about the fire. Is that what brought you and your sister to Cactus Patch?"

"Yeah."

Sensing Donny's reluctance to talk about the fire, Caleb quickly changed the subject. "Did you know the foot has more bones than any other part of the body?"

The dark look left Donny's face and he fired back a question of his own. "Did you know that if the sun blew up five minutes ago we wouldn't know it for another three minutes?"

Caleb responded just as rapidly, "Did you know that babies are born without knee-caps?"

After several moments of batting interesting and sometimes even amazing facts back and forth, Caleb squeezed Donny's ankle. "Any feeling here?"

"Sometimes it tingles," Donny said.

"What about here?"

"No."

Caleb checked the length of the leg all the way to the hip. "Any pain?"

"Sometimes. Mostly at night."

He replaced Donny's shoes and tied the laces. The boy appeared to have a partial lumbar spinal injury with some leg contraction.

"I can help you."

Doubt clouded Donny's face. "Help me how? Can you make me walk again?"

"No, I can't do that." Caleb sat back on

his heels. "I wish I could, but I can't. No one can do that."

Donny gripped the arms of his chair and leaned forward. "Then how are you gonna help me?"

"I can help you strengthen your muscles. That will make you more independent. I can teach you how to get in and out of bed by yourself. Use the facilities without help. Get in and out of your chair."

Donny's mouth twisted in disgust. "What good will that do? I'll still be crippled."

Caleb stood. "Only if you want to be."

"What is that supposed to mean?" Donny's eyes grew moist, but he was either too stubborn or too proud to give in to tears and glowered instead.

"You can choose to be a cripple or you can choose to be someone who just happens to have legs that don't work." Caleb hated to be tough on the boy, but mollycoddling would do him no favors.

Donny's face turned red and his nose flared. "What do you know? Have you ever been crippled?"

"No." Caleb studied him. Obviously he'd hit a nerve. "I've worked with patients with similar problems."

"That don't mean nothing! You've never had to sit in a chair all day. Or had to wait for your sister to dress you. Or been laughed at. You have no idea how awful that is."

Caleb rubbed the back of his neck. "You're right. I don't know what it's like to sit in a chair all day. But people laugh at me all the time for driving a motor buggy."

"That's not the same thing."

Humor failing, Caleb turned serious. "You're right. I have no idea what you're going through, but I do know this — you don't have much of a life. With God's help, I can change that."

Donny's lip curled and he suddenly looked older than his years. "Without my legs I can't do nothin'."

"What do you want to do?"

Donny waved away the question. "There's nothing I *can* do. Don't you understand?" His fingers curled around the arms of his chair and he seemed to deflate, his body shrinking. "I never got to run like the other kids or attend school. My sister taught me how to read and how to add and subtract."

So Molly wasn't only his caretaker, but also his teacher. "Let's suppose you can do anything you wanted. What would it be?"

Donny stared into space at something only he could see. "I keep having this dream."

Caleb waited a moment before prompting him. "Tell me about your dream."

115

Donny wrinkled his nose. "It's dumb."

"Dreams aren't dumb. Sometimes that's how God talks to us."

Donny studied him, his face filled with doubt. "How do you know that?"

"Says so in the Bible. That's how God talked to Abraham, Daniel, and Solomon, to name a few. He even talked to Mary and Joseph in dreams."

"Yeah, but those were important people," Donny said.

"In God's eyes, we're all important." Caleb tilted his head. "So tell me about your dream."

"In my dream I'm running." Donny's head bobbed slightly as if he was reliving it. After a while he added, "The wind is in my face and my hair is blowing." He reached for his book and flung it the length of the verandah. Magic lifted his head and stared at the book before resuming his nap.

"Why would God make me dream about something I can't do?" Donny asked. "Will you tell me that?"

"God sometimes uses dreams to warn of danger. That's how Joseph knew to flee to Egypt. God also uses dreams to reveal His plans for us. I dreamed about being a doctor long before I became one." After a slight pause he added, "Sometimes God uses

116

dreams to encourage us. That's what He did with Gideon."

Donny folded his arms and stuck out his lips. "Maybe God's warning me against listening to you."

"Or maybe He's showing you what would happen if you do."

"That's dumb." Donny's voice broke. "I can't run. I can't even walk."

Caleb grabbed the arms of the wheelchair, leaning forward until he was practically nose to nose with the boy. "You can do anything you want to do. You want to feel the wind in your face?" With a quick movement, he spun the wheelchair around. It was an older model with three metal wheels. The newer chairs had rubber tires and push rims for mobility, but this one lacked any such conveniences.

Grabbing hold of the hand bar, he tilted the chair onto the single wheel in back and steered it down the verandah steps, *thumpity-thump.* Magic jumped up, ready to play, and bounded down the steps after them.

"What are you doing?" Donny yelled, gripping the sides of his chair. "Stop!"

Ignoring him, Caleb pushed the chair around the courtyard, picking up speed as they circled the fountain.

Donny's initial cries of alarm soon gave

way to laughter. It was a tight little laugh at first that gradually turned into delighted guffaws.

"More, more," he shouted.

Grinning, Caleb spun him around, changed directions, and bolted forward, pushing the chair faster. "Brrrrooooooooom," he yelled, imitating the sound of a motor. Magic ran after them, barking.

"Whee," Donny cried, hair flying around his head. "It's just like my dream!"

Caleb swirled the chair around in a complete circle, and this time Donny howled with glee.

Molly raced across the desert as fast as her horse could carry her. *I'm coming, Donny. Hold on.* It was a beautiful warm day, the air crystal clear. Prairie dogs popped back into their holes as she raced by. Road-runners scurried to get out of her way. A turkey vulture circled overhead. Hurry, hurry. Had to keep going. Couldn't stop.

Taking care of Donny and working on the ranch was harder than she ever imagined. She was never at the right place at the right time. Whenever Ruckus or O.T. or Brodie needed her help with the horses or cattle, she was with Donny. Likewise, whenever

Donny wanted her, she was either riding the range or knee-deep in muck.

Poor Donny sometimes had to wait for hours before she could take him to the privy or move him to another location. He never complained, at least not verbally, but she sensed his anger and resentment increasing daily and this only added to her guilt.

She must have been out of her mind to think she could work on the ranch and still care for her brother. She wasn't even certain that the desert air was any more beneficial to Donny's lungs than Colorado's thin, dry air had been. Donny's wheezing spells seemed to be getting worse, not better, and it had done nothing to help her own night-time cough left over from the fires.

Nearing the ranch house, she spotted the doctor's automobile parked in front and alarm shot through her. Whenever the doctor came to check on Miss Walker's horse, he parked by the barn. Was something the matter with Donny?

Galloping up to the open gate, her jaw dropped. The doctor ran around the court-yard at full speed, pushing her brother's wheelchair, the little fluffy dog yipping at his heels. Yelling at the top of his lungs, Dr. Fairbanks made funny rumbling sounds. Had he gone mad?

119

She opened her mouth to protest but nothing came out. Instead, her thoughts whirled back in time to the day she stood watching in horror as her baby brother's carriage rolled down a hill. She was only eight at the time, but she remembered that day as if it were only yesterday.

Shaking the memory away, she yelled for the doctor to stop, but all the whooping, barking, laughing, and rattling of the wheelchair drowned out her voice.

She rode her horse into the courtyard. "Stop!" she shouted. "Do you hear me? Stop!"

Caleb halted the wheelchair and Donny's laughter faded away. All three males including the dog stared up at her.

She slid out of her saddle and wrapped the reins around the hitching post. Turning to face the doctor, she planted her hands at her waist. "What is the matter with you? He . . . he could have fallen." Even with the best of conditions the chair wasn't all that stable and had tipped over several times in the past.

Dr. Fairbanks frowned. "We were just having fun."

She glared up at him. He was even taller than she remembered and she was forced to lean her head back to meet his gaze. His poor judgment only confirmed her earlier opinion of his ability as a doctor. "At the risk of further injury?"

The doctor stepped away from the wheelchair. "It's true that your brother's well-being is endangered, but it's not from having fun."

"The only danger to my brother is you." If starting a stampede wasn't bad enough, now this. Donny let out a long, hacking cough. Worried, she hurried to his side. "Are you all right?"

His face scarlet, veins standing out on his neck, he didn't answer.

"Come on, I'll take you to your room." Grabbing the push handle, she wheeled him to the steps and stopped. Three steps. Only three steps led to the verandah, but they looked as formidable as a prison wall. Nothing made mountains out of molehills faster than a wheelchair.

Without a word, Dr. Fairbanks laid his hand on hers. "Let me."

His touch sent warm currents up her arm. Cheeks flaring, she let go of the wheelchair and stepped aside. With seemingly little effort, he turned the chair around, tilted it, and pulled it up the steps on its tiny back wheel with an ease Molly could only envy.

She followed behind. Reaching for the

pitcher on the table, she poured a glass of water and handed it to her brother. He took a sip and his coughed improved, but his chest rose and fell at an alarming rate.

"Thank you," she said to the doctor, her voice cool. "I can manage from here."

Dr. Fairbanks touched her arm, drawing her gaze to his. "I want to help. Your brother's condition will continue to deteriorate without medical intervention."

Overly aware of his touch, she moved away. "You know nothing about my brother's condition." Or history.

It had been a tough morning and she had no desire to argue. Everything she did that morning, from chasing calves to repairing fences, had met with criticism. She wasn't about to stand still while Dr. Caleb Fairbanks found fault with the way she cared for her brother.

"I know enough," he said. "I know that your brother has a partial lumbar spinal injury."

"If you know that much, then you must know his prognosis."

"Yes, but I can still help him if you'll let me."

She inhaled. She wanted to believe him, to believe that what he said was true. But there had been too many medical disappointments in the past. Too many broken promises. Too many times she'd seen her brother's hopes dashed, had her own spirit crushed. Right now it was all she could do to get through each day.

"I appreciate your concern but —"

The doctor pressed on. "We know a lot more today about such injuries, much more than we knew even a few years ago. I've witnessed some amazing results following manual therapy and —"

"The last doctor who suggested manual therapy wanted to whip his legs with a willow stick." The memory alone made her shudder.

"I would never hurt your brother."

Something in his voice — perhaps sincerity — made her study him. He really did have a kind face, a pleasant, open expression. She couldn't imagine him hurting anyone.

"Can you make him walk again?" she asked. "Can you do that?"

"No. I can't do that."

It wasn't what she wanted to hear, but at least he spoke the truth. Perhaps she had misjudged him. He was nothing like the charlatans in Dobson Creek who promised cures.

"Thank you for your honesty," she said

and she meant it. "But my brother has been through a lot these past few weeks. I don't know if you heard about the Dobson Creek fire." Donny still suffered nightmares from the fire. They both did. He didn't need the added stress of working with a doctor. Especially when there was no reason to believe that any sort of therapy would help.

"I heard about it," the doctor said. "About your brother —"

"My mind's made up." Was it his gentle tone or compassionate expression that made her perilously close to breaking down? "We have nothing more to discuss."

Not wanting to make a fool of herself, she gave the wheelchair an abrupt turn and pushed her brother into the house. "Good day, Doctor."

CHAPTER 10

"Come on, boy." Caleb lifted Magic out of the car and set him on the ground and together they walked into the blacksmith shop. They were greeted by a growling wolf-dog baring his teeth. Magic didn't know enough to be intimidated or even step back. Instead he perked his ears and gave a single bark in greeting.

The owner, a tall clean-shaven man dressed in a leather apron, greeted Caleb with a nod of his head. "That's enough, Homer." The wolf-dog stopped growling, but his golden-eyed gaze remained on the small pooch.

"I'm Dr. Fairbanks," Caleb said. "I'm staying with your aunt and uncle."

The smithy set his hammer on his work-bench, wiped his hands on a rag, and walked toward Caleb with an extended arm. "Been meaning to stop by and welcome you. Aunt Bessie told me she had taken in a boarder. Call me Luke. That there is Homer," he said, indicating the dog sniffing out Magic. The tails of both dogs wagged like two trainmen signaling one another.

Caleb shook Luke's hand before petting the larger dog. "Call me Caleb. That there is Magic."

"Pleased to know you." Luke glanced at the ball of fluff that was weaving in and out of Homer's legs. "How do you like livin' with my aunt and uncle?"

"Couldn't be happier. Your aunt is a terrific cook."

Luke grinned. "That she is. She also tends to interfere in everybody's business, and that means she's gonna meddle aplenty in yours."

"I'm afraid she'll be sorely disappointed. I don't have any business worth meddling into."

"Trust me, my aunt will find business that you didn't even know you had. You're safe for a while 'cause I'm getting married in a couple of weeks. Aunt Bessie's up to her brow in wedding preparations. Never knew taking a wife required so much fuss."

"Congratulations," Caleb said. "Married men seem to have less medical complaints than bachelors — along with less money."

Luke grinned. "I guess you gotta take the

126

good with the bad. What can I do for you?"

"I've been trying to get over here for days but my patients keep me hopping. Do you know anything about horseless carriages?"

Luke leaned against his workbench, arms folded. "Can't say that I do. Yours is the first one I've ever seen. You think they'll ever replace horses?"

"Money alone says they will. It's cheaper to run an automobile than to feed a horse, and parts can be replaced. A horseless buggy can outlast several horses, and if it breaks down you don't have to shoot it."

This brought a hearty laugh from the smithy. Pleased at finding an appreciative audience, Caleb continued, "That's not all. It's got a two-horse power engine and can go fifteen miles an hour providing the road is smooth and I'm going downhill."

Luke gave a low whistle. "I reckon that can make a big difference between life and death in a medical emergency."

Caleb nodded. "It sure can. The problem is, it tends to backfire and I don't know how to stop it. People hearing it think it's gunfire. I've already been shot at twice since arriving in town." A vision of a certain green-eyed beauty came to mind, which almost made him lose his train of thought. "The marshal just threatened to put me in jail for disturbing the peace. Would you look at it and tell me what you think?"

"I'll look, but like I said, I don't know nothin' about 'em." Luke followed Caleb outside.

In the short time that Caleb had been in the shop, someone had attached a big satin bow to the rear. He couldn't help but laugh. The entire town was practically covered in them.

"I'm afraid if I stand still for too long, your aunt will attach a bow to me," Caleb joked.

"There's no stopping Aunt Bessie," Luke said with obvious fondness. He walked around Bertha, checking her out from top to bottom. "That's a mighty good-looking piece of equipment, even without the bow. Why did you choose a gasoline engine over steam?"

"It's more economical to run," Caleb explained. "And there's less chance of fire. You can also start it quicker." It would take almost a half hour to heat water sufficiently to start a steam engine. A doctor on call couldn't afford to waste that amount of time.

"So when does it backfire?" Luke asked.

"Sometimes when I'm cranking it up. Other times it backfires for no good reason.

Mostly when I stop."

Luke stepped back. "Crank her up and let's see what we have."

Caleb slid the L-shaped pipe into the hole in front and turned it with all five fingers on one side of the handle for safety. The sparking device ignited with a bang, throwing the crank backward. Caleb was able to pull his hand back in time — but barely.

Hands on his waist, Luke shook his head. "Whoo-eee. That *fly*wheel sure does live up to its name." He lifted his voice to be heard over the loud rumbling sound.

Caleb rubbed his wrist. "It's a wonder I haven't lost an arm."

Bertha backfired and Luke jumped. Homer lowered his tail and darted through the open door of his owner's establishment. A woman coming out of Green's merchandise store dropped her basket of groceries and fled inside.

Magic pawed Caleb's trouser leg, ready for a ride, and Caleb lifted him into the back of the car.

Luke seemed oblivious to anything but the problem at hand. Dropping to his knees, he peered into the crankshaft opening. He struck Caleb as a man who did everything with careful consideration.

Luke waved his hand, indicating he was

finished, and Caleb turned off the engine. "So what do you think?"

"Sounds like too much fuel's getting into the sparking device." Elbow resting on his arm, Luke stroked his chin. "If we can figure out how to control the fuel, it should solve the problem."

Caleb nodded. "I'd sure appreciate anything you can do."

"I can also make a brace to keep the crank from kicking back. Probably won't keep you from gettin' shot, but it'll save you from a broken arm or two."

"I guess that's better than nothing," Caleb said. "Can you do anything about those bullet holes?"

"I'll see what I can do. I've got some orders ahead of you that I have to finish today. I can work on it tomorrow. Meanwhile, I'll figure out how to make a brace to keep the flywheel stable."

Caleb thanked him and bent in front of Bertha. A woman gasped and he looked up to see an audience staring at him. "It's perfectly safe," he assured the crowd. "Nothing to be afraid of. Now stand back." He waved his arm. "Stand waaay back."

Cactus Patch had a problem, which meant that Bessie Adams had a problem. Now that the nice doctor was staying at her house, she actually had two problems. For sure as the sky was blue the dear man needed a wife, but with the long hours he worked, he'd never find one on his own.

It was up to Bessie to find him the right woman, and that she had every intention of doing, *after* her nephew's wedding. First things first.

"I think you're making a big deal out of nothing," her sister, Lula-Belle, said that Tuesday morning after Bessie poured out her heart around the kitchen table. She was younger than Bessie by two years, but you'd never know it by her old-fashioned thinking. The drab clothes and tight corkscrew curls Lula-Belle favored didn't just assert prudery but a closed mind as well. The only concession Lula-Belle made to fashion was her ridiculous feathered hats.

"Nothing?" Bessie threw up her hands. She had just explained that the town's drinking problems could ruin Kate's and Luke's wedding, and all her sister could say was nothing?

Lula-Belle's mouth puckered. "I don't see what business it is of yours what men do with their time."

Bessie reached for the pitcher of lemonade. "Do you want Harvey Winkleman to

pass out at the piano like he did at Roy
Trumble's funeral?" Mercy. With all the
inebriated men at the funeral, it was a
miracle the undertaker didn't bury the
wrong person.

"There's nothing you can do about it,"
Lula-Belle said.

"Nonsense. There's plenty I can do."
Bessie filled Lula-Belle's glass. "I'm going
to insist that every saloon close the night
before the wedding. That way, not only will
our singer and pianist be sober, but the
guests will be too."

Lula-Belle's eyes opened wide. "How in
heaven's name do you plan to do that?"

"I don't know yet, but I'll figure out a
way."

Lula-Belle's springy curls bounced all over
her shaking head. "Every time you get a bee
in your bonnet, something goes wrong."

Bessie filled her own glass. "That's not
true."

"Isn't it? What about the time you decided
we needed to make our husbands take
notice of us? When you started getting all
fancied up, Sam thought you were sweet on
another man and it almost broke up your
marriage."

"This is different." Bessie set the pitcher
down. "This isn't about me. It's about our

nephew's wedding."

Lula-Belle reached for her glass. "I have a bad feeling about this."

"Oh butterball. You have a bad feeling about everything."

Molly hesitated in front of Donny's door, her heart heavy. Popping a lemon drop in her mouth to soothe her scratchy throat, she braced herself with a deep breath and knocked.

"Come in." His muffled voice sounded a mile away.

He lay faceup on the bed where she'd left him hours earlier. He didn't even bother to look at her when she entered the room. Instead he continued to stare at the ceiling, his face bathed in the yellow light of the kerosene lamp.

"Are you still angry with me?"

Donny said nothing and the silence was like a wall between them.

She sat on the edge of the bed and the springs squeaked beneath her weight. It hurt to stand but it even hurt to sit, and she rubbed her back. Never had she worked as hard as she had these last two weeks. She longed to collapse in bed but not before making peace with her brother.

Donny turned his head, his eyes dull as

tarnished copper. "Why won't you let the doctor help me?"

She inhaled. "Donny, you mean the world to me. If I lost you . . ." Nightmares of the fire continued to plague her. In her dreams she hadn't been able to reach him and she continued to wake every night in a cold sweat. "Dr. Fairbanks had no right to jeopardize your safety."

"He looks at me like a real person."

"You *are* a real person."

"Then stop looking at me like I'm some poor helpless child!"

She withered beneath his hostile look. "That's not how I think of you. It's not, Donny. Honest."

He stared at her but said nothing, and suddenly he didn't look like the boy she'd known so well — the boy she loved and cared for. Instead he looked like a stranger.

She'd noticed the physical changes — the chin stubble. The way his trousers barely reached midcalf. Then there was all that voice-cracking as he changed from tenor to baritone. She had become an expert at averting her eyes when she dressed him, looking away at just the right moment when he bathed. But this went far beyond bodily changes. It was as if he was about to cross some invisible line and leave her behind.

"You're smart and bright . . ." She reached for a dog-eared journal. "You have to be to understand this." Donny enjoyed reading his science magazines aloud and explaining the technical terms to her. "Read to me."

"I don't want to read."

"Then I'll read to you." She flipped through the pages. " 'It has long been imagined that the phenomenon of comet's tails is in some way due to a solar electrical repulsion.' " She looked up. "This makes my head want to explode."

"It's better than those sappy dime novels you read." He hugged himself and made a loud kissing sound to imitate a lurid cover.

"They're not sappy . . . Besides," she added with more than a little regret, "I'm too busy to read." The key to their future was the ranch. She could no longer waste time reading about true love. Such things existed only in books.

She tossed the journal on the bedside table and turned off the lamp.

"Molly."

"Yes?"

"When Dr. Fairbanks pushed me around the courtyard, it felt like I had legs."

She gripped the door handle and tried to breathe. The doctor had no right to interfere and had only made things worse. When she was only ten, a wealthy woman had invited her and the other miners' children to a grand house for Christmas dinner. Molly had never known people lived in such luxury, and the experience made it harder than ever to go back to the tent she called home. Sometimes ignorance really was bliss.

"Good night," she whispered.

CHAPTER 11

It was a hot Sunday morning but a slight breeze made the heat bearable and kept the flies away. Nearly three weeks had passed since Molly and Donny had arrived at the ranch, and it was hard to believe it was the middle of June already. Brodie said that July was the beginning of monsoon season, marked by high temperatures, wind, and rain, but for now the skies were clear.

Once she settled Donny on the verandah, Molly stood by his side and stretched, filling her lungs with fresh air.

After nonstop training of horses, rounding up cattle, and cleaning stables, things had finally settled down. The boss lady had left the previous day for Tombstone for a meeting about range rights and wouldn't be back until day after tomorrow.

Molly always knew when Miss Walker was gone. The cowboys behaved more leisurely, their usual stoic faces giving way to laughter as they joked among themselves. Even the horses seemed more relaxed, grazing peacefully . . . all except the little horse Donny called Orbit. The colt continued his strange habit of stepping sideways with his hind legs, his body circling around his lowered head. She still didn't know why he did it but she enjoyed watching him.

Laughing at Orbit's antics, she lifted her face to the sun, her eyes closed.

If she was lucky enough to inherit the ranch, this was how she would run it. She'd want the cowboys to call her Molly, not Miss Hatfield, and no one would have to wait for *her* to leave the ranch to take a day off from all but necessary chores. She shook the thought away. What good was it to dream? If the last couple of weeks were any indication, her chances of becoming Miss Walker's heiress were nil. Even Brodie said as much. Without the ranch she'd have nowhere to turn, no place to go.

Her gaze roamed over the land that, in a very short time, she'd come to love. She still couldn't get over the wide-open spaces. The vivid blue stretched from the yellows and pinks of the early morning sunrise all the way to the reds and oranges of the setting sun.

She no longer missed Dobson Creek, and

that surprised her. She didn't even miss the amazing variety of songbirds or the wild asters, lupines, and Indian paintbrushes that grew there. The desert flowers were so much more colorful and interesting. The blooms of the oddly shaped saguaros opened only after dark, and the waxy white and yellow flowers filled the night air with sweet fragrance. She especially liked the bright red ocotillo flowers.

God, this is the only real home we've ever known. Please don't let me mess it up. Whether or not God was listening or even cared, talking to Him was still a habit and brought her a measure of comfort.

Her prayer fell away with a sigh and she regarded her brother's sullen expression. "What do you want to do today?"

"Nothing," Donny muttered.

"We could play checkers." That never failed to cheer him, probably because she always let him win. "Or we could read to each other."

"I told you I don't want to do anything."

She chewed on her bottom lip. It seemed a pity to waste a whole day doing nothing. Earlier Ruckus had invited her to go to church with him and his wife, but she had declined. That was the last place she wanted to go.

She turned toward the house but a faint rumble made her stop. *Dr. Fairbanks.*

A strange fluttery feeling rushed through her. What was he doing here? He didn't generally check on Miss Walker's horse on a Sunday.

Like a protective mother, her first thought was to take Donny inside away from the doctor's prying eyes. She would have done exactly that had her brother not brightened and waved his arms to gain the doctor's attention.

Stunned by the sudden change in Donny, she swung her gaze to the road. Dr. Fairbanks pulled up in front of the house amid a cloud of smoke. The auto coughed and sputtered before finally falling quiet.

"Miss Hatfield. Donny," he called, waving. He jumped to the ground and bounded through the gate and courtyard and up the verandah steps, his dog at his heels. Appearing to be in jovial spirits, he tipped his hat and ruffled Donny's hair, making her brother grin.

Molly stooped to pet the fluffy ball greeting her with wagging tail.

"He's adorable," she said and laughed when the little dog tried to lick her face. It wasn't the kind of dog she'd expect a tall masculine man like the doctor to own.

"What's his name?"

"Magic," Dr. Fairbanks said. "And before you say anything, I didn't name him. In fact, I didn't even choose him. He chose me."

"Come here, boy," Donny called and Magic sprinted toward his chair.

Molly straightened. "He chose you?"

"Actually, I think he chose Bertha. I originally planned to drive all the way to Cactus Patch, so I stopped to purchase gasoline. When I wasn't looking, Magic somehow managed to climb into the car and curl up in the backseat. I didn't discover him there until twenty miles later. I turned around and drove all the way back to find his owner."

Molly studied the doctor with interest. Not many men would bother driving twenty miles to return a lost dog.

The doctor continued, "Unfortunately, Magic's owner had joined the Lord a week prior."

"So you decided to keep him."

He regarded her with clear, observant eyes. "It was more like he decided to keep me."

She glanced at her brother, who held Magic on his lap. "I guess that makes you a kept man."

"I've been called a lot worse." The corner

of the doctor's mouth quirked upward. "I hoped I'd find you here. I came to offer you both a ride to church."

It was the second invitation to church that day, but coming from the doctor it was even less welcome. Not only was the man a menace, he was unpredictable.

"You put my brother in danger, not once but twice. What makes you think I would go anywhere with you?"

Certainly not church. It had been years since she stepped foot in one. Not since her father's funeral. The elders explained that the presence of a dance hall girl would upset the delicate sensibilities of the town's "respectable citizens." For that reason, she was made to stand outside and peer through the open doorway with her brother. After the funeral she never went back.

"I came to apologize for my reckless behavior and am willing to be forgiven," the doctor said.

She might have been more ready to forgive had it not been for the twinkle in his eyes.

"Your idea of apologizing leaves a lot to be desired," she said. "And no, I will not go to church with you." God she might trust; church she did not.

"I originally intended to invite you both for an afternoon drive." Caleb flashed a devastating grin, teeth white next to his sun-bronzed skin. "I figured you'd say no to me, ma'am, but I didn't think you'd say no to the Lord."

"So now you presume to know how I think." She couldn't make up her mind whether to be annoyed or amused.

"If I'm wrong, I apologize." He tilted his head. "If not, your chariot awaits." He bowed from the waist. "And this charming and admittedly annoying driver is at your service."

She tried to maintain a cool demeanor but she had a hard time keeping a straight face. "Your modesty overwhelms me," she said. Why did she always feel like she was on the verge of losing control in his presence?

His grin widened. "I'll have to be more careful in the future. Did you know that modesty ruins more kidneys than whiskey?"

Donny gazed up at the doctor, his eyes bright with admiration. "And did you know that the moon has caused more insanity than syphilis?"

Molly's mouth dropped open. "Donny! We mustn't talk of such things."

Donny didn't look the least bit chagrined. "It's true."

"I believe it is, but your sister is right. Such talk should be left to doctors, moral reformers, and rumormongers." Caleb gave Donny's shoulder an affectionate squeeze and turned his attention to Molly. "About church . . . it's not every Sunday that the circuit preacher is in town."

"Sorry, not interested, but thank you anyway." She turned toward the house.

"I am."

Her brother's voice stopped her in her tracks. She stared at him in astonishment. "You never wanted to go to church before."

He glanced at the doctor. "I do now."

She leaned over the wheelchair and lowered her voice. "Remember what happened last time we went to church?"

"He'll protect us," Donny whispered back.

She caught her breath. Not only did Donny's faith in the doctor surprise her, but it was woefully misplaced.

"So what's the verdict?" Dr. Fairbanks asked.

She straightened. "Perhaps another time." She started toward the door again but Donny grabbed her skirt, beseeching her. They stared at each other for a moment before he released her.

"You don't have to come if you don't want to," he said.

She could hardly believe her ears. He was dismissing her? Just like that?

She met the doctor's gaze. His serious expression could not hide the warm light of triumph in his eyes. He had her over a barrel and he knew it.

"Your brother will be perfectly safe with me if you choose not to come." When she made no reply he added, "You can trust me."

Trust this man with Donny? How could she? At the moment she was having trouble trusting herself with him. The man could charm the bark off a tree.

"I'll go to church with you," she said. "I . . . just need to change." Her divided skirt and man's shirt would hardly pass muster in polite company, let alone church.

She dashed inside and up the stairs before realizing she was shaking. Her nerves were due to the prospect of walking into a church after she swore never to set foot in one again, and had nothing — absolutely nothing — to do with the kindhearted doctor.

If only she didn't feel that she was about to travel down an unfamiliar and maybe even a dangerous path.

CHAPTER 12

The vehicle jiggled, shimmied, and bounced down the bumpy road and it was all Molly could do to hang on or risk being tossed in the air.

Horseless carriage indeed! A bone-shaking monster was more like it. Why, oh why, had she agreed to ride in this dreadful, awful thing?

She gripped the side until her knuckles turned white, but nothing could prevent her teeth from rattling. But that wasn't the worst of it. Engine smoke stung her eyes and her throat closed in protest. The sickly reek of gasoline fumes and burning rubber made her want to gag. Ear-splitting vibrations pounded her head.

None of it seemed to bother her brother sitting in the backseat holding Magic in his arms. His smile reached from ear to ear.

Molly was just about to fling herself over the side when, mercifully, they pulled up to the church. Dr. Fairbanks parked behind a row of carriages, drawing curious stares from people standing outside. The engine made a strange choking sound before convulsing to a stop.

Molly slumped against the seat, fanning herself with her hand. Her stomach churned but whether from motion sickness or anxiety, she couldn't say. Probably both.

It was a surprisingly large church given the size of the town. The high adobe steeple looked like hands lifted in prayer. Stained-glass windows circled the building and a tidy cemetery spread out like a board game in back, the gravestones staggered like chessmen.

The doctor jumped to the ground and hurried around the front of the vehicle to her side. "See? Nothing to worry about. I got you both here safe and sound."

The quirk of his mouth told her he was enjoying himself at her expense. He held out his hand to help her from the buggy.

She took her time before placing her hand in his. "That . . . was the worst ride I've . . . ever . . . had," she huffed.

He leaned forward to whisper in her ear, his breath sending warm and surprisingly pleasant shivers down her spine. "Don't let Bertha hear you say that. You'll hurt her feelings."

She lowered her foot to the ground and, distracted by his nearness, lost her balance. His large hands nearly circled her narrow waist as he lifted her the rest of the way down, holding her in his arms until she gained her footing.

Before she had time to recover from the ride — or maybe even his touch — he had already reached for the wheelchair tied to the back.

Straightening her tilted blue hat that matched her bright blue frock, she swallowed hard in an effort to brace herself for the inevitable stares. Already a crowd gathered around them, but much to her surprise no one seemed to notice either her or Donny. Men, women, children — everyone — all gawked at the motor buggy.

"I say, old chap, how fast does it go?" asked a man with a British accent and dressed in a pin-striped suit and derby hat.

"Fifteen miles an hour on good roads," the doctor replied as he transported Donny from the backseat of the auto to the wheelchair. Molly envied the ease with which he was able to move her brother so quickly and smoothly while she had to struggle, more now than when he was younger.

A white-haired man discounted the claim

with a wave of his hand. "A horse can go that fast."

"Indefinitely?" Dr. Fairbanks asked.

"Of course not," the man admitted.

"I can go that speed for as long as the fuel lasts. Ten, twelve hours, it doesn't matter." His statement was met with a murmur of amazement.

A white-haired matron examined Bertha through a tortoiseshell lorgnette. "Unbelievable."

A man held a hearing horn to the side of the auto as if he expected it to say something. "Incredible."

Dr. Fairbanks pushed Donny's wheelchair away from the crowd. An older woman, dressed in a plum-colored gown better suited to someone half her age, broke away from a knot of people standing off to the side and hurried to greet them.

"There you are," she said to the doctor. She clapped her hands together and her triple chins shook like a stack of books about to topple over. Her felt sugar-bowl hat was surprisingly plain with none of the feathers or froufrou of other women's hats.

"I heard you leave the house early and I thought you had a medical emergency." Her gaze swept Molly up and down, curiosity carved into every buttery line of her pleasant face.

"Mrs. Adams, I want you to meet Miss Hatfield and her brother, Donny."

Mrs. Adams extended a bejeweled hand. "Pleased to meet you." She nodded at Donny. "You too, young man. But please, everyone calls me Aunt Bessie."

"She insists upon being called *aunt* whether or not you're related to her," Dr. Fairbanks explained in an aside.

Molly shook the woman's hand. "Please call me Molly."

Aunt Bessie was one of the few people who looked Donny in the eye. That alone would have been enough to earn Molly's approval if the woman's brightly colored dress hadn't already done so.

"Dr. Fairbanks was good enough to give us a ride to church," Molly said politely.

"Dr. Fairbanks is what his patients call him. You are obviously a friend and should call him by his given name, Caleb."

Molly blushed. "Well, I —"

"Molly," Caleb said, obviously approving the use of first names, "is staying at the ranch."

"Oh, so you're the one," Aunt Bessie exclaimed. "I heard Miss Walker had another heiress. That makes how many now?" She looked to Caleb for an answer but he simply shrugged.

"Don't ask me, I'm new in town," Caleb said.

"It's at least eight or nine," Aunt Bessie said in a chatty tone that suggested she had much to say on the subject. "Most didn't last but a day or two. Except for Kate Tenney, now betrothed to my nephew. You must meet her. I'm sure you two will have a lot to talk about."

"I'd like that," Molly said, though she had little time to socialize.

"She's a writer, you know," Aunt Bessie continued, lowering her voice to a conspirator's whisper. "She writes *dime* novels. You'll love the one that was banned in Boston."

Molly tried to suppress a giggle but couldn't. She'd never expected to meet anyone quite like the older woman, certainly not in church.

In a louder voice Aunt Bessie said, "You must come to the wedding. Your brother too. I'll send you an invitation."

Molly had no intention of attending the wedding, but Aunt Bessie was so warm and friendly she couldn't bring herself to decline, at least not to her face. Better to drop her a polite note later. "Thank you."

"Come along or all the good seats will be taken." Aunt Bessie slipped an arm through

Molly's and whispered, "You must tell me your secret for such lovely pink cheeks and red lips. Is it beet juice?"

"Carmine," Molly whispered back.

Aunt Bessie blinked. "Really? But it looks so natural."

"You have to brush it on with a light hand," Molly explained. Until recently, only actresses and prostitutes openly wore face paint. Respectable women wishing to obtain "natural beauty" were forced to kiss red crepe paper, pinch cheeks, and use burnt hair pins to darken lashes on the sly.

But that was gradually changing. Women in the workforce or living in large cities such as Denver shunned the pale skin that had been popular for most of the century. They openly wore rouge and tinted zinc oxide face powder, much to the disapproval of their elders. A woman could even purchase bust cream to enhance her figure.

"Where can I purchase carmine?" Aunt Bessie asked.

Molly was surprised by the question. Only young women painted. Surely Aunt Bessie wasn't serious about doing something that many still considered scandalous. "Montgomery Ward now carries cosmetics," Molly whispered back.

Aunt Bessie's eyes grew round as a child's

on Christmas morn. "I had no idea you could order such things by mail. Whatever will they think of next?"

They entered the church and Aunt Bessie hurried off to join her husband while Molly followed Caleb.

"I really like her," Molly said. If only more church people were as down-to-earth and friendly.

He grinned. "She does tend to grow on you, doesn't she?"

Whispered voices spoken behind gloved hands floated to her in bits and pieces.

"Who is that?"

". . . looks like a harlot."

"The nerve . . . in a house of worship no less."

If Caleb hadn't already parked her brother's wheelchair next to a wall out of the way of traffic, she would have left right then and there. Instead she followed him and took her place at the end of the pew between Caleb and Donny.

The horseless carriage no longer a diversion, she and Donny were clearly the center of attention. All around them people whispered and stared, just like they did at the church back home.

The wheelchair never failed to solicit attention, but what would she have done without it? When she was fourteen and Donny six, she played hooky from school to travel to Denver. There she met with a doctor known for miracle cures — some of the miners swore by him. That doctor studied Donny's medical records but gave her no hope. He did, however, offer her the use of a chair with wheels that had belonged to his deceased grandfather. She hadn't even known that such a chair existed and was ecstatic.

People stared at her as she pushed that chair through the streets of Denver to the stage depot. At first the Concord driver refused to allow the chair on the crowded coach. But she insisted and he finally relented after she greased his palm with a gold coin. For most of the journey, she hung out the window to keep her eye on the chair rattling and jostling in back of the coach with each rut of the road.

As she feared, the chair eventually fell off and she banged on the roof with pounding fists until the driver stopped. By the time she'd retrieved it, the stage had left her behind. She was forced to walk the remaining five miles pushing the chair uphill all the way.

Sheer hope got her up that mountainside. She was so certain that the chair would make a difference in Donny's life she would have swum across the ocean to get it to him. But after their first outing, it was two years before he agreed to sit in the chair again. He didn't like people gawking at him.

She couldn't blame him. Whenever she saw someone staring at him, it nearly broke her heart. She hated for people to judge him flawed when in reality he was only flawed physically. He had a sharp and inquiring mind and a good heart, but few people ever bothered to see beyond his useless legs.

The woman sitting on the pew in front of them kept glancing back at Donny. Irritated, Molly didn't even bother to lower her voice. "What do you think you're staring at?" Subtlety never worked with rude people.

The woman's mouth dropped open and she quickly swung her head around to face the front of the church, the feathers on her hat vibrating with what Molly hoped was humiliation. "Well, I never!"

Caleb laid a hand on Molly's lap, startling her. "She doesn't mean anything by it," he whispered in her ear. "She's just curious."

She pushed his hand away but only because she feared its heat would burn a hole through the fabric of her skirt. "Curious my . . ." Molly bit down on her lips.

The piano music stopped and an inebriated man weaved his way across the altar. He was hatless, and if that wasn't disturbing enough, his uncombed hair fell about his head like scattered feathers. Equally shocking, he was shoeless and one big toe poked through a hole in his black woolen sock. He'd obviously entered the church by mistake.

"Why don't the ushers remove him?" she whispered.

"I guess they want to hear what Reverend Bland has to say."

She blinked. "That's the preacher?"

Caleb hushed her with a finger to his mouth and she fell silent.

Reverend Bland slumped onto the podium. "Wel . . . wel . . . wel . . . come," he slurred.

The congregation stirred uneasily and whispered among themselves.

Caleb's gaze remained riveted upon the preacher. "Someone better grab him before he falls."

No sooner had he spoken than Reverend Bland swayed like a tree in the wind. "Lest us bray."

Caleb jumped up and hurried to the altar, catching the preacher just in time. Ruckus joined him and the two of them carted him away.

"What are we going to do now?" someone asked.

"Who's gonna preach?" asked another.

A man rose in front. Minus one leg, he walked to the pulpit on crutches. He was a tall slender man with ebony skin, kinky black hair, and a soulful face.

"As many of you know, my name's Washington. Jacob Washington. I'm not an ordained minister and I don't know how to preach," he said. "But I can tell you how God worked in my life."

He spoke in a calm, smooth voice that would normally encourage sleep, but the congregation listened with rapt attention.

He told how at the age of fifteen he was brought to America as a slave. "I ran away but they caught me and cut off my leg so I couldn't run again. But that didn't stop me. Nothing could do that because I had God on my side."

Molly glanced at her brother, who seemed completely captivated by the man and all that he uttered.

Caleb returned while the ushers took up the collection. "Is Reverend Bland all right?" she whispered.

"He will be. We took him to the infirmary to sleep it off."

"There's an infirmary in town?" she asked.

"It's actually a hotel room that's reserved for medical emergencies."

While the collection plate made its rounds, Mr. Washington sang. His voice was smooth as velvet, yet so haunting that it sent goose bumps down Molly's spine. "Swing low, sweet chariot . . . coming for to carry me home . . ."

Oh, if only she could sing like that.

Her brother gripped the arms of his chair, his knuckles white. "Is something the matter?" she whispered.

Donny looked at her. "He only has one leg. But I hardly noticed."

"Sometimes I don't notice yours either," she said.

"Yes, you do. You always notice."

She sucked in her breath and Caleb laid his hand on hers. "You okay?"

No, she was not okay. She felt the walls of the church closing in on her and she wanted to leave. "What you said about helping my brother," she whispered. "Did you mean it?"

Caleb's gaze met hers. "I can't make him walk again," he said, "but I can help him become more independent."

She pressed her lips together and blinked back a tear. Dare she believe him? Dare she chance more disappointment and discouragement?

158

A respectful silence followed Mr. Washington's song. He accepted the collection from the ushers and addressed the congregation.

"That beautiful hymn you just heard was originally meant as a secret code. It was how we black folks announced the arrival of 'conductors' to escort us slaves to the North. We had codes for everything disguised in hymns. When an attempt at freedom failed . . . when we had to regroup spiritually . . . when one of our brothers made it to the holy land . . . there was a hymn for every occurrence. We passed on good news and bad while singing God's praises.

"The Underground Railroad freed me from a plantation down south, but it is God that frees our hearts and souls." He lifted the collection basket aloft. "I'm living proof that all things are possible with God."

She glanced at Donny's profile. *"You always notice."* His words pierced her heart even as she thought about them. She leaned toward Caleb and whispered, "If . . . if I agree to let you help my brother . . . when will you be able to start working with him?"

Caleb leaned forward to glance at Donny. "The work has already begun," he whispered back.

■ ■ ■ ■

That night Caleb found Reverend Bland sitting on the edge of the bed in the hotel room used as the infirmary. Elbows on his lap, the preacher held his head and rocked back and forth, moaning in despair.

Caleb approached the bed and the preacher glanced up. Tears rolled down his florid cheeks but he didn't speak.

Caleb sat by his side and waited for the man to calm down. No sense trying to talk to him in his current state.

The preacher was the first patient to use the room since Caleb had taken over Dr. Masterson's practice. Caleb paid a hotel maid extra to boil the sheets and put fresh straw in the mattress. The walls and ceiling had been disinfected with carbolic acid and the sweet smell still lingered in the air even though the windows had been kept open.

Caleb dreamed of the day he could build a small hospital or clinic in town. Right now his main concern was the anguished man by his side.

A good twenty minutes passed before Reverend Bland uttered his first words. "How could I have been so foolish?"

Caleb felt sorry for the man. He knew how

to help the preacher physically, but pain that came from a tortured soul was beyond medical capabilities.

"My daughter . . ." Reverend Bland sobbed out the words and fell silent.

"What about your daughter?" Caleb pressed gently.

For an answer the preacher reached into his pocket, pulled out a crumbled telegram, and thrust it into Caleb's hand.

Caleb carefully spread the crinkled yellow paper across his lap. It appeared to be from Bland's wife and read, in part, that their daughter Elizabeth had died from smallpox.

A heavy weight settled in Caleb's chest. "I'm sorry." They were perhaps the most ineffective words in the English language, but he couldn't think of anything else to say.

"I wasn't even there to send my little girl to heaven with a good-bye kiss," the preacher lamented. "Or to comfort my wife." A sob escaped him before he continued. "Instead of praying for my daughter's soul, I drank myself to oblivion. Will God ever forgive me?"

The question surprised Caleb. As a doctor he had many doubts. He doubted his own abilities and sometimes even doubted the effectiveness of the medicine he dispensed.

But wasn't a preacher supposed to be secure in his faith? Wasn't that a requisite for the job?

"Forgiveness is the wonder of God's grace," Caleb said. "Isn't that what you preach?"

"It's nice to know that someone pays attention to what I preach." Reverend Bland studied Caleb with bloodshot eyes. "I'm not worried about God, I'm worried about *them*." He tossed a nod toward the window and staggered to his feet.

"Whoa," Caleb said. "You're not going anywhere yet."

"I have to apologize. I need to go to every family and ask for forgiveness."

Caleb studied the man. Physically he was a mess, but he was in worse shape mentally. "All right, but I drive."

Reverend Bland squinted. "You're going to make me ride in that rattletrap of yours?"

Caleb nodded. "Trust me. Nothing cures a hangover faster than a ride in a horseless carriage." He grinned. "Consider it penance."

CHAPTER 13

Eleanor Walker glared across the oak table. Eastern investor Mason Hampshire sat directly opposite her, his head wreathed with smoke from his pipe. He was surrounded on both sides by a motley group of men. Those unable to find a seat leaned against the wall.

The number of people he brought along for support amused Eleanor. Obviously he considered her a formidable foe — and rightfully so.

She only wished she didn't have to travel to Tombstone to show him just how formidable she could be when the welfare of her ranch was threatened. Tombstone was the county seat and that meant the town took on an air of importance it didn't deserve. It didn't even allow weapons within city limits, which was preposterous. What could be more useful in settling land disputes than the presence of a firearm? She felt naked without one by her side.

The only woman in a room of more than a dozen men, she alone knew how to raise cattle. Mr. Hampshire was a fraud, his only goal greed. The easterners in their silk shirts, single-breasted vests, and frock coats mopped their brows with silk handkerchiefs and loosened ascot ties. Their soft, bloated bodies were better suited for the plush velvet settees of Victorian parlors than hard leather western saddles.

The room was hot and stuffy and filled with the blue haze of smoke. Meant to be used by a lawyer conferring with a single client, the office wasn't large enough to air mob grievances.

Robert sat by her side, thoughtfully stroking his goatee. Though she and her banker friend didn't always see eye to eye, he never failed to take her side when it most mattered. Publicly, at least, they were of one mind. For that reason she was grateful that he had agreed to accompany her to Tombstone, if for no other reason but to give his support.

Her lawyer, Jesse Barker, sat at the head of the table. Since he'd agreed to let the battling foes air their differences in his office, he maintained the right to lead the meeting.

He banged a gavel on the table though it was totally unnecessary. No one had said a word since shuffling into the room. He stuck a quizzing glass in his right eye and proceeded to read the document in hand. His plaid suit and handlebar mustache were better suited to a Barnum and Bailey sideshow, but his ability to turn even the most elementary phrase into legal folderol never failed to amaze.

After completing his opening remarks, he pulled the quizzing glass away and glanced around the table. "Who would like to begin?"

Hampshire stood. "I will," he said, speaking in a New England accent. A robust, clean-shaven man with small beady eyes and hair plastered down with bay rum, he looked like a gambler on a winning streak. His gold watch chain spanned the front of his shiny vest from right pocket to left, looping through a buttonhole halfway between. He could command his men with a look or a snap of the fingers. Such was his authority that even the Arizona soil knew not to stray onto the polished toes of his spatted boots.

Someone pushed a document in front of him and he began to speak. "I plan to purchase several smaller ranches and combine them into one company. This will accommodate" — he glanced at the paperwork in front of him — "twenty thousand head of cattle. Though not as large as the C Company up north, it's an ambitious plan and I resent Miss Walker's claim that it would ruin the land. I see no justification for it. Anyone who thinks otherwise is a doddering fool." He took his seat.

Barker turned to Eleanor. "Miss Walker. Would you care to respond?"

"Of course I'll respond. That's why I'm here." Eleanor stood. She didn't need any prompt or document to say what *she* had to say. "This is not Montana or Wyoming, where it takes only forty acres to raise a single head of cattle. This is Arizona — a desert. Thanks to the ranches you referred to, the land is already overstocked, allowing little more than five acres per cow."

"And what would be a more reasonable number?" one of Mason Hampshire's associates asked.

Eleanor shot him a cold stare. "Ideally, I'd say sixty-five acres per cattle head. Fifty acres at the very least."

"Nonsense!" Hampshire thundered, banging his fist on the table.

"How do you expect anyone to make a profit?" someone shouted from the back of the room.

"You're not trying to make a profit," Eleanor said coolly, refusing to lose her composure. "You're trying to get rich while ruining the land for everyone else."

"That's ridiculous." A bald-headed man shot to his feet and pumped his fist in the air. "There's plenty of grass for everyone."

"That's only because we've had more rain than usual this past year," Eleanor argued. "I lost more than half my cattle in the last drought. Every rancher around here did. We all stand to lose many times that in the next drought if this overgrazing continues."

Everyone started talking at once. The lawyer pounded his gavel several times before restoring peace. "Let me clearly state the issue here so there's no misunderstanding what's at stake," he said, as if there could be any question. He then proceeded to complicate matters with a barrage of legal terms, turning overgrazing the land into a twenty-minute discourse punctuated with *therefores* and *wherebys*.

The moment he paused for breath everyone began talking at once.

"One at a time," he shouted with a bang of his gavel. "Miss Walker?"

Eleanor waited until she had everyone's attention before beginning. "I propose that before any decision is made, we form a cattle owners' association similar to the Cattle Raisers Association in Texas and invite every interested party to join."

Since organizing, Texan cattlemen had done an outstanding job stopping cattle rustling in the Lone Star state. A similar organization was clearly needed in Arizona Territory.

"If we all work together," she continued, "I'm certain we can come to some sort of agreement on how to raise cattle, stop cattle rustling, *and* protect the land."

She sat and glanced at Robert, who inclined his silver head. "I can't see you joining an association," he whispered.

She gave a slight shrug and said nothing. Forming an association such as she proposed would take time, perhaps even months, and she counted on that. Maybe by then the eastern investors would turn their sights elsewhere.

"I think a cattle association is a splendid idea," Barker said. Judging by her opponent's face, he didn't share the lawyer's enthusiasm for her idea. "I suggest we adjourn for lunch and discuss it further this afternoon."

"I suggest we adjourn permanently," Hampshire said.

Eleanor was inclined to agree. The meeting was a waste of time, with neither side willing to budge.

Barker glared at him. "Unless you wish to pay for my time, you'll show up after lunch."

Hampshire made no reply. Instead he stood and walked out of the room, followed by his men.

"What do you think?" she asked Robert as they left the lawyer's office.

"I think you're fighting a losing battle," he replied.

She arched an eyebrow. "Is that your idea of supporting me?"

"You wouldn't ask my opinion if you didn't want the truth."

He was right, of course. She trusted Ruckus and O.T. and even that new man, Brodie, but they were more inclined to tell her what she wanted to hear. "So what do you think I should do?"

"I don't know that there's anything you *can* do. You're waging a war against greed and I'm not sure that's a war you can win."

"If I don't win, the loser will be the land itself. If it's a war they want, it's a war they'll get."

Robert gave her a sideways glance. "I think you should sell the ranch."

She shook her head. She'd sooner set fire to the ranch than sell it. "After everything

I've been through these last forty years, do you honestly think I'd give up the ranch because of a greedy investor? Besides, I have a new girl to consider." To be honest, she should have let Molly go by now, but something held Eleanor back. Maybe she felt sorry for her. Or her brother. Good heavens! Could she be growing soft in her old age? Surely not!

"You can't blame me for trying." He crooked his elbow and she slipped her arm through his. Together they strolled along Allen toward Fourth Street.

He picked up the conversation. "It's not just eastern investors you're battling, it's changing times. I'm not sure that you're willing to be swept along with the tide."

"Some change is good," she said. "If it wasn't for the railroad, we'd still be making those long, weary cattle drives to Kansas."

"I suspect railroads will be the least of it. The new doctor in town is convinced that hooves are in danger of being replaced by rubber tires."

"Nonsense. No one in his right mind would choose rubber over steak."

He chuckled. "I was talking about horses," he said. "Speaking of steak, I could use a good sirloin about now. I have it on the best authority that the Can Can serves only the finest meat."

Eleanor smiled. She wouldn't think of eating anywhere that didn't serve Last Chance beef.

They reached the Can Can on the corner of Fourth. A billboard outside read "Fresh oysters and game in season." Humph. She would have to talk to the manager about advertising oysters over her beef.

Seemingly unaware of her annoyance, Robert held the door open for her. Eleanor stepped inside. Hampshire and his cronies were seated at a corner table, each nose buried in a bill of fare.

"Would you rather we eat elsewhere?" Robert asked.

"Certainly not," Eleanor said. "If we're lucky, my presence will ruin his appetite."

"It's your appetite I'm worried about," Robert said.

"Good, because I'm famished."

Chapter 14

Molly wasn't an expert on horses, but even she knew this particular mustang was special. Its silky hide was pure black, and at fifteen and a half hands he stood taller than most other mustangs. He ran with lightning speed around the corral, hooves barely touching the ground, mane flowing, tail high. The steed practically breathed fire.

Brodie had been trying to capture him for months and made no attempt to hide his pride at success. "And I didn't resort to no creasing," he said. He had no patience for mustangers who shot horses in the neck. If done right, it would stun them without causing serious injury, but Brodie was still against it, insisting that "creasing should be outlawed."

Molly agreed. "So how *did* you catch him?"

He glanced at her. "How do you think I caught him? I walked him down. Didn't let him stop for a second. Most horses can be walked down in several hours, but not this fella. Took me two days and two nights. By then he was so tired he practically begged me to capture him."

She couldn't imagine the stallion begging. Nor could she imagine anyone walking that length of time. Brodie was one tough bird.

"Watch his every move," Brodie said. "Every shift of the eye, twitch of the ear, flip of the tail means something."

Molly watched, but either the signs were too subtle to be seen at the horse's current speed or nonexistent. She switched the whip from her right hand to the left.

"Keep him going!" Brodie shouted.

Heart pounding, Molly snapped her whip and it whizzed through the air before hitting the ground. The horse circled past her with pounding hooves, his breath scalding the air.

"That's the way!"

The horse circled back. Molly readied her whip but it slipped from her gloved hand. She made a grab for it but the horse saw his chance and took it. Instead of making the turn, he plunged straight at her, ears pinned back, teeth bared.

Molly froze, legs rigid, mouth dry.

Brodie threw himself between her and the

maddened horse, his whip snapping through the air. The horse reared back, its powerful hooves missing her by inches.

Brodie grabbed hold of the mustang's lead rope and tied him to the fence.

Shaken, Molly ran her gloved hands down the sides of her split skirt to still her shaking body. Her heart was pounding so hard she could barely breathe. "I . . . I'm sorry."

Brodie whirled around to face her, his face red. "Sorry? What good is that gonna do?" Brodie threw down his whip. "If the boss lady makes you her new heiress, she won't be needing me." He stalked away.

She watched him walk away, tears scorching her eyes. She felt terrible. But it wasn't just the horse, it was everything. Exhaustion dogged her day and night. Every bone in her body ached and her hands were so sore she could hardly hold her hairbrush, let alone the whip. Even wearing gloves didn't help.

Caring for her brother and keeping up with the ranch work was harder than she ever imagined.

Swiping away a wayward tear, she marched to the windmill. She tossed her gloves aside and plunged her hands into the depths of the barrel, then splashed cold water on her face.

That's it. She'd had enough! Tomorrow she would ride into town and try to talk a saloon owner into hiring her. Then she'd quit this impossible job. The decision brought no relief. The thought of spending her nights in smoke-filled saloons with a bunch of inebriated men sickened her.

She leaned against the fence and prayed. *God, help me, hold me, tell me what You want me to do. Send me a sign.*

She squeezed her eyes tight. She always felt better when she sang. If only she could remember the words to the hymn Mr. Washington sang in church. Something about a chariot . . .

Sighing, she hummed "Little Brown Jug." The cheerful little drinking song was mild compared to some songs she knew. Still . . . she opened her eyes to make sure no one could hear her.

"Ha, ha, ha, you and me, little brown jug, don't I love thee!" Normally singing made her feel better but not today. She still had a night cough and her voice sounded like she'd swallowed a mouthful of pebbles. What saloon owner would hire her now?

A poke in the back startled her. Swinging around, she found herself face-to-face with the little blind colt Donny had named Orbit.

"Hello there," she said, reaching over the

fence to stroke his velvety soft nose. He bobbed his head up and down and pawed the ground as if to approve.

No one could tell by looking into his eyes that he was blind. He looked physically normal, and if it hadn't been for his odd behavior at times, she would never have guessed he was different in any way.

"You must have heard me singing," she said.

This little black horse had reached out to her and she felt an immediate kinship with him.

The colt's mother stood across the way watching. After a while she flipped her tail and whinnied. Orbit swung around, kicked up his back heels, and joyfully bounded toward the anxious mare.

Something Brodie said echoed in her mind. *"Horses can teach us a whole lot more than we can teach them."*

She would never forget her terror when that stallion had raced toward her. Now she knew how it felt to have one's legs fail. Was that how Donny felt during the fire? Or even on a daily basis?

Regret washed over her. Only that morning she had yelled at him for dawdling. Was that the lesson she was meant to learn from the wild stallion? To be more patient?

And the colt — *Is this the sign I prayed for? What am I to learn from this little blind horse? Please, God, help me understand* . . .

On Tuesday afternoon, Caleb drove to the ranch and found Donny in his room, reading.

"Ah, there you are," he said cheerfully, knocking on the half-open door. Magic didn't wait for an invitation. Already the dog had weaseled his way onto Donny's lap, his pink tongue all over Donny's face. The drawn curtains at the single window let in little light, but enough to see that Donny enjoyed the attention.

"Not good to read in the dark," Caleb said. Crossing to the window, he yanked open the curtains and the bright light pushed the gloom to the walls. He raised the heavy sash to let in fresh air before returning to Donny's side. He lifted Magic off Donny's lap and the dog curled up on the floor for a nap, tuckered out, no doubt, from all that face-licking.

"Did your sister tell you that I'd like to work with you? That is, if you'll let me."

Donny eyed him with a wary look. "She said something."

Something? That didn't sound too promising. "Good. We'll start slowly." He pulled a

177

chair in front of Donny's and sat.

Donny leveled Caleb with dark, glittering eyes. "What good will it do? I'm helpless," he grumbled. "Can't you see?"

Caleb studied him. What had happened since Sunday to put Donny on the defensive? "You're not helpless. You need help. That's a big difference. Everyone needs help. God made us that way to keep us connected to one another."

The youth glowered at him. "*You* don't need help."

"As a doctor, I probably need more help than anyone. I need help from other doctors, from scientists, from medicine, but mostly from God."

Donny folded his arms and frowned. "It's not the same thing."

"We can sit arguing about it or we can get to work. Your choice."

Donny obviously didn't know what to make of him, and that was good. Kept him off balance and less resistant. "Have it your way."

Donny sat limp as a rag doll as Caleb examined him from head to toe. As expected, Donny had a very limited range of motion in his legs, but it was his undeveloped chest and arm muscles that worried Caleb most. Until Donny built up those muscles, he would never be able to care for himself. But first he had to gain the boy's trust.

"Tell me about yourself. What do you like to do? Where do you like to go?"

Donny made a rude sound with his lips. "I can't do anything or go anywhere. I'm crippled."

"You're not crippled. Your legs don't work," Caleb said matter-of-factly, as if they were talking about something as mundane as the weather. "You just have to learn to do things a bit differently." He glanced at the stack of science books on the bedside table. Most of them had to do with astronomy.

"You don't need legs to study the sky. Or be an astronomer and discover another planet." Both hands on Donny's right foot, he flexed it up and down. "You can do anything you want with your hands, and your brain can take you anywhere you want to go."

Donny glared at him, his face red. "You're nothing but a snake oil doctor. Just like my sister said you were!"

"Molly said that, did she?" A memory of flashing green eyes and a pretty pink mouth came to mind, but he quickly shrugged it away. "So tell me, what's the hardest part of being in a wheelchair?"

"People acting as if I'm not there," he said, staring down at his pale legs.

"I'd hate that too," Caleb said.

"Actually, I hate it more when people do stare at me. They don't do it much," Donny said. "They mostly stare at my sister."

Caleb nodded. That Molly was something, all right. Even he couldn't help but stare at her. Just thinking about their first encounter made him smile. He was lucky she shot Bertha instead of him. Suddenly aware that Donny was giving him an odd look, Caleb cleared his throat.

He quickly finished his examination and handed Donny a piece of pipe ten inches in length. Donny seemed embarrassed about his legs. For that reason Caleb decided to work on his arms first so he would be less self-conscious.

"Raise it over your head like this." He demonstrated before handing Donny the pipe. "It'll build up the muscles in your arms and shoulders."

"I'm not doing that. I can't!" Donny threw the pipe down. Magic lifted his head off his paws and watched the lead bar roll across the tile floor.

Donny's body shook but whether from anger, frustration, or fear it was hard to say.

Caleb waited for Donny to calm down. Fifteen, twenty, thirty minutes passed and neither spoke. A breeze wafted through the windows, filling the room with a hint of sage. The curtains fluttered like the wings of a butterfly, but Donny remained motionless.

Finally, Caleb stood, picked the iron pipe off the floor, and set it next to the stack of books.

"Okay, you have a choice to make. Either you work with me or you don't. If you choose not to, then the chair you're sitting in will be your prison. If you work with me, that same chair will be your friend and will help you do whatever you want to do."

"I don't want to do anything."

"Not even go to the observatory in Flagstaff?"

Defiance crossed Donny's face. "How am I going to get there, eh?" He narrowed his eyes. "Tell me that."

"I plan on traveling to Flagstaff myself one day, but I'm not taking any prisoners."

Donny's face stilled but he said nothing and Caleb gathered his black leather case and headed for the door.

"Before you go . . ."

Hand on the doorknob, Caleb waited.

"Close the curtains."

Caleb released the doorknob and crossed to the window. "I still come to the ranch from time to time to check on Miss Walker's horse." It was no longer necessary, but he enjoyed the ride to the ranch and didn't want to consider that Molly was the real attraction. "If you change your mind, open the curtains and I'll know. If I see the curtains closed, I won't bother you."

He walked out of the room, shutting the door softly behind him. *Okay, God, don't hold back. Step in whenever You're ready and help me here.*

CHAPTER 15

Eleanor stomped into the house and hurried toward her office.

Surprised to find the crippled boy in the main room trying to reach for a hefty tome in her extensive library, she reached over his head for the book and handed it to him. "I'm afraid you'll find that dull reading. It's all about cattle."

"Cattle are pretty interesting," he replied. "I read all the books on the lower shelf."

That was a surprise. To her knowledge, no one had ever touched her books — certainly none of the many hopefuls who had answered her advertisement for an heiress.

"Have you now?"

His forehead wrinkled as if he feared he had done something wrong. "Did . . . did you know that eight pair of boots can be made from a single cowhide?"

Eleanor pulled off her leather gloves. "Good for a boot maker to know."

"And a single steer produces a hundred pounds of fat. That's a lot of candles."

"Is there a point to all this?"

He gnawed on his lower lip. "Meat doesn't even make up half of a steer's weight."

Eleanor slapped her gloves into the palm of her hand. "As far as I know, no one has figured out how to raise boneless cattle."

"According to what I read, the beef industry is expected to decline in the twentieth century."

The boy was losing her interest fast. "Now you sound like my banker."

"Yes, but there are other ways to make money," he said eagerly. "Beef tallow is already used for lubricating locomotives, and soon the fat will be used to make medicine and fuel, even glue and lady's paint." The boy studied her with eyes the same green color as his sister's. "It doesn't seem fair that you do all the work and someone else makes most of the profit."

"What happens after I sell my cattle is of no concern to me."

"It would be if you owned a meat packing house," he said.

The suggestion surprised her. During all the hours she'd spent discussing this very subject with Robert and her foreman, no one ever suggested the idea of the ranch owning its own packing house. She wasn't certain of the practicality or even if it was something to consider at her age, but she was impressed that one so young came up with the idea.

"What's your name?" Her abruptness of voice sent a shadow of worry across his face. If she wasn't so old she might consider working on her curt manner of speaking, but why bother at this late date? People eventually got used to her ways and no doubt this boy would too.

"My name is Donald but everyone calls me Donny."

"Donald it shall be. My main problem at the moment is other ranchers overstocking the land. That's what I have to think about."

"I'll think about it too."

She arched an eyebrow. "Will you now? Very well then. I'll let you get on with your thinking." She started toward her office.

"If you could look down from the sky, cattle would look like stars," he called after her.

She stopped at the threshold, hand on the door frame, and looked over her shoulder. "Stars?"

He shrugged. "You'd have to look at the earth from way up in the sky. Higher than a hawk."

"I imagine so."

"You might even be able to pick out a constellation, like the big dipper. But not if the cattle are all crammed together."

Eleanor arched a brow. "Yes, I can see where that might be a problem."

"Cattle should be spaced like stars. According to my calculations, one steer per sixty acres should last through a drought."

Eleanor laughed. Something about the boy was most appealing. "Surely you're not asking for a job?"

He practically shook with enthusiasm. "I'm good with figures, especially the ones with dollar signs. I even know how to calculate the distance to the sun."

"I'm sure some people will find that information most useful." She hesitated.

"*If* your sister works out" — doubtful at best — "perhaps we can find something for you to do."

An eager look brightened his face. "I'd . . . I'd like that. I'd like that a lot."

"Very well then." She walked into her office and closed the door. *Cattle are like stars? Constellations?* She shook her head. The idea wasn't any crazier than promising a wheelchair-bound boy a job.

Hampshire had called her a doddering fool. Good heavens. Perhaps he was right.

■ ■ ■ ■

Donny stared at the door long after Eleanor had shut herself in her office. A job on the ranch? He couldn't believe it. But Miss Walker didn't seem like the kind of person to say something she didn't mean.

He told the truth. He *was* good at numbers but only because he'd read that mathematics was a necessary skill for astronomers. Back in Dobson Creek he spent sleepless nights staring at the canvas ceiling, multiplying and dividing numbers in his head.

The first of every month he made his sister take him to the general store to purchase the latest science journal. He was able to teach himself basic trigonometry and calculus from the astronomical graphs printed inside. But that was when he still believed that it was only a matter of time before he would get up and walk.

He stopped believing in miracles the day his father died. Molly wasn't allowed in the church and he would always remember sitting outside in the cold while a pitiful small group of miners paid their respects.

Whether it was the reality of his father's death or the cruelty of other people, he didn't know, but his dream of becoming an astronomer no longer seemed possible.

Now his mind spun with exciting new possibilities. Never once had he considered working on a ranch.

The doc's voice sounded in his head. *"You can do anything you want to do."*

Was that true?

Dare he imagine himself working in the ranch office while his sister chased cattle and trained horses? Would Miss Walker trust him enough to pay the bills and make the money last until the next shipment of cattle sold? Would Molly then look at him differently — not just like her poor baby brother but like a man?

Rosita walked into the room, feather duster in hand. Seeing him, she backed away. She always tried to avoid him, but she wasn't alone in that regard. Both Rosita and her brother, Jose, treated him like he had the plague or something.

"Wait!" he called. "Don't go. I'm not going to ask you to come near. I just want you to . . . open the curtains in my room. Would you do that for me? Please."

Rosita nodded. She backed all the way out of the room before she turned and fled.

That night Molly knocked on her brother's

bedroom door. It was time to get him ready for bed, but she also wanted to talk to him. She didn't anticipate any difficulty in telling Donny her decision to find a saloon job. The hard part would come tomorrow when she tried to talk a saloon owner into hiring her. They'd want to hear her sing, naturally, and no matter how many hard candies she sucked, her voice still sounded froggy.

But that wasn't the only problem. Most proprietors didn't want her to just sing, they wanted her to entertain men in other ways. *Sinful* ways. She would rather starve to death than prostitute herself, but she couldn't let Donny go hungry. Never in a million years could she let him do without necessities. *Oh, God, please don't let it come to that.*

"Donny, I need to talk to you." She sat on the edge of his bed. "What are you reading?"

He held up the book so she could see the cover. "*Beef Bonanza: How to Get Rich on the Plains* by Gen. James S. Brisbin."

She made a face. She couldn't imagine anything duller.

"Wouldn't hurt you to read it," he said.

She stifled a yawn. She was so tired she could hardly keep her eyes open. And there wasn't a bone in her body that didn't hurt.

189

"Why this sudden interest in cattle?"

"Miss Walker said if you worked out, she might be able to find a job for me."

She stared at him. "A job?"

Donny frowned. "You don't have to look so surprised. I'm not a dunce. I'm good with numbers."

"I know you are, Donny. I didn't mean it that way." She tried to remember when she last saw Donny this excited. If only she didn't have to tell him their days on the ranch might be numbered. Surprised to see the curtains open, she walked over to the window to close them, stalling for time. A flash of lightning danced across the darkened sky, followed by a low rumbling.

"Leave them open," he said.

His request surprised her. Normally he kept the curtains closed day and night. "Are you sure?"

"Dr. Fairbanks said if I changed my mind and wanted him to help me, all I had to do was open the curtains."

"You want to work with him?" She couldn't believe this sudden change. Donny had been so against accepting the doctor's help.

"I like the doctor. He's funny."

"Funny?" She could think of many ways to describe Caleb, but funny was not one of

190

them. Tall, handsome, and . . . She quickly banished the thought.

"How do you mean, funny?" she asked.

"He drives a motor buggy and is always asking questions about the human body. I never know the answers, but he can't answer my questions either."

"Your questions?"

"About the stars and planets. He didn't even know the composition of the sun."

She smiled. "I bet he knows it now."

He nodded and grinned. "Leaving the curtains open is a secret code like the songs the slaves used to sing." His brows drew together. "I don't know if the doctor *can* help me, though."

"I have a feeling that if anyone can help you, it's Dr. Fairbanks."

He nodded. "What did you want to talk about? You said you wanted to talk to me."

A crash of thunder made her jump. "Oh . . . uh . . . it's not important. Let's get you ready for bed." She took the book out of his hand.

A half hour later she tucked him in and left the room, her mind racing. Donny working for Miss Walker? Never in her wildest dreams had she imagined anything like that.

But what if Miss Walker asked her to leave

the ranch? After what happened earlier with the wild mustang, that was entirely possible.

She hurried down the hall, determined to talk to Brodie — beg him on hands and knees if necessary. Somehow she had to make him give her one more chance — for Donny's sake.

She opened the front door. It was raining hard and already a river of mud and water separated the ranch house from the bunk-house and barn. Her talk with Brodie would have to wait.

Caleb almost missed the open curtains. For the better part of a week he'd checked Donny's window as he whizzed by and the curtains were always closed. He wasn't even sure they were open today. Maybe the breeze had simply blown them apart.

Since his horseless carriage could not go in reverse, he swung a wide circle. Careful to avoid the puddles left from last night's rainstorm, he pulled up in front of the ranch house for a closer look. Now that he had stopped the car, he realized there was no movement in the air. The wind that greeted the dawn had died down, leaving no question in his mind: the curtains were open. *Wide open.*

CHAPTER 16

Molly shifted in the saddle and took in her surroundings. She'd never before ridden out this far on the range. Had no idea that the Last Chance spread across such a wide area. Nor had she seen so many cattle at once since the day of the stampede.

She was still in Brodie's bad graces and it was a relief to take a break from his dark accusatory expressions. He had reluctantly agreed to give her another chance, but she had yet to prove she deserved it.

Since the incident with the stallion, she'd been relegated to cleaning stalls and grooming horses instead of training them. She didn't complain and had a lot to be grateful for now that Donny had agreed to let Caleb work with him.

With this thought she allowed herself to relax. She popped a lemon drop in her mouth to soothe her raw throat.

She rode at the tail end of a line of riders

trailing each other single file to protect the valuable grass as much as possible. Behind her, Ruckus drove a wagon filled with fence-mending equipment and salt licks.

It was July fourth — Independence Day. In years past, Dobson Creek had celebrated the holiday with great fanfare, and it was a shock to learn that it was business as usual on the ranch. Donny would be disappointed. He loved watching the parade, but mostly he liked the poppers, pinwheels, and double-headers that lit up the night skies.

How quickly time passed. It had been a little more than five weeks since she arrived at the ranch and the fire was now a distant though no less unpleasant memory.

Miss Walker took the lead today, followed by Stretch and Feedbag.

It was hard to believe it had rained last night. The ground looked bone dry but the cacti were fuller and the camphor-like odor of the creosote plant tickled Molly's nose. Nothing was prettier than the desert in bloom. Red, white, and yellow flowers dotted every cactus. Prairie dogs yipped and wild mustangs lifted their heads in wary watchfulness. How she wished Donny could see them!

Maybe one of the ranch hands would bring him out here, though she hesitated to ask. For the most part, the others avoided her brother.

Donny seemed to like the doctor and his asthma had greatly improved. More than that, he seemed happier and less frustrated. She still hadn't noticed any improvement in mobility, even though Donny did breathing and arm exercises every day.

Caleb said it would take time — but how much time? She grew more impatient with each passing day. How much longer could she keep up with both her ranch duties and care of her brother? *How much longer, Lord?*

Up ahead, Miss Walker and the ranch hands stopped. Stretch pulled out his gun and fired. Two wolves ran off. Shuddering, Molly urged her horse forward.

Some fifty or more dead cattle were scattered across the landscape. Molly stared at the carcasses in horror.

Ruckus jumped from the wagon and sauntered over to the nearest bovine already covered in flies. "Lightning got 'em," he announced.

"Let's hope that's the extent of the damage," Miss Walker said, and Molly marveled that the ranch owner could sound so calm. "Bury them. We don't want them attracting more wolves."

Ruckus nodded and hurried to move the

wagon closer to the scene.

Miss Walker glanced at Molly. "You come with me," she said in her usual clipped voice.

Molly didn't want to dig a bunch of graves, but riding alone with Miss Walker was hardly a welcome alternative. The woman was as intimidating as a charging bull.

Miss Walker rode by her side. "Your brother requires a lot more care than you implied when we first spoke."

Molly's heart thudded. Did Miss Walker intend to dismiss her? A short time ago she might have felt a sense of relief had the ranch owner sent her packing, but not now. Not with Donny having his heart set on working at the ranch.

"Caleb . . . Dr. Fairbanks is helping him to become more independent." If Miss Walker thought it odd that Molly used the doctor's given name, she kept it to herself.

"Brodie told me about the incident with the stallion."

Molly's hands tightened on the reins and her horse snorted. She forced herself to relax. "I . . . I assure you nothing like that will ever happen again."

Miss Walker studied her. Molly's stomach knotted and she shriveled under the withering glare. Had it been possible to disappear into a hole, she would have gladly done so.

"You could have been killed." The ranch owner pressed her heels into her horse's side and galloped off.

Molly watched her, not knowing what to think. Was that concern for her safety or simply a statement of fact? It was hard to know.

Miss Walker stopped a short distance away and Molly eased her horse alongside her. A line of cattle headed for a water trough by an enormous windmill. Not one steer had the familiar LC brand. Someone had cut the fence so that the cattle had free access to the ranch's water supply.

Several mustangs grazed nearby. One horse lay in the grass, body swollen and heaving in distress.

Next to her Miss Walker sat rigid in her saddle, her expression hidden beneath the shade of her wide-brimmed hat. "Now I know how my horse got strangles."

So far Baxter remained an isolated case, probably because Miss Walker had ordered her men to scrub every water and feeding trough on the property to prevent spreading the infection.

The air had grown uncommonly still all of a sudden, the huge windmill blades frozen as if painted onto the cloudless sky. It was as if nature held its breath waiting to see what Miss Walker would do or say next. The wait was short.

She pulled out her Colt and carefully aimed a shot at the base of the horse's ear, putting it out of its misery. The other horses took off running and the cattle scattered, bawling.

Miss Walker slid her weapon back into her holster.

Ears ringing from the pistol's report, Molly looked away from the unfortunate animal. "What do you plan on doing with those claim jumpers?"

"Claim jumpers!" The phrase hung between them so long Molly was certain she had said something wrong.

Finger to the brim, Miss Walker pushed her hat back. "Hmm. Never heard it put that way but that's a good name for them." After a moment she added, "If I knew what to do I'd have done it already." She leveled gray eyes at Molly. "What do they do about claim jumpers in Dobson Creek?"

"You mean other than lynching them?"

Miss Walker gave a hollow laugh. "Don't tempt me."

The touch of humor in Miss Walker's voice surprised Molly. Encouraged, she explained, "One man got rid of a bunch of lowly claim jumpers by salting the property several miles downstream."

"Salting?"

"He sprinkled gold dust around the ground and threw in a couple of nuggets for good measure. Then he started a rumor in town that he'd found the mother lode. I'm telling you, those rascals took off like a bunch of rabid wolves to make a claim."

"Hmm." Miss Walker's thoughtful gaze had none of the earlier rancor and Molly felt encouraged. A bellowing sound drew their attention to the distant fence through which a broad white face appeared. The bovine wasn't interested in them. Instead her attention was focused on a shaking bush. A young brown and white calf emerged from the shrub and bounded on spindly legs toward his mother.

After the two reunited, Miss Walker said, "I do believe you solved my problem." She quirked a thin gray brow. "Come on, we've got work to do." She turned her horse and raced back to where the men were busy digging a mass grave, and it was all Molly could do to keep up with her.

"Stop what you're doing!" Miss Walker rode up to Ruckus. "I want you to take a couple of those corpses and put them as close to the Bennett ranch as possible. Make certain there are no visible burn marks. Stretch? Where's Stretch?"

"I'm here, ma'am." Stretch pressed the spade of his shovel into the soil with his boot and leaned on the handle.

"Ride into town and let it be known that cattle are dying at the Last Chance Ranch due to disease. That should make them think twice before cutting my fence."

The men looked at each other and Ruckus rubbed his chin. "It could backfire," he said.

Miss Walker snapped a look in his direction. "Backfire how?"

"If buyers get wind that our cattle are diseased, they'll be less likely to purchase our beef."

Miss Walker considered this for a moment. "If we have to keep fighting for grass and water, our cattle will be too emaciated to sell."

Much discussion followed, but in the end, the ranch hands agreed the possible rewards were greater than the risks.

The brim of his Stetson pulled low, Stretch scratched the back of his head. "What disease do you have in mind, ma'am?"

"How about tick fever?" Feedbag said.

"Foot and mouth disease?" Stretch added.

"Gold fever?" Molly suggested, half-jokingly.

That got the men's attention. "The cattle died of gold fever?" Feedbag shook his head. "Never heard of such a thing."

"That's because no such thing exists," Miss Walker said. She thought for a moment. "The investors won't know what they're dealing with and that could be a good thing."

Feedbag shook his head. "They'll never go for it."

Stretch shrugged. "They might. Least for a while. That will give us time to repair the fences and come up with another plan."

"Very well," Miss Walker said. "Gold fever it is."

CHAPTER 17

Caleb turned his car down Main Street and blinked. Despite the early morning hour, a long line of people crowded the boardwalk from one end of the street to the other. It wasn't until he pulled up to his office that he realized the line began at his door. "What in blazes?"

He turned off the motor and the inevitable backfire rendered the crowd silent. Something about the cool morning air made Bertha want to get in the last word.

A horse neighed and tried to pull away from the hitching post. Magic barked and wagged his tail and waited for Caleb's command.

"Come on, boy." He climbed out of the motor buggy and lifted Magic to the ground. The moment Caleb stepped up to the front of the line, everyone began talking at once. Something about gold fever . . .

Unable to make heads or tails out of their

babble, Caleb waved his arms. "Quiet! One at a time." He pointed to the owner of the mercantile store. "Suppose you tell me what's got folks all riled up."

Mr. Green assumed an air of importance, his spectacles riding the tip of his nose. "There's an epidemic of gold fever, and me and the others want to get ourselves one of them shots so we don't get it too."

Caleb rubbed a hand across the back of his neck. Gold fever or its equivalent was probably the oldest disease known to mankind, the main symptom being greed, but it was the first he'd heard of it being a medical problem.

"If you want a cure for gold fever, you're in the wrong place," he said, lifting his voice to be heard at the far end of the line. "Church has a better cure than I do."

"We ain't talking about *that* kind of gold fever," another man yelled out. "We're talking about the kind that kills animals."

Mr. Green nodded. "Hundreds of Last Chance cattle have died."

That was news to Caleb. He was at the ranch yesterday working with Donny and no one mentioned a word to him about dead cattle.

"Yeah," someone yelled. "And we don't want to catch it." He rolled up the sleeve of his shirt. "So we're ready to be evaporated."

The crowd murmured agreement.

"I think you mean vaccinated," Caleb said, shaking his head. The very same people who refused to be vaccinated for small pox or malaria now demanded to be vaccinated for a disease that, as far as he knew, didn't physically exist.

"You can't catch a disease from steer unless you eat the meat."

"You catch chicken pox from chickens," someone argued.

"Not true," Caleb said, but everyone started talking at once again and drowned him out. Some people still didn't believe that germs caused infection, nor understood that viruses and bacteria led to disease. Almost every new discovery in the medical field was met with skepticism and resistance, even among some doctors and scientists.

"Quiet!" He waited until he had their attention. "I'll check this out and if there is any danger to you and your families, I will let you know."

He stepped into his office amid a chorus of protests and after Magic skittered inside, slammed the door shut.

Molly stood as far away from the mare as the horse stall allowed and didn't move.

This was the first Brodie had allowed her to work with horses since the day she froze in front of the stallion. Her job was to get the horse used to being around people, nothing more.

The paint stared at her for maybe two or three minutes before turning her head away with a swish of her tail. Molly took another step closer and the horse regarded her again. Her ears flickered and she pawed the ground.

Training a wild horse required infinite patience, and that had never been Molly's strong suit. Whenever she showed impatience as a child, her father would always say, "All in God's time, child, all in God's time." It was his stock answer for everything.

"When will we live in a real house?" she'd asked him, weary of the tent they called home.

"All in God's time."

"When will Mama get well?"

"All in God's time."

God's time wasn't her time and after her mother's death, she wondered if such a thing even existed. It irritated her that her father accepted no responsibility for what happened or didn't happen. Instead of saving his hard-earned money for a house, he spent it foolishly at saloons and gambling halls, leaving them precious little to live on.

She tried to learn patience — prayed almost daily to accept her lot in life without complaint. But her annoyance grew along with exhaustion.

When Donny dawdled over the wash sink or took forever to brush his teeth, it was hard not to snap at him. Her body ached so much that she was sorely tempted at times to leave him in his wheelchair rather than battle him into bed.

Caleb insisted Donny had made progress, but in what way? He required constant care and still couldn't do anything much for himself. If anything, he seemed more helpless with each passing day . . . or perhaps she simply expected more of him.

She shook her thoughts away but the guilt remained, shrouding her like a second skin. She could walk and Donny could not. She could run and dance and jump and hop, but Donny could not. She squeezed her eyes tight. Nothing she wanted, nothing she wished for, was more important than caring for Donny and making certain he always had a home.

Sighing, she took another step closer to the mare. Predictably, the animal lifted its head and gazed at her.

"Talk to her," Brodie had instructed. *"Let*

her get used to your voice."

And so she sang, her voice barely more than a whisper. Stopping to clear her throat, she dug in her pocket for a lemon drop and popped it in her mouth. After a couple of minutes she tried again. This time her voice sounded smoother.

She sang just as she did each morning for Orbit. "Ha, ha, ha, you and me, little brown horse, don't I love thee!" Lately she'd started changing some of the words to the saloon songs to make them less bawdy, and she wondered why she hadn't thought to do so before.

She sang softly at first so as not to strain her voice or startle the mare. She ventured a dance step or two. The horse continued to graze on hay, paying her no mind. Encouraged, she took a couple of side steps, sashayed her hips, kicked up her leg, and turned. "Ha, ha, ha, you and me . . ."

Caleb walked toward the stables looking for Molly. Surely she could explain the rumors in town. Donny knew nothing about dead cattle or gold fever.

Caleb hated to admit it but the stables drew him like a magnet, and every chance he got, he went there. He enjoyed making Molly happy. It didn't take much. The least bit of encouragement he offered on her brother's progress made her eyes sparkle and brought a beautiful wide smile to her face.

He'd exaggerated Donny's progress, God forgive him, but he couldn't help it. Molly looked so forlorn at times, so downhearted and worried. How could he possibly tell her the truth? How could he let her know that Donny's progress was slow if not altogether nonexistent?

He heard the voice before he saw the singer but knew immediately that it belonged to Molly. Her voice sounded smoky but no less sweet. He'd never heard the song sung with so much passion and enthusiasm.

"Ha, ha, ha . . ."

Grinning, he walked with quiet steps until he spotted her inside the stall. Not only was she singing but dancing and his grin widened. Hands on her waist, she moved with easy grace, shaking her shoulders and swaying her hips. Her red shirtwaist was as bright as the flower of an ocotillo. Wisps of hair had worked loose from her braided bun. "The Little Brown Jug" never sounded so good — or looked so tempting.

She finished her song and he clapped. She spun around, her green eyes as dark as the disapproval on her face. He wasn't sure what he'd done wrong, but she came charging at him like a raging bull.

She let herself out of the horse stall and swung around to face him. "Don't ever do that again while I'm training a horse."

"That's what you were doing? Training a horse?" They sure did do things different out here in Arizona Territory. "I think the horse can manage the steps but I'm not sure about the shoulder movements."

She stared at him for a full moment before bursting into laughter. "Everyone has trouble with the shoulder movements," she said.

He grinned back at her. "I knew you were a singer, but I didn't know you were also a dancer."

She arched a fine eyebrow. "How did you know I was a singer?"

He shrugged. "Small town."

Her face softened. "I'm sorry. I shouldn't have yelled. Teaching that paint to get used to my voice is part of her training."

"Lucky horse," he said.

Her pretty pink cheeks grew a shade darker. Aware that he stared, he said, "I heard that you had some trouble out here."

She looked confused. "Trouble?"

"With the cattle. Something about thousands dying of . . . gold fever." He tilted his head. "I thought that particular affliction was unique to us humans."

She laughed. "Thousands, eh? So our plan worked."

"Plan?"

She studied him. "Swear you won't breathe a word of this to anyone."

"Anything you say to me will be treated in the strictest of confidence."

"Even though I'm not your patient?" she asked.

"Your brother is."

She seemed satisfied with his answer and quickly explained about the ranch's dispute with eastern investors. "Miss Walker is against a big cattle company moving in. The ones already here keep cutting our fences and using our water. She thinks that's why Baxter got sick."

"She could be right." None of the other ranchers had complained about sick horses, but that wasn't too surprising. Illness could ruin a ranch's reputation and hurt cattle sales. For that reason, ranchers often didn't speak up until a problem got out of hand. Miss Walker was the exception.

"When we found fifty steers killed by lightning, we decided to spread the rumor that they died from disease. We hoped it would stop the other ranchers from trespassing."

"Did your plan work?" he asked.

"It has so far. We haven't found a cut fence in a week." She angled her head as she looked up at him. "How did you hear about it?"

"From a long line of people waiting in front of my office demanding a vaccination against gold fever."

Her eyes sparkled like an emerald sea. "Wait till Miss Walker hears about that." She glanced toward the ranch house. "How is Donny doing?"

"He's making progress." He inhaled. There he went again, but he couldn't seem to help it. If only he could change the way her brother regarded himself. Instead of focusing on what he could do or was capable of doing, Donny saw only his disabilities.

Instead of the smile he hoped for, a flash of impatience flitted across her face.

"You say that every time," she said.

"Have you noticed no improvement?"

She thought for a moment. "Not really. Except maybe his breathing. He's not wheezing as much."

"Ah, you see? Progress. Once we complete therapy, his breathing will improve even more. I'm convinced of it."

"Are you saying that strengthening his muscles will improve his asthma?" she asked.

On more familiar ground, he elaborated. "We don't know what causes asthma but we have a pretty good idea what triggers it. I've noticed in some of my patients that anxiety or worry or even stress can cause breathing difficulties."

"Is that why coming to Arizona seemed to affect his breathing?"

"Possibly. A new environment uncertainty about the future . . . any of those things can cause his bronchial tubes to tense."

She bit her lower lip. "I don't mean to sound ungrateful or impatient. It's just that . . . others have promised miracles and nothing worked."

Her words stabbed at his conscience. Was that what he was doing? Promising something he could not deliver? "I'm not in the business of miracles. I leave such wonders to God. But I am a big believer in the human spirit. Your brother's a fine lad with a good mind. Don't underestimate him."

"Is that what you think I'm doing?"

He nodded toward the horse stall. "What do you see when you look at that horse?"

"What do I see? I see a fine animal with a strong spirit. I see a great deal of potential.

But what has this got to do with my brother?"

"Do you know what I see when I look at that horse? I see an animal with spindly legs and complicated intestines that should have been extinct thousands of years ago."

Her mouth dropped open. "That's . . . ridiculous."

"Not any more ridiculous than looking at Donny and seeing only his imperfect legs."

"You're wrong," she snapped. "That's not all I see."

He reached for her hands. "Molly, look at me. People act how they're expected to act."

She pulled away. "I don't expect him to act helpless!"

"He's not helpless, Molly. He's scared."

"Scared?" She grew still. "Of what?"

"Of losing you."

"That's ridiculous!"

"Is it?" He studied her. He'd committed to helping Donny, but perhaps Molly had a greater need. Caring for Donny under the best of circumstances would be difficult enough for anyone, but she had a full-time job. On a ranch, no less. Though she tried her best to hide her worry and fatigue, he could see what it was doing to her. Such a heavy burden would tax the hardiest of men.

"What would happen if you lived a normal

213

life?" He trod on dangerous ground and already he felt her resistance. Whenever he got too personal, she either pulled away or put a wall between them. Even so, someone had to step in before she destroyed herself.

And then he took the biggest chance of all. "If you were to, say . . . marry?"

If the question surprised her, she gave no indication. "That's not going to happen," she said without hesitation, as if she had thought long and hard on the subject.

He stared at her, incredulous. "How can you be so certain?" *A beautiful woman like you?*

"Marriage means children and I couldn't handle another child."

He frowned. "Donny's not a child."

"You know what I mean. Even my mother —" She looked away, but not before he saw the pain in her eyes, the tremor of her lips, the clenching of her fists.

A protective surge rushed through him. He wanted to reach out to her. He wanted to take her in his arms and hold her and make the pain go away. "What about your mother?" he asked gently.

It took her a moment to lift her gaze to his, the pain no longer visible. But he had seen and he knew.

She shook her head. "Nothing. It doesn't

matter. I just meant that Donny needs a lot of care."

Sometimes unspoken words were the loudest, and he heard Molly's loud and clear. Her mother was so overwhelmed with caring for her son she neglected her daughter.

"And you plan to throw your life away because of him?" As a doctor he tried never to sound critical or disapproving, but today professional discipline failed him and both had crept into his voice.

Her eyes widened and she took a step back. "I'm not throwing my life away. This is the first real home Donny and I ever had." At the sound of galloping hooves outside, Molly lowered her voice. "If I can secure Donny's future at this ranch, he'll never have to go into one of those horrid asylums."

Miss Walker marched into the barn in full riding gear, spurs jangling. "There you are, Doctor. Did Miss Hatfield tell you that we think we know how Baxter got infected?"

Caleb pulled his gaze away from Molly and turned to the ranch owner. "Yes, she did."

"How much longer must I keep him quarantined?"

"I think we can safely say there's no

215

danger of him infecting your other horses." The diagnosis had been proven correct and abscesses had formed as predicted. They popped on their own and almost immediately the horse showed improvement. For safety's sake, he'd insisted they keep Baxter isolated for a couple of weeks.

"I'll take one last look at him if you like," he said.

"Come along, then." Miss Walker strode toward Baxter's stall with long hurried strides, but Caleb was hesitant to follow.

He lowered his voice to a near whisper. "Molly, I know you care for your brother but —"

"You better not keep Miss Walker waiting." She let herself back into the stall and closed the gate between them. She stared at him for a moment before turning away.

There was so much more he wanted to say to her if only she would let him. "Molly . . ."

Miss Walker called to him. "Well? Are you coming?"

Long after Caleb left and the sound of his auto had faded away, Molly stood inside the stall thinking about what he said. As if sensing a change in her, the paint stared at her with wary regard and refused to let her get too close.

Molly tried to sing but it was no use. Her heart wasn't in it.

"What would happen if you lived a normal life? If you were, say . . . to marry?"

Stop it! she screamed silently, but it was no use. Caleb's words kept bouncing around in her head, seeming to resonate from the very barn walls until she feared she was losing her mind.

She clenched her fists. How dare him! How dare Caleb make her want things she had no business wanting. This might not be a *normal* life but it was *her* life — and it was the only one she deserved.

CHAPTER 18

Molly couldn't stop coughing. The cough that started during the Dobson Creek fire had grown progressively worse. At first she only coughed at night, but the hot, dry monsoon winds that tore across the desert set her to coughing for most of the day. A dark haze of sand and dust filled the air and she made Donny sit inside all day — something he hated to do.

Her throat was sore and her chest hurt and she worried about Donny catching her cough.

It wasn't the initial illness she worried about as much as the asthma attack that inevitably followed even the slightest infection.

The cough was annoying for another reason. If the clanking windmill and banging barn door didn't distract the horses enough, Molly's hacking spells put them on edge.

Brodie didn't say anything about her cough, but he made no effort to hide his displeasure at her being late. He disapproved of the number of times she sneaked away to care for her brother and he made no bones about it. Today was no different.

"Now that you're back maybe we can git some work done."

"I'm sorry I'm late but Donny —"

"The only thing I'm interested in is these here horses," he retorted. He tugged on his rawhide hat, kicked a small rock with his scuffed boot, and ambled away.

She heaved a sigh and followed him into the corral. How could a man with infinite patience for horses have so little tolerance for people?

Whirlwinds of sand raced by and a new horse Brodie called Blackie kicked up his hind legs and bolted around the corral in a frenzy. It was all Brodie could do to contain him. Keeping one eye on the battle between horse and man, Molly worked with a more placid, though head-shy, mare named Starburst.

It was a day for distractions. When the wind finally died down and the horses grew calm, Caleb arrived to work with Donny. His motor buggy backfired, sending the horses into another panic. Orbit didn't help matters. Hearing Caleb's auto, Orbit hoofed the fence and whinnied loudly until his friend Magic joined him. Nuzzling each other, the dog and horse then took off running side by side.

Molly laughed at the two animal friends, bringing a sharp glance from Brodie.

Sighing, she gently slid a bridle over Starburst's face and waited for the mare to lower her head before slipping the bit in her mouth and buckling the straps. Starburst took the bit well for the first time, but when Molly coughed, the startled mare took off running with her nose up in the air.

"She'll learn that it's more comfortable with her nose down," Brodie called.

Molly had learned a lot about horses in her short time on the ranch. Each teaching method had to be adjusted according to the personality of the horse. Lightning was a runner, Blaze a kicker, and Starburst easily spooked. The new pinto was docile for the most part but was given to sudden outbursts of energy when least expected. Then there was Blackie who was as unpredictable as the weather.

Her favorite horse, though, was Orbit. Each morning she stood by the fence and sang to him and he never failed to come galloping up to her. His antics made her smile, but it was his unfettered joy for life that she liked best.

The mare soon grew tired and stopped running. Molly hacked through another coughing spell and the skittish horse took off again.

"You gotta do something about that frog," Brodie grumbled.

"I'm trying," she said. Rosita had plied her with honey and some sort of cactus juice that tasted sour but felt soothing to her throat.

"Better let the doc have a look." He tossed a nod in the direction of the ranch house just as Caleb emerged from the courtyard. Molly was surprised to see him leave so soon. His session with Donny had lasted for a mere twenty minutes. Her brother had been in a bad mood at lunchtime, which was why she was late. Was he still being difficult?

"I don't need a doctor." She'd purposely avoided Caleb since their meeting in the barn. His nearness distracted and confused her and she needed her full wits to get through each day.

"Let him decide." Before she could protest, Brodie waved until he got Caleb's attention.

"I told you I don't need —" But it was too late. Caleb tossed something into his auto and jogged over to where they stood.

He greeted them both and glanced at the horses. "Is there a problem?"

"Nope," Brodie said. "At least not with the horses. But Molly here is having some throat trouble."

"Oh?" Caleb's glance sharpened as he studied her.

Molly glared at Brodie who shrugged and walked away. She cleared her voice. "It's just a little cough."

"It doesn't hurt to take a look." Caleb motioned toward the ranch house. "We better go inside."

She started to argue but changed her mind. With a shrug she marched to the house, pulling off her gloves as she walked. Moments later she settled upon a leather chair in the large room. Just being out of the dust-filled air made it easier to breathe and already she felt better.

Donny was in his room and Miss Walker was out on the range. There was no sign of either Rosita or Jose. It was just her and Caleb.

"How long have you had the cough?" he asked. Though he acted completely professional, she felt oddly shy in front of him.

She wasn't used to talking about herself to a doctor or anyone else. It was always about Donny.

"Since the fire."

He bent over her, probing her neck with his fingers. His touch sent warm shivers racing through her, his large hands surprisingly gentle.

"Open and say ah," he said.

She did as he asked and he peered inside her mouth. He was so close she could smell the faint scent of gasoline and the stronger fragrance of bay rum and leather.

His gaze met hers for an instant. "Does it hurt when you swallow?"

"A little," she admitted.

He pulled out his stethoscope and hesitated. Lines deepened on his brow and he cleared his throat. "I need to check your lungs."

Warmth rushed to her cheeks and she gave herself a mental shake. It was only a medical examination — nothing more.

"Would you mind unbuttoning the top buttons?" he asked.

She nodded and fumbled with a shaking hand. Slowly she unbuttoned two buttons, exposing her upper chest. He waited for her to complete the task before moving closer. She swallowed hard and lifted her chin, determined not to let him know how much his nearness affected her.

Caleb pressed the chest piece against the ivory skin below her neck. She didn't flinch or even blush like most of his other female patients. For some odd reason, that made his job even more difficult.

Beneath her shirtwaist she wore an eyelet-trimmed camisole embroidered with tiny blue flowers. He sucked in his breath and looked away.

Moving the chest piece, his hand accidentally brushed against her bosom. A soft gasp escaped her and her gaze met his.

"Sorry," he said. In his haste to set her mind at ease, his voice sounded harsh. Ragged.

She lowered her lids and her dark lashes swept her cheekbones. She said nothing, but his ear pieces picked up the quickening of heartbeats.

Examining a woman was never easy. Caleb's college professors taught that protecting a woman's modesty was of utmost importance, even more important than her health. Caleb didn't agree, but he was nonetheless obliged to examine women fully dressed and deliver babies blind, keeping a mother's modesty intact while he fumbled beneath a blanket.

But no woman had been as hard to examine as Molly — not because she was fully dressed but because she made him feel less of a physician and more of a man. Never before had he been so conscious of where he put the chest piece or placed his hands as he was at that moment.

He tried concentrating solely on the patient but it was the woman who commanded his attention. He observed things about her not previously noticed or detected — things not relevant to a medical examination.

Her eyes were an ever-changing sea turning from light to dark green seemingly on a whim. Today they looked like polished jade with little flecks of gold in their depths. One fine brow was arched a tad higher than the other. Her nose turned slightly upward like the corners of her mouth. The dimples on her cheeks looked even more intriguing up close.

"Did you know that lungs are the only organs in the body that can float in water?" He normally asked trivia questions to relax patients or divert their attention. In this case, it was the physician who needed calming and distracting.

Her gaze lifted to his and her dimples

deepened. "I'm sure that information will come in useful one day."

He grinned back at her. Her faint fragrance engulfed him and he envisioned himself in a field of lilacs. Instead of lowering her gaze she looked at him with bold regard, two circles of pink on her cheeks.

"Cough for me."

She did what he asked and he drew back, pulling the stethoscope away and stuffing it back in his bag. "You have a bronchial infection. It doesn't sound too serious." He reached into the depths of his bag and pulled out a brown vial. "Take this two times a day."

She took the glass bottle from him. Their fingers touched briefly before she quickly pulled away. "What happens if I don't take it?"

"You'll either get better or you won't."

She gave a girlish giggle and he recalled the graceful way she danced that day in the barn, could almost hear the musical sound of her voice. Finding himself staring, he quickly averted his gaze and stooped to pick up his leather bag.

"Thank you." She followed him to the entry hall and he turned so suddenly to face her, she bumped into him. His hand shot out to steady her, his fingers curling around her elbow.

"Sorry," she said, stepping away from him.

His hand dropped to his side. "It was my fault." Lost again in the depths of her green eyes, he gave himself a mental shake.

"Uh . . . if there's no improvement in a day or two, let me know."

She nodded. "How . . . how was your session with Donny?" Her voice softened when she said her brother's name but a shadow of worry settled on her forehead. It was all he could do not to chase it away with a touch of his hand.

"It went very well." It wasn't exactly a lie but neither was it accurate. They had a setback today — nothing to be concerned about — or at least that's what he hoped. Donny had refused to get into his chair by himself. Maybe tomorrow.

"You didn't work with him as long as you usually do," she said.

"I . . . have to get back to town." Fearing she may have picked up his hesitation, he quickly added, "I'll try to make up the time tomorrow."

Her face lit up with a smile and something stirred inside, something sweet and tender and dear. Moments passed and still they stared at each other. She was the first to recover or at least look away. "I best not

227

keep you any longer."

He didn't want to leave but there really was no reason to stay. "Get some rest." With that he turned and hurried out the door.

Still shaken from her encounter with Caleb, Molly stood by the fence watching Orbit. Something was wrong. Normally the colt was in constant movement. Never before had she seen him stand so still. His mother stood a short distance away, seemingly unconcerned about her offspring's odd behavior.

The brilliant orange sun was low in the western sky, casting purple shadows over the desert. The wind had died down but the distant mountains were still hidden behind a haze of dust.

Orbit wandered slowly over to his mother, but instead of letting him nurse, she pushed him away with a jab of her nose.

Molly's mouth dropped open. What was going on?

She waved her arm, motioning Brodie over to the fence. Brodie finished unsaddling his horse before joining her.

"I just saw Orbit's mother push him away. She won't let him nurse."

Brodie didn't seem surprised. He leaned on the fence and gazed at the two horses in the distance just as the mare forced the young horse away a second time.

Brodie pushed his hat back. "Looks like she's tired of taking care of him."

"You mean she can turn on him, just like that?" Could nature really be that cruel?

"He's more dependent on his mother than most foals. Guess you might say he's out-stayed his welcome."

Once again Orbit tried to approach the mare. This time she nipped him and Orbit ran away with a high-pitched whinny.

Molly gripped the fence. "We've got to do something before she hurts him."

"Better get him out of there." Brodie walked away.

"Wait," she called. "What do I do then?"

"Wean him," Brodie called back. "Teach him how to take care of himself."

Molly stared after him. How in the world was she supposed to do that?

CHAPTER 19

Molly was very much on Caleb's mind when he drove to the ranch a few days later. He wanted to help her but didn't know how. One thing was clear: She couldn't keep up her frantic pace very much longer. Something had to give.

He looked for her as he pulled in front of the ranch house and turned off the engine. The loud boom from Bertha's tailpipe bounced like a cannon fire. Horses whinnied and a squawking chicken took off in a flurry of feathers. Magic placed his front paws on the dash and barked. There was no sign of Molly and he frowned. Today was Wednesday and that was the day she worked with the horses. He knew her schedule like he knew his own.

His office hours were nine to two, which left afternoons free to work with Donny unless there was an emergency. A rash of late-night medical calls, mostly women delivering babies plus an unexpected death, had interfered with his sleep for almost a week. Two nights previous, he'd nodded off while driving and had nearly run Bertha into a ditch.

Though some older citizens still regarded him with suspicion, he had enough patients to keep him busy, many with lung conditions. The prevalence of breathing problems puzzled him until Matt Corrigan, editor of the *Cactus Patch Gazette,* explained that most had the condition prior to moving to the territory.

"Everyone knows that the desert is good for what ails you," Corrigan said. "It's a regular sanitarium."

Not all patients flourished in the desert. Little Jimmy didn't. Nor did Miss Whitehead, a hypochondriac whose long and lengthy "organ recitals" were every bit as tiresome as a recital of *Gray's Anatomy.*

But his most challenging patient by far was Donny. Caleb had known working with Donny wouldn't be easy, but it turned out to be far more difficult than he imagined. It wasn't just the problem of getting muscles that hadn't been worked in years, if ever, to move. The real difficulty was getting Donny to see past his disability, and he had reached a plateau.

Today Donny's stubborn expression came within minutes of Caleb's arrival.

Without a word, Caleb attempted to lift Donny out of his chair. "Let go of me," Donny said. "What are you doing?" He struggled but his weak muscles were no match for Caleb.

Caleb set Donny on the floor and rolled him over, facedown. Donny wasn't even strong enough to raise himself on his arms. All he could do was turn his head and look up at him in confusion and maybe even fear. He looked as helpless as an upside-down desert tortoise.

"Wait till I tell my sister!"

"I'll tell her myself and save you the trouble." Caleb felt sorry for the youth but he knew of no other way to break through Donny's resistance. "Let me see you get into your chair."

"I can't. You know I can't."

Caleb sat on his haunches next to Donny's side. "You can learn."

Magic rolled on his back next to Donny, paws in the air. It wasn't often that someone was on the floor at his level and he meant to make the most of it.

"See? Even Magic agrees that you can learn." Magic's antics usually made Donny laugh, but not today. "Getting into your chair by yourself is an important step. Eventually you'll be able to dress without help and use the privy in private. You'll be able to do a great many things."

"I can't! Don't you understand? I'm crippled!" Head down, he slammed his fists against the floor and his face turned red.

"What do you think you're doing?"

At the sound of Molly's voice, Caleb stood to find Molly glaring at him, her green eyes smoldering with fury.

"This is part of his training and —"

"Pick him up. Now!" She waited in seething silence until Caleb had returned Donny to his chair. "I wish to speak to you outside," she said, her tone leaving no room for argument. She stormed from the room.

Caleb squeezed Donny's shoulder. "Think about what I said." He glanced at Magic curled up by the wheelchair and left the room, hoping to quell the confrontation with Molly he knew awaited him. Somehow he had to make her understand his methods. Each step forward was followed by two steps back, but he had no intention of giving up and he didn't want her to give up either.

She stood on the verandah, hands on her hips, looking ready to fight him tooth and nail. Normally she wore a man's shirt but today a yellow shirtwaist topped her divided skirt. The bright color offered a startling contrast to the dark look on her face. He could almost feel sparks flying out of her. Anger had never looked so enticing.

"How dare you treat my brother like an animal!" she fumed.

Caleb drew back in surprise. "Is that what you think I'm doing?"

"What else can I think? You said you would help him. You said he had improved. From what I can see, all you've done is make matters worse!"

"All right, I admit it. I haven't been completely honest with you about his progress, but I *will* help him. I *am* helping him. We're close to a breakthrough."

"Making my brother lie helpless on the floor is no breakthrough."

"That's just it, Molly. Your brother *is* helpless."

"You don't need to tell me that," she snapped.

"What I'm trying to say is that he doesn't have to be."

"Your services are no longer required," she said, her voice edged in ice. "I think it would be better if you just leave." She turned but he grabbed her by the wrist and drew her close.

"What are you afraid of, Molly? Are you

afraid that if your brother becomes more self-sufficient he won't need you? Is that why you keep him confined?"

Color drained from her face and she pulled her arm away. "How dare you! You know nothing about me or my brother."

"I know enough," he said. "I know you treat him like a child and —"

Something seemed to snap inside her and she came at him with flying fists. He caught her by both arms. Her thick dark lashes flew up and they stared at each other, her flesh soft and smooth beneath his touch.

He felt a stirring inside. He wanted to bury his head in her wealth of dark hair, to follow her sweet, warm breath to its source. God help him!

Something like a flame passed between them and she shuddered as if she felt it too. The moment passed and she pulled away.

"Send me your bill," she said, surprising him with her calm, controlled voice. Had she not felt what he felt?

"I don't want your money."

"Then we have no further business." She raced into the house. Magic barely had time to scoot outside before she slammed the door shut.

Caleb stared at the space she no longer occupied. Molly was gone but he could still smell her fragrance, still remember the unexpected thrill that shot through him just before she pulled free of his grasp.

Now I've done it. It wasn't the first time he'd lost a patient for lack of tact. But none of the patients he'd lost in the past bothered him more than losing Donny. He hated to admit it, but losing Molly was what he regretted most.

Donny sat on the verandah where Molly had left him earlier that day. Gaze focused on the corral in the distance, he squinted against the bright afternoon sun. A black mustang ran from one end of the corral to the other, tail high and mane flowing. Molly stood with rope in hand, forcing the horse to keep running.

The horse's name was Lightning because he tried to run away from every new experience.

"We have to teach it that running away is not the answer," Molly explained when Donny had questioned her.

He secretly wished the horse would run away and take him along. He almost imagined himself seated high above the pounding hooves. He often thought of the day the doctor pushed him around the courtyard. It was almost as if he were running, as if his wheels had become legs and his flapping arms had become wings. Running might not help Lightning, but it would be the answer to Donny's prayers.

He reached into the side of his chair and pulled out the iron pipe he kept there. The doctor said that if he built up his arms and chest muscles, he would take him to the Flagstaff observatory. Though the doctor now stayed away, Donny meant him to keep his promise. So day after day he pumped the iron up and down. Even at night when sleep escaped him, he lay in bed and worked with the pipe, raising his arms to the ceiling.

It hurt, though — it hurt a lot. Sometimes his muscles and shoulders felt so sore he could hardly sleep.

Both hands on the pipe, he lifted it over his head, counting each up-and-down movement. Today he made it all the way to eight before his muscles began to burn.

Tucking the pipe back into the seat, he breathed out and held his breath. The doctor said he needed to build up his lung capacity, and that might help his asthma. The breathing exercises were harder to do than the physical ones and so far the longest he could hold his breath was only a few seconds.

Donny reached his arms over the chair arms and grabbed hold of the wheels. In the past, he'd not been strong enough to move the wheelchair himself, but now he managed to move it a couple of inches along the verandah's wooden boards.

Sweating, he rested a moment and waited until he caught his breath before trying again. He pressed down on the wheels with everything he had. This time his chair caught on a loose board. He jerked his torso back and forth.

"Come on, come on." The chair suddenly lunged forward, picking up speed as it rolled toward the steps.

He fumbled with the wheels. "Stop," he gasped. "Stop!"

The front wheel hit the top step with a bump. The chair tilted, pitching him forward. He sailed over the steps and hit the ground hard.

Molly stifled a yawn. She'd spent the last two nights sleeping in Orbit's stall trying to calm him. The first night away from his mother Orbit paced all night, his loud whinnies keeping the cowhands awake and upsetting the other horses.

She held up her hand. Orbit poked at the hay in her palm. "Come on, you can do it.

It's good. Yum, yum."

This time, instead of pulling away, Orbit took the hay in his mouth.

Molly grinned. "See? I told you it was good to eat." While the horse chewed, Molly reached for another handful of hay.

Ruckus ran into the stables, shouting, "Molly, quick, you're needed at the house."

"Why? What's wrong?" she gasped, but Ruckus had vanished as quickly as he'd come. Dropping the hay, she shot out of the stall, slammed the gate shut, and ran. A group of cowboys were gathered in front of the verandah. Alarmed by the overturned wheelchair, a cold knot of fear caught in her throat.

Heart beating madly, she pushed through the circle of cowhands. "What happened, what —"

Donny lay sprawled on the ground. His eyes were open but he looked deathly white. She dropped to her knees by his side. "Donny, speak to me. Oh, *God.*"

"Looks like he fell down the steps," Stretch said. "We found him all laid out like Sunday's going-to-meeting suit."

She leaned closer. "Tell me where it hurts."

Donny turned his head toward her.

239

"Molly, I flew. I flew through the air like a bird."

She checked his head, neck, and back, but he didn't seem to be injured.

"Would you like us to take him to his room, ma'am?" Stretch asked.

"Yes, please."

Stretch knuckled Wishbone on the arm. "Give me a hand."

Stretch lifted Donny under the arms, Wishbone grabbed his feet, and they carried Donny up the steps and into the house.

"I flew like an eagle," Donny called.

Next to her, Brodie turned the wheelchair upright. "Where do you want me to put it?"

"On the verandah will be fine," she said.

He stood looking at the ground, rubbing the back of his neck beneath his ponytail. "He's gonna be all right," he said, and after a moment's hesitation added, "He's tough like his sister."

It was the first civil word he'd spoken to her since the day she'd frozen in front of the stallion.

"Thank you, Brodie." She hurried up the steps and into the house.

Caleb sat at the table in the small but tidy kitchen eating breakfast, Aunt Bessie in the chair opposite. She wore a blue and white flannelette wrapper with a drawstring waist, but it wasn't her apparel that grabbed his attention. It was her face. Something about it looked . . .

Paint.

Catching himself staring, he lowered his gaze to his plate. "You make the best cackleberries I've ever eaten." He mopped up the yellow yolk with a piece of fresh-baked bread.

"Why, thank you, Caleb." Aunt Bessie smoothed her wrapper.

Something in her voice caught his attention. Obviously she had something on her mind. "Everything all right?"

"Not entirely. As you know, my nephew is getting married next week."

"It's the talk of the town," Caleb assured her, knowing she would be pleased.

She gave him a quick smile that faded into a frown. "I don't know if you've noticed, but Cactus Patch has a serious alcohol problem."

Indeed, he had noticed. Hardly a morning went by that he wasn't greeted by a steady stream of men wanting relief from hangovers. A doctor could almost build a practice solely on treating town drunks.

"I'm afraid it's a problem in most western towns," he said. Boredom, economic problems, and loneliness were all contributing factors.

Aunt Bessie let out a sigh. "Not only do I have to worry about the preacher staying sober but my singer and pianist as well. Somehow I have to find a way to keep the three of them sober."

"I don't think you have to worry about Reverend Bland."

"Maybe so, but keeping the other two sober is like trying to rub the V off a liberty head nickel. Is there anything you can do to cure them of drinking?"

"You mean like a vaccination?" Had she not looked so serious he might have laughed, but he didn't want to hurt her feelings. Some people had a strange idea about what vaccinations could do. One man had even asked him to vaccinate a wife addicted to ordering from the Montgomery Ward catalog. "I'm afraid not."

Aunt Bessie pushed a gray strand of hair behind her ear and cleared her throat. "Are you planning to bring Molly to the wedding?"

His heart thumped. "I hadn't thought about it."

"What a lovely girl." She gave him a motherly smile. "A pity that she's got her heart set on becoming Miss Walker's heiress." Her lips puckered as if the very thought was distasteful.

"I'm aware of Molly's plans."

"And did you also know that Miss Walker forbids anyone inheriting the ranch to marry?"

His fork froze in midair. "Forbids?"

"Have you ever heard anything more ridiculous in your life? It goes against nature. Why, the good Lord must be shaking in His boots at such nonsense."

"I'm sure you're right." Caleb placed his fork on his plate and dabbed his mouth with a napkin. "What would happen if Moll . . . Miss Hatfield . . . were to marry?"

"She would lose her rights to the ranch. It's all legal, even though it goes against God's will. I hear Miss Walker doesn't do anything without her lawyer."

Caleb sat perfectly still. Why would anyone — especially someone like Molly — agree to such a thing?

Donny! Practically everything she did was for her brother, including forfeiting any sort of happiness for herself.

Aunt Bessie leaned toward him as if sensing she'd lost his attention. "It's probably for the best. I don't know that she would make any man a good wife. I heard that she was a dance hall girl back in Dobson Creek."

He knew she was a singer but a dance hall girl? It would certainly explain a lot about her, including her choice of attire and the graceful way she moved. He still warmed to the memory of her singing and dancing in the barn.

"I take it you don't think a dance hall girl would make a good wife?"

"Mercy! Don't get me wrong. I believe in keeping an open mind, but you don't want to open it so far as to come unhinged."

"I should say not," he said lightly.

"Why, even Luke's fiancée had a questionable background, but I never held that against her. It seems to go with the times, doesn't it? Backgrounds just aren't what they used to be."

"I have a hard time believing Miss Tenney led a less than spotless life." The few times he'd run into the blacksmith's fiancée, she'd looked like a lady. Spoke like one too.

"Looks can be deceiving. You'd never know by looking at her that she writes dime novels, and one was even banned in Boston. Still, I told myself open mind, open mind. But a dance hall girl . . ." She shook her head.

"Just exactly what kind of wife does

your . . . open mind think I need?" he asked, curious.

"A fine doctor like you needs a good, upright Christian woman," she said.

"Absolutely," he agreed, preferably one with green eyes. Startled by the unbidden thought, he dropped his fork and reached for his coffee cup.

Aunt Bessie continued, "She has to be kind and considerate and willing to let you put your patients' needs before her own."

He took a sip of the hot brew. "Nothing less would do," he murmured. And she must have the voice of an angel. Yet another memory of Molly singing flashed in his head.

"Fortunately, I happen to know a couple of young women who fit the bill. If you like, I'd be happy to invite one or even both to Sunday dinner."

Caleb stood and cleared his plate, setting it in the sink. "That's very kind of you, but a bit premature. I'm not ready to take a wife." That much was true, but since Aunt Bessie looked about to argue the point, he quickly grabbed a Meat Fibrine Dog Cake and walked outside to feed Magic.

Molly was nothing more than a distraction. Pretty as a picture, she was, with the voice of an angel, but a distraction nonetheless. If he told himself that enough times, he might even come to believe it.

CHAPTER 20

Molly let herself into the doctor's office, setting off a jangle of merry bells.

"I'll be right with you," Caleb called from behind a half-open door.

She swallowed hard and sat on one of the chairs lining one wall. Just being in his office made her feel . . . what? Nervous? Anxious? Confused?

She'd thought long and hard about making this trip but didn't know what else to do. Caleb was the only doctor in town.

Still shaken by Donny's accident, she blamed Caleb for filling his head with all those crazy notions. Thank God he hadn't been seriously injured when his wheelchair flew down the steps, but there had been other incidents just as worrisome. Only that morning she found him on the bedroom floor. She was a nervous wreck worrying about what her brother would do next.

The door sprang all the way open and Caleb filled the doorway. He seemed to sap the very air out of the room with his presence and suddenly she couldn't breathe.

His hair was mussed and he looked tired, as if he'd been up all night. Faint lines lightly etched his normally smooth face and his shirt and trousers were wrinkled as if he'd slept in them.

He looked surprised to see her. "Molly. Is everything all right?"

She stood with a casualness she didn't feel. Somehow he always made her feel like a confused schoolgirl who didn't know her own mind. She dug her fingers into the velvet fringe handbag and fought for control. The handbag didn't go with her divided skirt, checkered shirt, and wide-brimmed hat, but it was the only one she owned.

"No, it's not all right."

He frowned. "Come inside." He stepped aside to let her into the examination room and then led her into his office. Magic greeted her with wagging tail and she stooped to pet him.

"Have a seat."

She straightened and decided to remain standing. "I won't take up much of your time." Perhaps if she remained standing she could keep her wits about her.

"How is your cough?"

"Much improved, thank you." She cleared her throat. "I . . . I apologize for my . . . behavior the other day . . . about Donny. You did what you thought best."

Caleb sat on the edge of his desk, arms folded across his broad chest. "So did you."

"At least we're in accord about something," she said.

"We both want what's best for your brother. We just have different ideas on how to achieve it." He studied her and her cheeks grew warm under his scrutiny. "Since you're here, may I assume that you're having second thoughts about dismissing me?"

"You assume incorrectly." She sounded unbearably prim even to her own ears.

"What a pity. So why *are* you here?"

"I'm here because I ran out of Donny's asthma medicine."

He dropped his relaxed easy manner and assumed an air of professionalism. "What do you usually give him?"

"Nitrate of Amyl."

He grimaced. "That's a dangerous drug." He rose to reach into a high cabinet. "Try this," he said, closing the cabinet door. "It's safer and just as effective." He handed her a small bottle labeled Vial of Lobelia. "How is Donny otherwise?"

249

She slipped the medication into her hand-bag. "He's fine now, no thanks to you."

"What did I do?"

"You put all those fancy ideas into his head. Now he thinks he can fly."

Caleb's eyebrows rose. "Fly?"

"Just the other day he took a tumble from the verandah. He could have been seriously injured. Fortunately, he didn't suffer more than a few bumps and bruises. And this morning" — she shuddered at the memory — "this morning I found him on the floor of his room."

"And you think I had something to do with all this?"

She took a deep breath. "He's not been the same since you worked with him. He's more moody and difficult to handle. You put all those ideas into his head."

Caleb shook his head. "I didn't put them there. Becoming more independent is part of growing up."

"If he injures himself he won't have a chance to grow up."

He reached for both her hands, and warm shivers shot up her arms.

"Molly, I want to help."

Her breath caught in her chest and she couldn't think, let alone speak.

He stared down at her calloused palms

before meeting her gaze. Feeling self-conscious, she pulled her hands away.

"Let me work with him," he said. "I can teach him safe ways to move."

Something in his eyes made her hesitate. He looked at her more like a friend than a doctor, and this only added to her turmoil. "He's the only family I have," she whispered at last. "If anything happens to him . . ."

"I'll do my best to make sure nothing does."

"I don't know . . ."

"I'm not promising miracles, but I can help him. From what you say, I've already helped. Admit it."

"Maybe. I don't know." She shook her head. "I used to trust Donny to stay where I put him, but no more."

He folded his arms. "That's not necessarily a bad thing."

Wanting to believe what he said was true, her resistance crumbled. "I can't pay much."

He shrugged. "Seeing Donny improve will be payment enough."

"And you won't treat him like an animal."

"Never did, never will."

"I don't want him on the floor," she said.

His jaw tightened. "If I'm to help your brother, I have to do it my way. If you question my methods or limit the way I do

251

things, then nothing will get accomplished. I'll work your brother hard, and I expect him to give me everything he's got in return. If my expectations seem harsh, it's only for Donny's own good."

Oddly enough Brodie expressed a similar opinion about training horses. Brodie's methods seemed harsh at times, but he got results. Still, she wasn't sure she had the stomach for what Caleb proposed.

"If I agree to your . . . conditions, will you agree to mine?"

Caleb slid off the desk, standing tall in front of her, but she did not back down. "Probably not," he said, "but go on."

"You will work with Donny only in my presence." Tough training methods might work on horses, but her brother required a gentler approach.

"Absolutely not."

"He's my brother."

"I'm his doctor."

"Only if I say so!"

They stood practically toe to toe. If she wasn't so much shorter, their noses would have touched.

"Sorry. I can't work under your conditions," he said.

Surprised at his unwillingness to meet her demands, she refused to back down. "Then we have no further business."

His expression changed, like the closing of a door. "The medicine I gave you should help with the asthma. Have him drink tea. Don't know what it is exactly, but there's something in tea that seems to help asthmatics."

"Thank you," she said, slipping the strings of her handbag over her wrist. The room was small, but the two of them seemed miles apart and she regretted it more than she could say.

She looked away from his steady gaze and turned.

She let herself out but stood for several moments on the boardwalk in front of his office. She was shaking, but whether from disappointment or something else, she didn't know. Loud voices wafted from the saloon across the way, followed by a gunshot. The marshal practically sprang out of his office and raced across the street.

Shuddering, Molly walked around a drunken man sprawled facedown in the dirt. She'd grown accustomed to such sights in Dobson Creek and never given it much thought. Today the man's self-imposed helplessness filled her with disgust.

CHAPTER 21

Bessie hunkered beneath a corner table at the Desert Rose Saloon and put a finger to her mouth. "Shh." She motioned her sister closer.

Lula-Belle rolled her eyes but crawled to Bessie's side, bumping her head on the table's underside.

Bessie had chosen this particular spot to hide because the table was occupied by Hank Gristle, slumped in the chair passed out cold. Since the man didn't look to be much company, she figured others would avoid his table. So far she was proved right.

"This is the most ridiculous thing you've ever come up with," Lula-Belle whispered, rubbing her head. "And that's saying a lot."

"Quit your bellyaching," Bessie said. "It's for a good cause." She'd do anything for her two nephews. "I want Luke's wedding to be perfect."

And she meant to see that it was. Bessie

knew from the moment she'd set eyes on Kate Tenney that she was the right woman for her nephew. Luke tended to be thick-headed at times, just like her husband, Sam. For that reason it took a great deal of persuasion on Bessie's part to bring him and Kate together, but it was worth every anxious moment she'd gone through. She'd promised her dying sister all those years ago to take care of her two boys and that's what she'd done. Was still doing, although Michael, the youngest of the two brothers, still required work.

Like all the saloons in town, the Desert Rose Saloon was long and narrow. Since taxes were based on lot frontage, not length, some saloons were little more than a door wide and a hundred or more feet long.

The smell of whiskey and cactus wine permeated the air and the blue haze of smoke burned her eyes. She was covered in sawdust and her knees, back, and chair warmer hurt like crazy. What a person had to go through just to put on a decent wedding!

It was early yet and the saloon was only half full. Others would soon arrive. It was a rare night that every saloon in town wasn't packed to the gills. Miners, cowboys, husbands, fathers, Christians, and non-

255

Christians — pretty much every man in town showed up sooner or later.

Fortunately, that didn't include her husband, Sam, or Lula-Belle's husband, Murphy, but only because they couldn't keep their eyes open much pass seven p.m. It appeared that the only cure for alcohol was old age.

She glanced around the room at men in various stages of stupor and was sickened. "What a crying shame they can't figure out a better use of their time," she whispered.

"I was just thinking the same about us," Lula-Belle whispered back.

Little Jimmy Trotter's father, Harvey, sat in a corner next to a half-empty whiskey bottle. A farmer by trade, he wore a plaid shirt under denim overalls. The same sun that burned his skin dark brown had bleached his hair pale yellow.

Bessie shook her head. *The man finds out his son has some sort of blood cancer and instead of turning to the Lord he turns to booze.*

It didn't help that Reverend Bland drank himself silly following the death of his little girl. Some men used the preacher's lapse as an excuse to justify their own disgraceful behavior.

"Okay, now that you dragged me in here,

what are you planning to do?" Lula-Belle asked in a hushed voice.

That was just it; Bessie didn't have a plan. Never before having stepped foot in a saloon, she hadn't the faintest idea how to convince the owner to close his doors on the eve of the wedding.

She glanced outside, wondering if they should just leave. Then she saw something that lifted her spirits. That new woman, Molly Hatfield, just walked past the saloon. Now if that wasn't an answer to prayer, nothing was.

"Stay here."

Before Lula-Belle had a chance to protest, Bessie crawled out from under the table and hurried outside. "Molly!"

Molly turned and greeted her with a smile. "Why, Mrs. —"

"Aunt Bessie."

"Aunt Bessie, how nice to see you."

Lula-Belle came barreling out of the saloon like she was being chased by wolves. "How dare you take off and leave me in there by myself!" Upon spotting Molly, she tried to gather her dignity but it was too late.

Molly looked from one to the other. "You were in the saloon?"

Bessie saw no point in denying it. "Yes,

we were, but it was for a good cause." She lowered her voice. "Since you were once, eh . . . worked in a saloon . . . I wonder if you would be kind enough to assist us?"

"Yes, of course," Molly said, curiosity written all over her face. "How can I help?"

Bessie quickly explained the problem. "So you see, if something isn't done, the wedding will be ruined."

"Oh, I hope not," Molly said. "How do you plan to get your singer and piano player to stay sober?"

"That's just it," Bessie said. "I don't have a plan. I was hoping you would help us come up with one."

"Have you talked with them and explained . . ."

"That's a great idea. Come with me." Aunt Bessie grabbed Molly's arm and practically dragged her to the batwing doors. "Aren't you coming, Lula-Belle?"

"You got Molly, you don't need me." Lula-Belle hobbled away, rocking side to side like a child's hobby horse.

Bessie led Molly inside and ducked beneath the table, motioning Molly to join her. Molly looked momentarily startled but she nonetheless dropped down on all fours and scrambled beneath the table, earning Bessie's approval.

"Panhandle is the town piano player and he's due any moment," Bessie explained, keeping her voice low. "He rides into town the same time every day."

She arranged her bulky form until she could clearly see the bar by peering between Hank's legs. She poked Molly with her elbow. "There he is."

Molly, on hands and knees, stared at him.

Bessie whispered, "He can only play when he's sober." Right now he was so drunk he couldn't hit the ground with his hat in three tries. "If Panhandle is here, Winkleman can't be far behind. He agreed to sing at the wedding." He and Panhandle were thicker than feathers in a pillow. "Winkleman has a lovely smooth voice — that is, when he's not three sheets to the wind."

Panhandle bow-legged his way across the room, bellied up to the bar, and lifted a shabby boot onto the shiny brass foot rail. Randy Sprocket, the saloon keeper, placed a shot glass on the polished bar and reached for a bottle of whiskey.

Molly moved her head until it practically touched Bessie's. "Okay, here's what you do."

She whispered her plan. "Is that clear?"

Bessie nodded. Mercy. The girl wasn't just pretty, she also had a good head on her shoulders. Still, what she proposed was a bit more daring than Bessie was prepared for. "You have to come with me."

Molly nodded. "Just let me know when you're ready."

Bessie gathered her wits about her and braced herself with a deep breath. "Now."

She struggled to her feet like a newborn colt, her creaking bones hollering in protest. In her anxiety to reach the bar, she accidentally knocked Gristle off his chair. Gasping, she dropped by his side. A few blurry-eyed men glanced at her but were too far gone to concern themselves with a woman who may or may not have killed a man.

Frantic, Bessie checked Gristle's pulse and head. Sprawled on the floor he continued to snore away, seeming none the worse for wear.

"I think he's okay," Molly said.

Blowing out her breath, Bessie stood, brushed the sawdust off her skirt, stepped around Gristle, and sauntered over to Panhandle with as much dignity and authority as she could muster. Molly was right behind her and the two of them surrounded the man at the bar like two determined bookends.

A painting of a naked woman hung on the

wall behind the bar, looming over the bottles of liquor arranged on a shelf. Averting her eyes, Bessie gave her head a determined toss. She would match her purple gown and carefully applied carmine and complexion powder with the bare-skinned woman in the portrait any day.

Molly signaled with a slight nod of the head that Bessie was to speak first. "Hello, Panhandle."

Clearly smitten with Molly, Panhandle managed to pull his gaze away from her long enough to give Bessie a quick glance. "Bessie."

He was one of the few men in town who didn't bother covering up his pox marks with a beard. He liked to brag that he had as many pox marks on his face as the piano had keys. Bessie suspected that before his face was disfigured by disease he had been a handsome man. Nothing about his appearance suggested he was a piano player, except perhaps his long tapered fingers.

He downed his whiskey in one quick swallow. He then wiped his mouth with the back of his hand. "Does your" — he struggled to find the word — "m-mister know you're here?" he slurred.

Molly answered his question with a question. "Does your missus know *you're* here?"

He caught the saloon keeper's attention with a wagging finger and pointed to his empty glass. "Where . . . where else would I be?"

"Home with your family," Bessie said. He had three children but he and his wife had lost two to diphtheria. He hadn't been the same since.

Sprocket slung a dirty rag over his shoulder, picked up a half-empty bottle, and filled Panhandle's glass.

Panhandle gulped down his drink and the bartender immediately replenished it. "That's ex-exactly where *you* thould be."

"For your information, I have an equal right to be here," Bessie said. "We both do," she said, indicating Molly.

Panhandle laughed in her face, squinting through unfocused eyes. "The only way you're ever gonna get equal rights, Bess, is to thacrifice some."

"I'm not much for sacrificing," Bessie admitted.

"I'm sure that Mr. . . . eh . . . Panhandle isn't much for sacrifice himself," Molly said.

Panhandle turned his head toward Molly. "What makes you say that?"

"A discerning man like yourself would demand only the best," Molly explained with a flutter of eyelashes. "Which is why we're surprised that you would patronize *this* particular saloon."

Panhandle lifted his glass. "Why wouldn't I? It has the highest p-poker thakes in town."

Molly shrugged. "That's fine if you don't mind drinking watered-down whiskey."

Panhandle stared at the amber liquid in his glass, his face turning an alarming shade of red. "Watered?"

"I thought you knew," Bessie said, emulating Molly's calm demeanor the best she could by pretending to study a fingernail. Mercy, her heart pounded to beat the band and Molly looked cool as a block of ice. How did she do that?

Panhandle frowned. He then took a sip of his drink, swooshed it around in his mouth, and slammed the glass onto the bar. "You're right."

Bessie glanced up at the tin ceiling and feigned a look of childlike innocence. Molly's idea worked! It was amazing how a mere suggestion could sway a man's opinion about almost anything. God forgive her and Molly the lie, but it was for a good cause.

Panhandle pulled away from the bar. "It's the last thime I thum in here." He staggered away without paying.

"Hey, where you going?" the saloon keeper called. "You owe me."

"I don't owe you nothin'," Panhandle slurred. "These two ladies here sed you're messin' with the kick. Gonna get me thum good thuff."

Sprocket slammed the bottle on the counter and glared at Bessie and Molly. "Why'd you tell him that? This whiskey is pure as gold."

"*Fool's* gold you mean," Molly said, staring him straight in the face.

Sprocket got all red and looked guilty as a two-timing husband. Bessie was taken aback. The whiskey *was* watered down, but how in the world did Molly know that?

"What do you want?" Sprocket demanded. "Money?"

"Tell him, Aunt Bessie," Molly said.

Bessie went to put her foot on the brass foot railing and accidentally turned over a spittoon. Sidestepping the spilled tobacco juice, she leaned on the bar, hands clasped beneath her neatly stacked chins. "My nephew is getting married next Saturday."

The saloon keeper wiped the bar with a dirty rag, purposely knocking against Bessie's arm. "You're losing your touch, Bessie. The wedding hasn't yet been declared a national holiday."

Bessie gave him a closed-mouth smile. "I'm working on it."

Sprocket shook his head. "I think the heat addled your think box." He glanced at Molly. "Yours too."

Bessie pulled her arms off the bar, all pretenses gone. "And your whiskey is watered down."

"But it's not too late to make amends," Molly added.

He squinted. "What's that supposed to mean?"

Molly leaned forward. "It means that you will stop cheating your customers and . . . you will close by three p.m. Friday and stay closed until after Saturday's wedding ceremony."

The saloon keeper's hooked beak practically met Molly's dainty upturned nose. Despite his menacing look, Molly didn't seem the least bit intimidated.

"Let me get this straight. You want me to lose a whole day's business just because of a blasted wedding?"

"You already lost one customer's business," Molly said.

"For your information, I've got expenses to pay. We have more than eight hundred residents in this town. That means the saloon tax is now fifty dollars a quarter — double what it was only a few years ago."

Bessie had no sympathy for the man. He

and the other saloon owners in town had wrecked more families than all the loose women put together.

Molly didn't look sympathetic either. She looked downright determined — Bessie's kind of woman.

"Men are fussy about their whiskey," Molly said, clearly an expert in such matters. "If they suspect that you're charging full price for watered whiskey, you'll end up closing your doors permanently."

Tom Mason set his glass on the bar next to Molly with a leer in her direction. He was as tall as he was wide, his legs and arms as round and firm as tree trunks. A known troublemaker, hardly a day went by that the marshal didn't have to lock him up for disturbing the peace. "What's that you said?"

"Don't pay any attention to her," Sprocket muttered. "You can't believe anything an old gossip says."

"It's only gossip if it's not true," Bessie argued. She then repeated Molly's claim for Mason's benefit.

"Why, you —" Mason grabbed hold of Sprocket's shirt and dragged him over the counter in one swift move.

This gave the other customers an excuse to rise to their feet and start swinging.

Quick as a flash, fists flew every which way. Chairs whizzed across the room. Tables overturned. Cards, chips, and glasses crashed to the floor. A bullet hit the naked woman where no sun should shine and the painting crashed to the floor.

Nodding approval at the woman's demise, Bessie ducked and weaved her way around the brawling men, but before she could escape, a man grabbed her.

"Let me go!" she yelled, hitting him with her fists.

Out of the corner of her eye she saw Molly climb up on the bar. What in the world? As quickly as it started, the fight ended. It took Bessie a moment to know why. Molly was singing. Not only was she belting out a bawdy drinking song, she was swinging her shapely hips in a way that . . . well, she was swinging her shapely hips.

The man holding Bessie became so engrossed he seemed to have forgotten her. She pulled away and he made no move to stop her.

Bessie was no expert on dance hall girls, heavens, no! But unless she missed her guess, Molly wasn't half bad and even the saloon keeper looked enamored.

The men tapped their feet and clapped their hands. When Molly finished singing she let one of the men help her to the floor.

She stood a chair upright and leaned over the bar. "Do we have a deal?" she asked in a loud husky voice.

The saloon keeper waved his dirty rag in surrender. "Okay, okay, you win. I'll close Friday at six."

"Three," Molly said.

"Five."

They settled on four.

Bessie couldn't believe it. "We did it," she all but crowed after leaving the saloon. She lifted her hand in the air and Molly's hand touched hers with a resounding clap.

"We were lucky." Molly brushed the sawdust off her skirt. "But we could have gotten ourselves killed."

"Yes, but it was for a good cause." Bessie started down the boardwalk just as the marshal came running up the street — late to the party as usual. "Come along, Molly."

Molly hurried to catch up to her. "Where are we going?"

"Where do you think?" Bessie replied. She couldn't resist sashaying Molly-style as she ambled along the boardwalk. "To the Golden Eagle Saloon. I'm not about to let one little bar fight stop me. Get ready to sing and, eh . . . swing those hips."

CHAPTER 22

Molly didn't want to go to the wedding. She didn't even know the "happy couple," as everyone referred to them. She'd never met the groom and had caught a glimpse of the bride for only a brief moment.

But it wasn't just the wedding, it was the church. Just the memory of being forced to stand outside during her father's funeral filled her with rage. And the few times she'd stepped foot in the Cactus Patch church confirmed her opinion: churchgoers were a bunch of hypocrites! *Sorry, God, but it's true.*

There were exceptions, of course, Aunt Bessie being one. But even her friendly smile couldn't make up for all the judgmental glares from other worshippers. Still, she had no intention of letting Aunt Bessie down, not after their mutual escapades and knowing how much the wedding meant to her.

Never had Molly seen so much fuss over a

wedding. The way the ranch hands talked about the nuptials was unnatural. If a miner ever went to a wedding, he was either the groom or dragged there at gunpoint — sometimes both. It struck her as odd that the ranch hands looked forward to the event and couldn't stop talking about the bride-to-be.

"That Kate was really somethin'," Ruckus said. "I never saw anyone have so much trouble stayin' on a horse."

He wasn't the only one enamored with the woman named Kate. Stretch told about the time she read them a novel. "A love story," he said, without embarrassment. "And she writ every word herself."

Even Wishbone got into the act. "Remember the time she climbed the windmill?"

"And the time she was chased by a javelina," one of the other ranch hands added.

Molly was tired of all the talk about the wonderful, divine Kate. "Why isn't Miss Walker going to the wedding?"

Ruckus shook his head. "I don't think the boss lady will ever forgive her for givin' up the ranch for marriage."

"She doesn't have to worry about me runnin' off and marrying." Since singing at the Cactus Patch saloons, she'd worked even harder to learn ranching and could now ride and rope with the best of them. She didn't want to go back to being a dance hall girl — she couldn't. All those leering men. All those horrible drunks. She shuddered. It was the ranch or nothing. Had to be.

Nothing could stop her now. Not even her silly schoolgirl crush on the handsome and charming Caleb Fairbanks.

Ruckus insisted that he and his wife, Sylvia, drive her and Donny to the church. She debated on what to wear and settled on her yellow dress with puffed sleeves. The modest neckline made up for the bright — some might even say bold — color. People would stare. They always did, but it was better they stare at her than Donny. Protecting her brother was all that mattered. It was uppermost in her mind practically every waking moment.

Donny wore his dark pants and white shirt and a tie made from rattlesnake skin that Ruckus loaned him.

People were milling outside the church when they arrived, greeting friends and sharing news. All talk stopped when Molly stepped down from the buckboard. She didn't recognize any of the men staring at her, but they certainly seemed to know her. A few men winked and tried to talk to her but were yanked back by glaring wives. Molly glared back. If it hadn't been for her and Aunt Bessie, most of these men would have been in no condition to attend the wedding. This was the thanks she got.

Cactus Patch churchgoers were every bit as narrow-minded as they had been back home in Dobson Creek and she wanted no part of them.

Seething, Molly held her head high and walked past the crowd, drawing attention away from her brother with an ease that only came with practice. Her feigned poise deserted her the moment she spotted Caleb.

Heart skipping a beat, she met his gaze with a hesitant look, the last encounter in his office a sword hanging over their heads. Had he heard how she and Aunt Bessie forced the saloons to close down? Not that it mattered. Of course it didn't.

He tipped his hat politely, keeping his thoughts hidden behind hooded eyes. She walked by him with a slight nod that belied her churning emotions.

A short while later she tossed a glance over her shoulder to find him still watching her. Cheeks flaring, she quickly followed Ruckus and the wheelchair into the vestibule.

■ ■ ■ ■

Bessie had arrived at the church early that day. There was little left to do except re-arrange a basket of flowers, straighten a bow, and drape a satin ribbon over the piano. The church had never looked so lovely. Dressed to the nines in her very best green taffeta frock, face deftly painted, she bustled up the aisle in a swish of swirling, rustling skirts.

The door flew open and her sister rushed into the chapel like a hen chased by a fox, feathers and tightly wound curls all aflutter. "Bessie, you won't believe the news. Mr. Winkleman is dead!"

Bessie gasped. "Are you sure?"

Lula-Belle gave an indignant nod. "Of course I'm sure. Heard it with my own two ears."

"But that's not possible," Bessie wailed. "I just talked to him yesterday. Told him what I wanted him to sing."

"From what I hear, dying doesn't take all that long," Lula-Belle said in a hushed voice. "You can do it in less than a day. An hour if necessary."

Winkleman dead? It was shocking but not all that surprising. Something about wed-

273

dings gave him cold feet. He'd left a bride at the altar not once but twice, but never did Bessie imagine he would go to such extremes to avoid a wedding not his own.

Her husband, Sam, opened the door just wide enough to stick his head through. "Are we ready?" he asked.

"Not yet," Bessie said, waving him away. She spun around to face her sister. "How did he die?"

"According to Mr. Green, Mr. Winkleman died of sobriety." Lula-Belle spoke in a hushed voice, one generally saved for funerals, hangovers, and sleeping babies.

"That's the most ridiculous thing I've ever heard. How is it possible for a man to die from *not* drinking?"

"Mr. Green said that sobriety was hard on the heart and even harder on the family."

Bessie made a face. "So is planning a wedding, but you don't see me kicking the bucket."

Lula-Belle's brow creased like a folded fan. "Mr. Green blames you for insisting the saloons close last night."

"Mr. Green blames me for Governor Hughes's removal." Just because she supported the governor's prohibition stance was no reason to think she had anything to do with his political troubles.

Determined not to let Winkleman's demise ruin the wedding, Bessie paced back and forth. "We'll just have to do the best we can without him. As long as we still have a piano player . . ."

"Eh."

Bessie stopped pacing. "Go on, get it out. What is it?"

"Mr. Green isn't the only one to blame you for Mr. Winkleman's death. Panhandle does too."

Bessie made a face. "I don't care who he blames as long as he plays the piano."

Lula-Belle threw up her hands. "That's just it. He refuses to attend the wedding. That leaves you without a piano player *or* a singer."

Bessie pressed a palm on her forehead. "Wait till I get my hands on Panhandle. Just wait!"

Sam peeked around the open door and again she waved him away. She traced a path up and down the aisle of the still-empty church, wringing her hands and bemoaning her misfortune. Sam's voice could be heard placating impatient guests.

What a fine kettle of fish! What did she ever do to deserve this? No wedding could proceed without music. Why, oh why, didn't things ever work out as planned?

"What about Mr. Washington?"

"He went to Flagstaff on business." Lula-Belle stared at the oak door, her eyes wide with dismay. "What are you going to do?"

"I don't know. I'm thinking. I'm thinking."

Lula-Belle straightened her outlandish feathered hat. "Well, think faster. The guests are growing restless."

Bessie suddenly brightened. "Molly!"

"What?"

"Molly sings."

Lula-Belle looked horrified. "The dance hall girl?"

"If you can sing in a saloon, you can sing anywhere." She started up the aisle. "Close your mouth and come along."

CHAPTER 23

The moment the church doors flew open, guests streamed inside the sanctuary, pushing past Donny's wheelchair as if it didn't exist.

"Watch where you're going!" Molly snapped. "Of all the rude —" It nearly broke her heart to see her brother treated like a piece of furniture.

After everyone else had entered the church and the way was clear, Ruckus pushed Donny's wheelchair inside. Molly followed behind, aware that all eyes were on her.

The church was crowded with practically every seat taken, but Ruckus located an empty pew in back with room for the wheelchair. It was hot and Ruckus's wife handed Molly a fan, which helped a little. After getting Donny settled, Ruckus left to escort the bride down the aisle.

Caleb sat several rows in front, his broad shoulders practically touching the guests seated on either side of him, and it was all Molly could do to keep from staring at him.

Just then Aunt Bessie burst through the door and ran up the aisle, her face so flushed it looked like a bad case of sunburn. Her bright green dress was better suited for a woman half her age and made her generous figure look even more rounded. Her gaze traveled from pew to pew, hat to hat, stopping when it got to Molly. She then threaded her way along one row of seated guests to Molly's side.

"I need your help," she whispered. "I need you to sing."

Molly wouldn't have been more surprised had she been asked to stand in for the preacher. "But . . . I don't know any . . . wedding songs." She didn't even know any Christian songs for that matter.

"That's all right. Just sing something romantic," Aunt Bessie said. "But don't wiggle your hips."

"But . . . but . . ."

Bessie looked around. "You don't by chance play the piano, do you?"

"No, I'm sorry —"

"I do," Donny said, raising his hand shoulder high.

"Shh," Molly cautioned but already too late.

Aunt Bessie practically danced with joy.

Molly shot Donny a warning glance before quickly trying to save them both from embarrassment. "He can't read music. He can only play a few songs by ear." None of which were appropriate for a wedding.

"That's quite all right," Aunt Bessie assured her. "Beggars can't be choosers, can they?" She gave a thin little laugh before growing serious. "You're an answer to my prayers. Both you and your brother. Come, come."

Aunt Bessie hurried away and stood in front of the altar. She clapped her hands to get everyone's attention. "As you may know, Mr. Winkleman is no longer with us. May God bless his soul. And our piano player . . . is indisposed."

An uncharitable female voice floated up from the back of the church. "Hammered, more like it."

"I say we should close all saloons permanently," another woman stated.

A loud murmur concurred. Things were clearly out of control and Molly felt sorry for Aunt Bessie.

Bessie lifted her voice to be heard over the clamoring crowd. "Please, we'll talk about that later. Right now we have a wedding to think about, and Miss Hatfield and her brother have graciously volunteered to help out."

No sooner had Aunt Bessie made the announcement than all eyes turned in Molly's direction. One woman looked appalled and another glared at her grinning husband.

Aunt Bessie moved the piano stool to make room for Donny's wheelchair. "Come, come. Don't be shy. We're already late getting started."

Molly's heart fluttered and she felt a sinking feeling inside. She was hardly the answer to anyone's prayer. But since Stretch had already wheeled Donny to the piano, nothing could be done but to make the best of things.

Molly walked up the aisle and took her place by Donny's side, flushing from the weight of a hundred gazes. She felt out of place. Singing in front of a bunch of intoxicated miners was one thing; singing to a staid and sober group of churchgoers was entirely something else.

She leaned over the piano. "I wish you hadn't volunteered!" she whispered.

Donny looked confused. "I didn't want you singing by yourself," he whispered back.

Molly felt a tug inside and her anger melted away. Her brother had been trying to protect her.

Aunt Bessie lifted her hand, indicating it was time to begin. "We're ready," she called, her voice shrill with excitement.

Molly's brain raced. Donny didn't know how to read music so the hymnal on the piano stand was of no use. Unfortunately, his limited range ruled out anything resembling appropriate wedding or church music. The least offensive song he knew, perhaps, was "John Brown's Body." Why, oh why, hadn't she paid more attention to his musical education?

Panic rose inside. "I don't know what to sing," she said beneath her breath.

"How about this?" He played several notes and Molly's knees practically buckled. "Not that one!"

He continued to play the prelude. "That's my favorite," he argued. "And everyone loves the way you sing it."

He was right: it was her most requested song, but it was never meant to be sung in church.

Forcing a smile for the benefit of the wedding guests, she stood by the piano, her mind scrambling. *What's another word for drink?*

She opened her mouth to sing, "Think, think, think . . ." The piano was almost as out of tune as the one she sang to nightly at

Big Jim's.

"Old Ben Harrington could do nothing but think . . ."

Aunt Bessie looked confused, as did some of the female wedding guests. No doubt they wondered why *thinking* caused Ben to stumble and fall. Most of the men, however, recognized the ditty and some even laughed out loud, much to the annoyance of the women by their sides.

Donny played with great gusto, his fingers rippling over the yellow keys as easily as leaves blowing in the wind. He hit plenty of wrong notes, but since the piano was out of tune anyway, it didn't much matter.

She sang all four painful stanzas, substituting any word that might be deemed offensive. "So he threw out his frisky pug," she sang, instead of whiskey jug. "And old Ben Harrington never thank again." *Thought;* she meant to say that he never *thought* again.

After Molly finished the song, an uneasy silence filled the church. Aunt Bessie's smile was forced. Even the feathers on Aunt Lula-Belle's hat were frozen in place.

Finally someone clapped, the hollow sound of palm against palm bouncing off the rafters. It took Molly a moment to determine her appreciative audience of one was Caleb. A warm flush crept up her neck. Others followed his lead, though the male guests were remarkably more enthusiastic than the women.

Reverend Bland, who had been standing by the wall, coughed and took his place in front of the altar. He looked remarkably different than the last time Molly had seen him. His pants were neatly pressed, as was his frock coat. One would never guess by appearances that he'd been any less than a respectable preacher.

He was followed to the altar by a nice-looking man in a dark suit who was obviously the groom. The preacher stared at Molly for a moment before turning his gaze to the back of the church.

Aunt Bessie signaled with a nod of her head that it was time for the bride to make her appearance.

"Play 'Poker, Whiskey, and Women,' " Molly whispered. It was another drinking song but at least it was a march. She only hoped no one recognized the tune. As soon as Donny started playing, the guests rose and faced the back. The door flew open and Kate Tenney, looking absolutely radiant in a simple ivory gown, walked down the aisle with Ruckus by her side, her steps in perfect sync to the drinking song.

The bride's fitted bodice gave way to delicately puffed sleeves. The skirt flared from the waist to the hem. Her blond hair was brushed away from her face, falling down her back in a cluster of curls secured by a silk tulle veil decorated with white ribbon bows.

She took her place by her handsome groom, greeting him with a beautiful smile so filled with love it gave Molly goose bumps. She recalled seeing her parents exchange a similar look, and though she'd been too young at the time to know what it meant, she'd never forgotten. But that was before Donny's accident, before her family was ripped apart.

The bride and groom turned to face the preacher.

"Dearly beloved . . ."

After the vows were exchanged, guests streamed outside to another tinny encore of "Poker, Whiskey, and Women." When the church was nearly empty, Molly leaned toward her brother.

"I hope you're satisfied. Now we're the laughingstocks of Cactus Patch."

Donny's puzzled expression looked genuine. "Everyone looked so hot and miserable before the wedding. I thought it would make them laugh. It would have, too, if you hadn't changed the words. It didn't make any sense the way you sang it."

"This is a church and —"

"Ben Harrington was a thinker, eh?"

She whirled at the sound of a male voice to find Caleb behind her, a gleam of humor in his eyes. She should have known that he wouldn't let the song pass without comment.

"My brother knows only a limited number of songs," she said stiffly.

"Ah, but he plays them so well." He gazed at Donny. "You didn't tell me you could play the piano." He swung his gaze back to her. "Music talent runs in the family."

To hide her reddening cheeks, she moved toward Donny.

"Allow me," Caleb said. He gripped the handlebar on the back of the wheelchair, pulled it away from the piano, and pushed it up the aisle.

"I must say, you two know how to make a solemn occasion . . . interesting. I don't think I ever enjoyed a wedding more."

She fell in step by his side and glanced at him askew. As far as she could tell, he wasn't just being nice; he meant what he said. "I hope Aunt Bessie wasn't upset."

He grinned. "The only thing she cares

about is adding a new notch to her match-making belt."

Ruckus and his wife stood in line outside the church, waiting to wish the bride and groom well. One woman stepped out of the church and walked a wide circle to avoid Molly. She gave Donny a pitying glance but he didn't seem to notice. He was too busy plying Caleb with questions.

"Do you know how many parts there are in a piano?"

"I haven't the slightest idea," Caleb said, his humor-filled eyes on Molly.

"More than twelve hundred. And do you know a piano's real name?"

"Pianoforte," Caleb said, and both he and Donny laughed as if sharing some sort of private joke. How did Caleb do that? How did he always manage to make Donny laugh?

Aunt Bessie bustled over to them, her sister, Lula-Belle, padding behind like a faithful dog. "Thank you for saving the day," Aunt Bessie said graciously. "I don't think I've heard such a . . . uh, lively tune played on that old piano."

"If it was a funeral it would have awakened the dead," Lula-Belle muttered.

"It's the first time I've been in church when everyone was wide awake," Bessie said, glowering at her sister. She patted Molly on the arm. "And it wasn't only because the guests were sober. You really do have a lovely voice, dear. Everyone enjoyed hearing you sing."

"Especially the men," Lula-Belle added, the outlandish feathers on her hat seeming to vibrate with disapproval.

Bessie frowned at her sister and pulled Molly aside. "How do I look?" She waved her hand in front of her painted face.

"You look beautiful."

Aunt Bessie looked pleased. "Isn't it amazing how a little paint can make a woman look so natural?"

Molly laughed and the two sisters tottered off to greet the other guests just as Ruckus wandered over.

"Are you ready to go?" he asked. "Bessie has planned cake and punch back at her house, and I thought we could get an early start before the stampede."

Aware that Caleb was watching her, Molly hesitated. A man started toward her but his wife jerked him away. She was used to being treated as an outcast, but for some reason it hurt more here in Cactus Patch than it ever did in Dobson Creek. She wanted to go back to the ranch in the worst possible way, but it hardly seemed fair to

Ruckus and his wife to spoil their fun.

Caleb stepped forward. "Why don't you go on ahead? Molly wishes to return to the ranch and I'll be happy to drive her and her brother there."

Her mouth dropped open. She didn't know what she resented more: Caleb's ability to read her thoughts or the way he took charge.

Caleb met her startled gaze with a look of satisfaction. "Thanks to last night's closing of saloons, the fine citizens of our town seem to be experiencing a streak of good health. If this keeps up I'll be able to work with Donny both today *and* tomorrow."

"Tomorrow?" she asked with innocent sweetness. "You plan to work on the Sabbath?"

"I believe God makes allowances for doctors," he said without missing a beat.

Ruckus looked from Caleb to Molly as if sensing the undercurrents that flowed between them. "Are you sure you want to miss the party?"

"It's for the best," she said, meeting Caleb's amused smile with a frown.

"Very well." Ruckus turned to his wife. "Come along, my dear." Ruckus and Sylvia headed for their buckboard and other guests followed suit.

"Thank you for giving me an excuse to avoid the reception," Caleb said with a slight bow. He walked behind Donny and pushed the chair down the church path. "I was never one for parties. I only came to the wedding because Aunt Bessie insisted."

Molly fell in step by Caleb's side. "Glad to be of help," she said for Donny's benefit. Beneath her breath she added, "How dare you make decisions for me."

"Are you saying you wanted to go to the reception?" he asked.

"That's not the point and you know it. Furthermore, you're not working with Donny."

"I believe he has something to say about that," he whispered back.

"I'm his sister!"

"And I'm the only doctor in town. That makes me *his* doctor. But of course, you'll have to give me full rein. That's my one and only condition."

"I have no intention —"

"Do we get to ride in Bertha?" Donny asked, seeming oblivious to the argument raging behind him.

Caleb gave her a knowing smile. "Bertha it is. Unless your sister objects."

He put her on the spot and he knew it. "What exactly do you mean by full rein?"

He grinned. "I knew you'd see the light."

"I never said —"

Before she could finish her denial, he bolted ahead, the wheelchair rattling and bouncing and Donny laughing all the way.

Molly watched with conflicting emotions. She wasn't one to give in, especially on matters that concerned her brother, but something told her that this was one fight she couldn't win. And maybe, oddly enough, she didn't even want to try.

Molly stood outside her brother's bedroom door, hands clenched. Donny's frustrated protests coming from within made her want to scream.

Several times she raised her hand to knock and put a stop to the session. Each time she decided against it. Before starting the session Caleb had made her promise to give him full rein and not interfere, but it was harder than she thought.

"I'm not doing that!" Donny yelled. "I can't."

Caleb's voice remained calm and patient. "Can't or won't?"

She couldn't make out what Donny said next and the silence that followed was almost as unbearable as the protests.

Something hit the door with a thud and

she jumped back. The door flew open and Caleb stared at her a moment before brushing past her.

"Donny?" she whispered, rushing into the room. "What's going on? What's the matter?"

Donny refused to look at her. "Go away."

"Donny, talk to me. Tell me what happened."

"I said go away!"

She left the room to chase after Caleb, but she reached the road just in time to see the tail end of his auto disappear in a cloud of dust.

CHAPTER 24

Molly circled the corral astride a horse named Midnight under Brodie's watchful eye. Midnight was a black horse with a star-shaped white spot on his forehead and had one white leg.

She tried to ignore Caleb's vehicle parked in front of the ranch house. It had been nearly a week since Caleb stormed out of the house. She never thought to see him again but she was wrong. He was back the very next day and every day since, schedule permitting. He had even driven her and Donny to church Sunday.

She didn't ask for Donny's progress report, and neither Caleb nor Donny volunteered one. It was better that way. Avoiding the subject meant less chance of half-truths leading to false hope.

Still, she watched for signs of improvement. She couldn't help herself. Did Donny seem stronger or was that wishful thinking?

Did he seem happier, more content, less given to mood swings?

Brodie's voice was like a knife cutting through her thoughts. "Keep the circle small. Don't let him pivot."

How to turn was one of the first lessons a horse had to learn. Another important lesson was how to back up correctly.

The horse's natural inclination was to turn to the left and Molly had to train him to turn to the right.

"Watch his head," Brodie called. The horse's head had to be tilted with the nose slightly to the outside. "Keep the reins low."

Molly rode the horse at an easy pace, alternating between a slow trot and walk until Midnight turned smoothly with little prodding.

"Not bad," Brodie said as she dismounted. "Not bad at all. Never thought I'd live to say this, but you have a way with horses."

The unexpected compliment made her smile. "I have a good teacher," she said.

Brodie ran a hand along the horse's neck. "Too bad you're so distracted. If Miss Walker is crazy enough to make you her heiress, you better figure out what to do about your brother. You can't take care of him and run a ranch."

Unable to deny the truth of Brodie's statement, she said nothing.

Brodie grabbed hold of Midnight's reins. "I think he's had enough for today. Tomorrow we'll teach him how to back up."

Brodie led the horse away and she leaned her back against the fence, elbows resting on the top slat. In the distance the red tile roof of the ranch house glistened in the hot afternoon sun. Yellow rays glanced off Caleb's motor buggy. Caleb had not left yet. That had to be a good sign. If Caleb succeeded in doing what he said he would do, life would be so much easier. But that was a very big *if.*

Pushing her thoughts away, she walked to the fence to watch Orbit and Magic play. The two friends never failed to make her smile. Today Orbit came bounding toward her even before she had a chance to sing, Magic nipping at his heels.

Donny sat in his chair gasping for air. He hadn't been able to crawl to his chair or anywhere close to it, but he had made progress.

"I moved," he gasped.

Doc Fairbanks nodded. "Yes, you did."

It took Donny several moments to catch his breath. "You promised to take me to Flagstaff."

The doctor shook his head. "You're not ready yet. It took you forty minutes to move a couple of inches. You gotta do better than that. You also have to learn to dress yourself and manage the privy. When we travel to Flagstaff, I'm not waiting on you."

"I don't want you waiting on me." Donny folded his arms across his chest. There was no pleasing the man. "Tomorrow I'll move a foot, maybe even farther."

"A foot won't get you in the chair."

"A foot is as good as a mile when you're a —"

Doc raised a dark eyebrow and waited.

Donny bit his lip to stifle a grin. "You thought I was going to say cripple, didn't you?"

"Were you?"

"What I was about to say is when you're under the thumb of a slave-driving, ninny-hammering, know-it-all doctor!"

Doc Fairbanks thought for a moment, then shrugged. "I can't say that's a better choice of words, but it will do. For now." He tossed a nod at the door. "How about some fresh air? It'll help you breathe better. It might even improve your disposition."

"Fresh air is your remedy for everything." The doc hardly ever walked into a room without flinging open a window.

"Fresh air and sunshine are God's greatest healing gifts." Without waiting for an answer Fairbanks pushed him through the house and outside, settling him in a shady spot on the verandah. "See you tomorrow."

"Don't remind me," Donny said, though secretly he looked forward to it. The doctor made him work hard but Donny liked him. Liked him a lot. He liked the company and the way the doc treated him like a real person. He even liked stumping Fairbanks with questions. The doctor knew a lot about science and the human body, but he didn't know much about astronomy or cattle.

He watched Caleb walk to his car. He admired the way the doc carried himself, his shoulders back and head held high, his easy stride. That's how Donny would walk if he could. Even now, he straightened his back and held his head aloft to imitate the doctor.

You could tell a lot by the way people walked. Some people judged others by their profession or how they dressed, but Donny judged people by the way they walked. Miss Walker didn't walk as much as march, her boots hammering the floor like a carpenter with a stubborn nail. Rosita scurried around like a scared little mouse. Stretch bopped his head back and forth like a long-necked bird, and Feedbag's feet splayed out at ninety-degree angles.

Molly didn't walk as much as glide. Or at least she did when she wasn't worried about him. Then she walked as if she carried a weight on her shoulders. She tried to hide it, but he wasn't fooled. He knew he was a burden.

She didn't look like she was carrying a load now. The moment she spotted the doctor she waved, her feet barely touching the ground as she hurried toward Bertha, a bright smile on her face. Donny almost expected her to jump in the air like Orbit.

Watching her, he frowned. It didn't look like his sister but it was. No mistaking that. But why did she look so different?

Doc Fairbanks turned to face her and the two talked. Donny couldn't make out what they said, but something in the way they stood and looked at each other caught his attention. It was as if some invisible thread bound them together with a single knot.

Squinting, Donny leaned forward for a better look. The doc and his sister laughed and there was something . . . but what?

It took him a moment to figure it out. Caleb *liked* his sister and she *liked* him back. Donny gripped the arms of his chair. Why had it taken him so long to see what was as clear as the nose on his face? Now he knew why the doctor worked him so hard. The sooner Donny became independent, the sooner the doc could steal Molly away.

A cold sweat broke out on Donny's forehead. He swallowed hard but already his breathing had become labored. A doctor in Dobson Creek had advised Molly to put him in an institution. For weeks Donny had nightmares about such a place. Even now, his body grew cold just thinking about it. Molly promised him she would never put him away, but what if she fell in love and got married? What then?

He mustn't let that happen. He mustn't let anyone take his sister away. Not even the funny and kind Doc Fairbanks.

Molly led Caleb to the far corral and called to Orbit. Both Orbit and Magic came running. Caleb talked soothingly to the young horse and petted him gently before taking his head in both hands. He studied first one eye and then the other. Magic watched with every bit of anxiety that Molly felt.

"What do you think? Is it moon blindness?" She'd heard of the disease but had no real knowledge of what it was.

After a moment Caleb released the horse. "It's not moon sickness," he said. "And it's not cataracts. It looks like both retinas are detached."

"Can anything be done?" she asked.

"I'm afraid not. It's a congenital problem." He gave her a look of apology. "I'm sorry, Molly. I wish I had better news for you."

"I wish you did too."

Magic barked and Caleb lifted him over the fence. The horse and dog chased each other around the corral. No one would ever guess by appearances alone that the little fellow lived in a world of darkness.

She rested her folded hands on the fence. "Is he in any pain?"

"No, he's not."

Relief washed over her. She couldn't stand to think Orbit was hurting in any way. "What's going to happen to him?"

Caleb turned to face her, his back to the fence, his dark brows slanted. "It's hard to say. I guess it will depend on Miss Walker."

That's exactly what Molly feared. The ranch woman wasn't about to keep a horse that didn't earn its keep and Orbit couldn't survive in the wild. A shiver ran through her and Caleb touched her arm.

"Are you okay?"

She nodded, her skin tingling beneath his hand. "I . . . I better let you get back to town."

He released her arm but the warmth of his touch remained. "I'm sorry I can't do more."

She smiled up at him and his gaze held hers. "You're doing enough already." When he made no reply, she added, "Thank you."

He gave her a smile that sent her pulse racing. "Donny did good today. We're making progress."

"You aren't just saying that, are you? So I won't worry?"

"I'm not just saying it. I swear."

She chewed on her lip. "He still needs a great deal of help."

"Be patient," he said. "Miracles take a while."

She sighed. Her father always said that everything happened in *God's* time. What about *her* time? Why couldn't things happen faster? Why did she always have to wait?

"I would feel better if you'd let me pay you for your efforts." At least if she paid him she would have some control. If nothing else she would have more say in the matter. "I can't afford much, but I do draw a small salary from Miss Walker."

He shook his head. "I don't want your money."

"Why not? What do you get out of this? Coming here day after day." Surely he had better things to do, other patients requiring care.

"When I was in medical school I met many war veterans in wheelchairs from both the North and South. Most had spent their lives in institutions or soldiers' homes. I remember one man in particular. His name was Ben Watson. He was a brilliant man, a mathematician, forced to spend a lifetime in a crowded soldiers' home, his mind wasted. By the time I met Mr. Watson it was too late to do anything for him, but it's not too late for Donny."

She sucked in her breath, wishing she could believe what he said was true.

"I better get back to town," he said.

She nodded, though she hated to see him go.

He whistled and Magic came running. He reached for the dog, lifting him over the fence and onto the ground. By the time she and Caleb reached the car, Magic was already in the front seat. The dog's ability to climb into the high-framed vehicle by himself never failed to amaze her.

Molly stepped back while Caleb cranked. The car roared to life, shaking like dice in a gambler's hand.

He heaved himself into the driver's seat. "Molly, don't worry," he said, lifting his voice to be heard. "A man walks in many ways. Your brother hasn't yet found his way of walking but he will."

Molly watched him drive away. *Please, God, let him be right. Please help my brother find his way.*

Eleanor stood by the fence watching Molly teach a horse to back. It wasn't something horses liked to do, but this one followed Molly's commands without hesitation.

"Back," Molly called, popping the horse on the chest with a rope. She backed the horse through a muddy puddle, all the way to the fence.

Brodie stood next to Eleanor. "She's good. She started out bad but caught on real quick. Has a real knack with the horses, she does."

Eleanor was well aware of the girl's natural abilities, but running a ranch required more than simply having a way with horses. "I need someone who can devote herself fully to the ranch. She can't do that and care for her brother."

"I worry about that too. But she's determined. I'll give her that much."

Determination was good but it only went so far. If she hadn't felt so sorry for the girl and her brother, Eleanor would have sent them packing long ago.

She grimaced at the thought. It wasn't like her to feel sorry for anyone — not where the ranch was concerned. Could this new softer side be yet another symptom of advancing age?

"Determination never ran a ranch," she said, her voice curt. Where the ranch was concerned, divided loyalties never worked. It was all or nothing.

"No, ma'am, I reckon not."

A thriving ranch was living proof that choices made in the past — some of them painful and demanding great personal sacrifice — had been worth every drop of blood and sweat shed through the years. The ranch gave her life meaning. Without it, all would be for naught . . . her life an utter waste.

Eleanor spun around and walked away. Molly was the eighth woman to answer her advertisement for an heiress — or was it the ninth? Surely there had to be someone out there who could take over the ranch should — heaven forbid — something happen to her.

Caleb blinked and rubbed his forehead. It was late, almost midnight. Medical books were piled high on his desk. He'd spent the last several hours skimming through the thick tomes searching for information on leukemia.

Magic, curled on the floor in front of the desk, looked up from time to time as if to say, *Hey, it's past my bedtime.* Getting no response, the dog laid his head down on crossed paws and watched Caleb with soulful eyes.

Caleb ran his finger down the page. Europeans named it *"weisses blut."* White blood. No known cure existed for the disease.

A combination of arsenic trioxide and potassium bicarbonate, called "Fowler's Solution," brought red blood count back to normal, but it was only a temporary reprieve. Once treatment stopped, the white blood count soared again. Long-term use of the drug led to arsenic poisoning. In this case the cure, however temporary, really was worse than the disease.

Heart heavy, he turned off the gas lamp. Tomorrow he would send a telegraph to his professor in Boston and ask for the latest research on the disease.

His old mentor often said that God heals but doctors get the credit. Caleb had seen his share of miracles. Every doctor honest enough to admit it had seen miraculous cures. But it was the non-miracles that puzzled him, when God chose not to intervene. Those were the times that made him question his ability as a doctor and as a man of faith.

Magic padded after him through the waiting room and outside. The cool night air barely penetrated Caleb's dark mood.

Banjo music drifted down Main from one of the saloons. Raucous laughter rolled out of another. Despite Aunt Bessie's best efforts, saloon owners refused to stay closed on Sundays and still sold alcohol to youths.

Several drunks staggered along the boardwalk singing a tuneless song. Earlier, gunfire had sent the marshal racing to the far end of town.

A woman Caleb recognized as the barber's wife waltzed into a saloon and reappeared moments later, dragging her husband out by the ear.

A drunk lay on the boardwalk, snoring soundly and reeking of whiskey.

Caleb wasn't a drinking man, but at the moment he envied the man his oblivion.

CHAPTER 25

Donny fed Orbit a fresh garden carrot. Earlier Molly had tied Orbit to the verandah railing so that Donny could talk to him, and the little black horse was good company.

"You like that, eh?"

The horse's head bobbed up and down. He then poked his nose around looking for more.

"That's enough for you today."

Donny ran his hand along the horse's neck and sighed. The horse's future was in as much jeopardy as his own. He could still picture his sister and Doc together, the way they laughed and looked at each other. The way his sister fairly danced when she walked.

It scared him. It scared him so much he could hardly breathe. If she married, she would put him away and he would never see her again. He'd rather die than live in an asylum and lose the only family he had left.

But what could he do about it? Stop working with the doctor? He hated the idea of not seeing Doc Fairbanks. He looked forward to their sessions. The doctor made him work hard, but already Donny felt the difference in his arms and shoulders.

Still, he loved Molly more than anything else in the world. He had no choice. He must stop the doctor from coming to the ranch or risk losing her.

Donny rehearsed what to say and how to say it. He didn't want to hurt the doctor's feelings or seem ungrateful.

The moment he heard Bertha in the distance, he practiced his speech. *It's not fair to take you away from your other patients.* Donny grimaced. Doc Fairbanks would never believe his sudden concern for others.

I'm not doing any more exercises. They hurt too much. No, he had used that too many times in the past and it never worked. The doctor simply shrugged and made him work harder.

Think, think. *I can't continue working with you because . . . because . . .*

When Doc's automobile pulled up in front, Donny almost panicked. Nothing he could think to say seemed right.

Doc Fairbanks jogged up to the verandah. "Sorry I'm late." He bounded up the steps. "Let's get to work."

"I'm not working. I'm done."

"Done, eh?" Doc Fairbanks petted Orbit. The little horse whinnied and moved his head from side to side. He turned to Donny. "What do you say we go for a drive? I'll even let you steer."

Surprised, Donny gaped at him. Expecting an argument, he was caught off guard. Steer? Did he say steer? "Are . . . are you serious?"

Doc Fairbanks studied him with intense eyes and Donny felt like he was under a microscope. "It looks like you could use some sunshine and fresh air."

Hesitating, Donny's mind whirled. Was this a trick to get closer to Molly? "I'm crippled." It was his standard answer for everything.

"You steer with your hands, not your feet. I'll work the brakes and gas pedal. All you have to do is stay on the road."

It was an irresistible offer, and though everything inside him shouted no, his nodding head said yes.

Moments later Donny was situated in the driver's seat, his hand on the steering column. Caleb cranked the motor and leaped into the passenger seat.

"A couple of things," Caleb shouted over the engine noise. "Don't oversteer. It's also common courtesy to assist any horse and buggy you run off the road. Understood?"

"How do I assist anyone if I can't walk?"

"As long as you can talk, you can assist, and if you can't assist, offer an apology for the inconvenience you caused." Doc glanced around to make sure the way was clear. "Just remember, the motor provides the power but the driver — that would be you — provides the brains. Ready?"

"Ready!" Donny's heart raced with excitement. Mouth dry, he grasped the steering shaft with a shaking hand. Magic barked from the backseat as if to announce he was ready too.

Doc arranged himself so that he could reach the gas pedal. "Here we go!"

The car lurched forward, throwing Donny back against his seat. It was harder to steer than it looked. The car veered either left or right with every bump in the road and it was all Donny could do to stay on the road.

One hand on the dash, the doc stared straight ahead. "I haven't been so nervous since performing my first surgery."

Donny brushed the sweat off his forehead with his free arm. "I don't know what you're nervous about," he yelled back. "I'm the one driving."

Doc laughed. "Hold on," he shouted. He gave the engine more gas and Bertha picked up speed.

Donny couldn't remember ever having more fun. "Faster!" he cried. "I want to go faster."

On the road ahead he spotted Molly on horseback. She moved to the side of the road to let them pass. Both he and the doctor waved as they drove by and her jaw dropped.

Donny laughed. He'd hate to be in the doctor's shoes when Molly got hold of him. Knowing his sister, she would probably ban him from coming to the ranch.

The thought tickled him to the core. He couldn't have planned things more perfectly had he tried.

Gripping the reins of her horse, Molly spun her head around to stare at the departing vehicle. She could have sworn —

No, it couldn't have been. She was seeing things. A desert mirage! Still, it sure did look like Donny was driving.

She kept her gaze focused on the departing vehicle. It suddenly veered off the road and sped across the rough terrain, rocking up and down like a boat in stormy seas. Heart in her throat, Molly watched, not knowing what to do.

The motor buggy barely missed a haying machine but drove straight into a wall of newly mowed hay before stopping. Bales of hay tumbled down, burying the occupants.

"Gid-up!" Urging her horse into a full run, Molly's pulse raced as fast as Starburst's flying hooves.

Caleb was already out of the vehicle by the time she arrived and greeted her with a boyish grin. "He's fine. He's not hurt." He lifted a bale from the backseat and tossed it away.

"No thanks to you!" She slid off her horse and rushed to Donny's side.

Donny sat in the driver's seat holding Magic and laughing. The little dog licked his face and this made Donny laugh harder.

Thinking her brother in shock, she gently shook him. "Donny, it's all right."

"Did you see me, did you see me? I was driving!"

She lifted Magic out of Donny's arms and set him on the ground. "Yes, yes, I did see but —"

"I was driving," he shouted again as if she hadn't heard him the first time. He fingered the dashboard like a mother touching a newborn baby.

She curled her fingers into balls and glared at Caleb's back.

"Now look what you've done."

He tossed another bale of hay away before turning to face her. "What I've done?"

"He's hysterical," she sputtered.

"He's happy."

"He could have been injured or —"

"But he wasn't. He oversteered. It's easy to do. I've done it myself. Next time he'll do better. Won't you, buddy?"

The warm way he addressed her brother drained away her anger. "There won't be a next time. It's . . . it's too dangerous. Kindly take him back to the ranch. And you steer."

She had forgotten to stake her horse in her eagerness to get to Donny, and Starburst had wandered a short distance away to where a clump of grass bravely pressed through the dry cracked ground.

Caleb followed her, waiting to resume the argument until they were out of Donny's earshot. "Would you prefer that he spend the rest of his life confined to a wheelchair? Why don't you just put him in an institution like an injured war veteran? He'll be really safe then."

"I don't need to put him anywhere. I can keep him safe here on the ranch. If you would stop interfering and stop —" She walked up to Starburst and grabbed her rein. *And stop making me believe you can help Donny.*

"Stop what?" Caleb asked. "Stop treating him like a real person?"

"Stop thinking you know everything about my brother and me. You know nothing about us. If you did, you wouldn't —"

"Wouldn't what? What wouldn't I do, Molly?"

You wouldn't want anything to do with me. Out loud she said, "Just leave us alone." Tears burned her eyes but she refused to give in to them.

"Molly, don't." He pulled her into his arms. "Trust me," he whispered into her hair. He held her close, stroking her back.

Twisting in his arms, she sought to break free, but he only tightened his hold. "Trust me," he repeated.

Whether it was his warm embrace or gentle plea she didn't know, but all at once her resistance drained away. She laid her head in the hollow of his shoulder and clutched the sleeve of his shirt. She trusted him and that was part of the problem. What she didn't trust were the feelings he stirred inside.

■ ■ ■ ■

Donny rested his head on the back of the seat, his fingers still wrapped around the steering column. He still couldn't believe it. He actually steered a horseless carriage. He needed practice. Still . . .

He gazed up at the sky and imagined himself in all sorts of places. The Grand Canyon and the Flagstaff observatory . . . the big cities he'd read about . . . the oceans, both the Pacific and the Atlantic. He'd always wanted to see an ocean.

All too soon the visions in his head popped like soap bubbles. He would never see those places and the sooner he accepted his fate the better.

Brushing straw away from his pants, he glanced around.

Molly's horse grazed a short distance away but he couldn't see either her or the doc. Eyes narrowed against the bright sun, he scanned the desert until a movement caught his attention. He'd mistaken Doc for a cactus.

He leaned forward for a better look and his heart stood still. Was that Molly? In the doctor's arms? Donny wiggled around in the seat and shaded his eyes against the sun.

314

It was Molly all right. No question.

Donny's chest felt as if someone had tied a rope around him. His throat closed and he gasped for air.

He'd been tricked. The doctor took him driving for one reason and one reason alone: to get closer to Molly. That's all the doctor cared about. He wanted Molly all to himself.

Well, it wasn't going to happen. Nothing meant more to Donny than his sister. Not the horseless buggy and not even the Flagstaff observatory. His sister was his world and he had no intention of letting the doctor take her away. Not now, not ever.

He wrapped his hand around the rubber ball and blew the horn as hard as he could.

That night Molly tossed Donny's nightshirt on the bed. He was obviously still angry with her, but that was no excuse for his childish behavior. Exhausted after a hard day's work, she was in no mood for games.

"You could at least help by taking off your shirt." He'd done nothing since arriving back at the ranch but sit in his chair limp as a rag doll.

"I *am* helping you."

"No, you're not. A wooden statue would be more help." She tried to calm down.

315

Arguing with him never got her anywhere. "I know you're disappointed because I forbade you to drive again. But it's for your own good. You could have been hurt."

Donny folded his arms across his chest. "I didn't want to steer it. Doc Fairbanks made me."

"Hmm." It wasn't like Donny to place blame on others. "It didn't look like you protested too much."

"I don't want to ride in his old car and I don't want to work with him anymore."

She sank down on his bed and leveled her gaze at him. "Donny, he's helping you. He says you're making progress."

"No, I'm not. He just wants you to think that so that he can —"

She quirked a brow. "What, Donny, what does he want me to think?"

"Never mind. Nothing." He looked away.

She reached for his arm but he pulled back. Too tired to fight him, she stood. "All right, have it your way. Sleep in your clothes. See if I care."

She left the room and he didn't try to stop her. She hated leaving him in his chair all night, but she could no longer move him without his cooperation. When he was a child she could lift him in her arms and carry him. Those days were long gone. She stood in the hall hoping he'd call her back, but minutes passed without a single sound coming from his room.

She headed for the stairs when the unmistakable clatter of Caleb's auto buggy made her heart skip a beat.

CHAPTER 26

What was Caleb doing here this time of night? She had nothing more to say to him. But now that he was here, he could jolly well deal with Donny!

Fearing the bell would disturb Miss Walker, she hurried to the front door and ripped it open before Caleb had a chance to ring.

"Hello, Molly," he said. In the dim light he looked serious. His eyes reflected light from the gas lamp and his gaze bored into her like burning coals.

She glared at him. "It's late and thanks to you my brother won't let me put him to bed. Now you can deal with him."

She kept her voice loud enough to be heard over the idling motor car yet not so loud as to disturb the other residents. Miss Walker had been working in her office since supper, and Rosita and Jose had already retired for the night.

His jaw tightened. "We'll deal with him later. Right now, you and I need to talk."

"We have nothing left to —"

He stepped forward. With a single swoop he lifted her off her feet, tossed her over his shoulder, and carried her down the steps and through the courtyard.

Shock quickly yielded to fury. "Let me go," she raged. "How dare you!" She pounded her fists against his back but he kept moving. "Put me down!"

He dumped her unceremoniously into the back of the carriage. Before she could make her escape, the auto took off, throwing her against the seat.

"Stop!" she ordered. They hit a rut in the road and Molly's entire body left the seat before bouncing back down. "Do you hear me?"

Caleb ignored her and kept driving, his head outlined by the flickering carriage lights. Overhead stars shimmered in the black velvet sky as if doing some sort of wild dance. A trembling full moon had risen over the mountains, casting a silvery glow on the desert floor.

The car shook and rattled and Molly feared it would split in two. Fumes burned her eyes and the smell of burning rubber filled her nose. "If you don't stop I'll . . . I'll jump."

She swung at his shoulder just as the car hit a bump in the road. Missing her target, she fell back, breathing hard.

She peered over the side at the ground whizzing by them and changed her mind about jumping. She was furious with Caleb, but not furious enough to risk life or limb. Instead, she flung her body back against the seat in a fit of pique. She cried out whenever they hit a rough patch of road, but mostly she seethed in silence.

The cool night air blew in her face, a welcome relief after the heat of the day. Hair pins worked free from her bun and loose hair whipped around her head.

At long last Bertha came to a rolling stop. It was about time. She didn't even wait for Caleb to turn off the motor before climbing out of the car. Legs shaking, her boots sank into soft ground. She didn't know where she was and didn't care. She'd walk home if it took her all night.

"Mooooooo."

Startled, she jumped, her back pressed against the side of the car. Now she knew why Caleb had stopped. Cattle blocked the road, but she'd been too upset to notice until now.

"Don't turn off the motor," she cried.

No sooner were the words out of her mouth than the car rumbled and coughed, then stalled of its own accord. She met Caleb's gaze and she knew by the horrified look on his face that he feared a backfire too.

She held her breath until her chest felt ready to explode. One minute. Two. Bertha didn't make a sound and the cattle stayed calm. Molly slumped against the auto, hand on her chest to still her pounding heart.

Grinning, Caleb scrambled over the side to join her.

"It looks like we're stuck here for a while," he said cheerfully. Cattle milled around them in every direction, the air filled with the smell of heated hides.

He leaned against his vehicle, arms folded. "I guess this is as good a place as any to talk."

She glared up at him. The glow of the carriage lights lit his face and his eyes shone like polished gems.

"I have nothing to say to you."

"Shh. Keep your voice down," he cautioned. "We don't want to spook our friends here."

"It wouldn't be the first time you started a stampede," she replied, though she was careful to keep her voice low.

"And I'm going to do my best not to start another," he said.

"That gives me small comfort, seeing that we may be stuck here all night," she hissed beneath her breath.

"Look on the bright side. You're stuck with me."

She bit back the retort springing to her lips. She didn't want to argue. Not here and not with him.

Several moments of silence passed, punctuated by low moos and shuffling hooves. Curious beeves stopped to check the still-flickering carriage lanterns before moving away.

Caleb finally spoke. "Molly, I can't work with your brother unless you're honest with me."

"He doesn't want to work with you."

"All right, I can accept that. I think he's making a big mistake, but if that's what he wants I'll respect his wishes. Right now, I'm concerned about you. There's something you're not telling me and I want to know what it is."

His gentle gaze seemed to reach into her very soul. Instinctively, she lowered her lashes, blocking out his probing eyes and protecting her long-held secret. Something

Brodie said came to mind. *"You gotta teach a horse to use his instincts to take care of himself."* That's what she wanted to do — and her instincts told her to run. Only she couldn't. She was hedged in on all sides by cattle.

He brushed away a strand of her hair and ran a knuckle tenderly up the side of her face. The gentleness of his touch wrapped around her like a warm blanket. She prayed for strength even as she felt herself growing weak. How did he always manage to do this? Confuse her to the point that she didn't even know her own mind.

"I apologize," he said. He looked and sounded sincere and the last of her defenses melted away. "I should have talked to you before taking Donny for a ride. I wasn't thinking. I have a patient who is growing more sickly every day and I guess I was looking for an escape."

"Oh, Caleb, I'm so sorry." She studied his face. "Do you want to talk about it?"

"All I can tell you is that my patient is a child and" — his voice broke — "it doesn't look good."

The sadness in his voice touched her deeply. She pressed her hand against his face. "Why does God let these things happen?" She wanted to believe in a good and caring God, but at times like this it was so very, very hard.

Caleb covered her hand with his. "I guess God wants to see what we're made of, and right now I feel like I'm made of straw."

"That's not true, Caleb. You're one of the strongest men I've ever met. Certainly you're the kindest and most generous." Their gazes locked and it seemed like nothing existed but the two of them. "You give so much of your time caring for others — helping Donny. Yet you ask for nothing in return."

"Don't make me out to be a saint," he said. "I do want something in return, more than any man has the right to ask. I want to see your brother live a full and happy life. I want to look into a worried mother's eyes and tell her that her child will be all right. I want to lift a drunk out of a gutter and cure his pain." He fell silent for a moment before adding, "I want you and me to be more than just friends."

Her senses jolted as if hot water had suddenly poured through her veins. Speechless, she pulled her hand away. Not even the bellowing of a dozen calves drowned out the sound of her pounding heart.

He lowered his voice. "But that's not what *you* want, is it?"

Her mouth went dry. "No. No, it's not." She spoke the truth. Of course it was the truth. Why, then, did it feel like such a lie?

"Because of Donny."

It was a statement, not a question, but still she nodded. "He's in the wheelchair because of me." She didn't want to tell him what happened that long-ago day, didn't want to tell anyone, but she had to make him understand why they could never be more than friends.

"Go on," he said gently.

"I . . ." Her eyes filled with tears. "I'm responsible for his accident. Isn't that enough? I did that to him."

She searched his face, certain to find the same condemnation observed so often on her mother's face. Instead he pulled her into his arms and held her close. Something broke loose inside and the barriers around her heart crumbled away. The needy child within felt comfort in his arms, the needy woman felt protected. Head on his chest, she breathed in his fragrance, absorbing his very essence. The spicy scent of bay rum aftershave filled her head, chasing away the smell of heated hides and burning rubber.

"How, Molly? How are you responsible?" he murmured in her ear. When she didn't answer, he added, "Sometimes it helps to

325

talk. To let it all out."

"I — I was pushing his carriage and it got away from me." She spoke slowly because turning the horrible memories into words brought almost unbearable pain. "It rolled down the hill and I could do nothing" — her voice broke in a sob and he tightened his hold — "nothing to stop it."

"You couldn't have been but a child," Caleb said quietly. He lifted her chin and gazed into her face, his eyebrows raised inquiringly. "How old were you?"

A shiver of awareness ran through her. "I was eight. Old enough to know better."

His eyes widened beneath his arched brows. "Molly, you were a child."

She stiffened. "Don't," she whispered. "Don't try to make it sound like I'm blameless. I should have known better. I should have protected him. Instead, I stopped to look at a doll in a store window and . . ."

She forced herself to breathe but she couldn't stop the tears or even the words. A dam had burst open and words tumbled out of her mouth so fast she could hardly keep up.

"It was cold that day. It was about to snow. I remember because I wore a thin dress. I had taken off my coat to cover Donny." It was a week before Christmas, and she'd stopped to admire a decorated tree in a store window, only to be mesmerized by a doll beneath a pine branch.

The porcelain doll had a rosy-cheeked face, a delicate bow-like mouth, and blue eyes that appeared to follow her wherever she moved. It was dressed in a cotton dress and high-button shoes with a big straw hat atop a head full of honey curls. She had never seen a doll more beautiful or lifelike.

As she talked, memories assailed her until she could no longer keep up with her thoughts. The doll. The carriage rolling away. The horror. "I screamed and a stranger ran after it."

Caleb's gaze never wavered from her face, not even when a calf brushed against them with its tail. He pushed tendrils of hair away from her forehead and murmured soothing words in her ear.

"It's all right. Let it out."

In her mind's eye she could see that long-ago day. Some of the details were vague but not Donny's limp body. She could see him so clearly it was as if everything that happened played out before her eyes again.

"Donny lay sprawled on the ground. He never made a sound. I tried to get to him but a crowd had gathered and I couldn't get through. I . . . I was certain he was dead."

He lay in a coma for several days and no one knew if he would live. Her father never blamed her but her mother certainly did. Her mother had waited years to bear a son but she hadn't bargained on becoming a nursemaid.

No longer did her mother tuck her in bed at night or brush her hair or help with her stitchery. She no longer existed in her mother's eyes. Molly had begged for forgiveness, even on her mother's deathbed, but none ever came.

Molly could hardly blame her. Not only did the accident change Donny's life, it changed all their lives. Her parents' marriage suffered as well. Mama and Papa argued over Donny's care and her father stayed away days at a time. Donny's accident was like a hatchet splitting the family apart.

When her tears were spent, Caleb held her face between his hands and gazed into her eyes. He brushed his mouth against her forehead and kissed the tip of her nose. She trembled at the sweetness of his lips against her flesh, at the tenderness in his eyes, but nothing prepared her for the moment he kissed her fully on the mouth.

Blood pounded through her veins. His mouth demanded a response in kind and she earnestly kissed him back. Rising on tiptoes, she flung her arms around his neck. He pulled her closer still and it seemed as if their very hearts embraced.

At that moment, nothing seemed to exist outside the circle of his arms, not the lowing cattle nor the silvery moon stealing a silent path across the sky. Not even Donny.

When he lifted his mouth away, disappointment flooded through her. "How many cattle does Miss Walker own?" he asked, his hot breath mingling with hers.

An odd question under the circumstances but she replied, "Nearly two thousand."

He gave her a crooked smile and her heart practically flipped. "Excellent." Once again his kisses blocked out everything except for the exquisite sensations.

In between kisses they talked. He told her about his dream of one day opening a clinic. "And I want one of those machines that take pictures of the bones," he said.

She couldn't imagine such a thing possible, but she shared his enthusiasm. She told him about Dobson Creek and how she came to sing at Big Jim's. "When Papa took ill and could no longer work at the mines, Big Jim was the only one who would hire me. He was Pa's friend and I think he did it as a favor. I didn't even know I could sing until I took the job."

"You have a beautiful voice, Molly," he said. "I wish you'd consider singing at church. We need a singer like you. I'm sure you could learn some hymns."

Sing at church? Normally she would have laughed at the idea, but not tonight. Tonight anything seemed possible — even photographing patients' bones and singing in a choir.

It was after midnight when the last steer moved away and Caleb was able to take her home. She sat in the front seat and this time hardly noticed the bumpy ride. She floated on air. Neither of them spoke during the drive back to the ranch house. Talking over Bertha was never easy. Tonight it was impossible because she was too busy reliving the memory of Caleb's embrace.

His kisses were nothing like the stolen kisses of miners' sons or the occasional slobbering kiss of some drunk who unexpectedly grabbed her at Big Jim's. Nothing about Caleb was what she had come to expect from a man.

Parking a distance from the ranch house to avoid disturbing the residents, Caleb walked her to the verandah. His eyes shone like jewels in the moonlight, his hand at her waist felt warm and reassuring.

All too soon they reached the front door. "Good night," she whispered, but before she could enter the house he pulled her back and swung her around in his arms once again. He leaned forward to kiss her good night and she quickly closed the distance between them.

And then she heard it, a voice calling from the open window of Donny's bedroom. "Mol-ly."

In the blink of an eye, the magic vanished. In a single heartbeat, sanity returned and reality slapped her in the face.

She pulled out of Caleb's arms and turned to the door.

"Wait," he called softly. "When can I see you again?"

She stopped at the threshold, her back toward him. Such a simple question, yet it held a world of meaning. He didn't want to *see* her again; he wanted to hold her again, kiss her again, and she wanted him to do all those things.

"Molly!" Donny's voice was like thunder in her ears and she feared he would wake the others.

She couldn't see Caleb's face and he couldn't see hers. Couldn't see how much she hurt. Couldn't see her dying inside.

"We can't. Not like this." Somehow she found the strength to step inside and close the door. Somehow she managed to keep her tears at bay as she felt her way through the darkened hall to Donny's room. Somehow she managed to walk into her brother's room when all she wanted was to rush back into Caleb's arms.

"What . . . what took . . . you so long?" Donny gasped between wheezy breaths. "I've been calling you."

"I'm sorry." She felt her way across the room. The lamp had burned out. Fumbling in the dark, she ran her fingers across the bedside table until she found the safety matches. She refueled the lamp and lit it with trembling fingers.

Donny was still in his chair where she'd left him. Even in the yellow glow his lips looked blue. She reached for his medicine and spilled some on the floor as she counted out the prescribed number of drops. She held the handkerchief to his face, and as he breathed in the soothing fumes she willed the pounding of her heart to cease.

He pushed her hand away, breathing a bit more easily. "I heard . . . Bertha." He looked up at her, his face filled with accusations, and she quickly turned her back so he couldn't see her face.

"Yes, Dr. Fairbanks and I . . . were talking."

"But it's late," he said.

"Yes, so we need to get you to bed so we can both get some sleep."

"Are you sick? Is that why the doc was here so late?"

She closed her eyes. If heartsickness was a disease, then yes, she was ill. "No," she said. "I'm well."

After settling Donny in bed, she tiptoed quietly up the stairs to her room. It was no use trying to sleep. Instead she stood on the balcony, gazing at the moonlit landscape.

She felt different, not at all like herself. It was as if someone had reached inside and rearranged every organ in her body. Outside, nothing had changed; she was still responsible for her brother's care, but with one major difference.

She always knew the sacrifices she would have to make to ensure Donny's future, the biggest being any sort of a normal life for herself. It was a sacrifice she'd been willing to make. Had no qualms about making.

Until now.

CHAPTER 27

During the next week Molly tried her best to avoid Caleb. It was easier that way. His presence only confused her, made her want things she had no business wanting. Made her ache inside.

Riding always cleared her mind and she talked Brodie into letting her take an appaloosa for its first ride outside the corral. The horse's name was Big Spot. A mild-mannered horse, he was brown all over except for a white spot that looked like someone had splashed whitewash on his back.

Brodie cautioned her to take it slow and not try anything fancy. "You gotta watch these well-mannered horses, especially when they insist upon letting you go over a fence first."

Big Spot did no such thing and Molly put the horse through his paces with no trouble. She took her time heading back to the ranch. It was hot but a slight breeze cooled her flushed face.

Spotting Caleb sitting atop the corral fence waiting for her, she reined in the horse abruptly. Apparently he had no intention of giving up. Avoiding him only postponed the inevitable. Bracing herself with a deep breath, she pressed her legs against Big Spot's sides and the horse trotted toward the barn.

Caleb waited for her to unsaddle the horse and lead him to pasture before pulling away from the fence. He stopped behind her, his shadow closing the distance between them.

"You've been avoiding me."

She pretended to play with the gate catch and said nothing. In the adjacent corral, Orbit hung his head over the fence to nuzzle Magic. Orbit whickered, Magic barked, and the two took off, romping alongside the fence. Even as she watched she felt the heat of Caleb's gaze.

"And now you won't even look at me," he said at last.

She turned to face him. Big mistake. "About the other night. You were right. It did help to talk to someone." *To talk to you.*

"I'll always be here to listen, if that's what you want."

It wasn't what she wanted, but it was all

she could have. Silence stretched between them before she trusted herself to speak enough to change the subject. "How . . . how is the little patient you told me about?"

He grimaced as if in pain and she longed to hold him as he held her on that memorable moonlit night.

"Not well."

Studying him, she thought of all the negative prognoses she'd received on Donny's condition. She felt sure that Caleb would never be distant and cold to his patients as Donny's doctors had seemed to her. Yet how could a doctor survive otherwise?

"I'm praying for him," she said. "And I'm praying for you too."

He nodded. "Right now I can use all the prayers I can get."

She took a deep breath. "You're a good friend, Caleb. I never told anyone else what happened. Only you."

A muscle quivered at his jaw but thankfully he kept his distance. "That's a big burden to carry around."

"Yes, it is. I —" She glanced around. Where was Brodie when she needed him? "I better get back to work."

"Are we not going to talk about it?" He took a step forward. "Are we not going to talk about what happened the other night?"

She backed away. She didn't want to think about the other night, but the truth was she hadn't been able to think of anything else. "Nothing can come of it. I have Donny to think about."

"And I have a new practice."

"I guess that's the answer, then." She looked away. "Neither of us can afford to be distracted."

"Drat, Molly! Why are you making things so difficult?"

She stared up at him. "You're the one making things difficult. My life is the ranch now and I can't think of anything else."

He grabbed her by the wrist, startling her. "Because I can't give you what you have here?"

"This ranch is Donny's security. He'll never want for a thing. He'll always have a home."

"He'll always have a home with me." Caleb released her. "You both will. That is, if you will have me."

She stared at him. "You . . . you can't mean that."

"I mean it," he said.

Momentarily speechless, she shook her head. "You have no idea what you're saying. After my brother's accident my parents . . . it broke them apart. Things were never the same between them."

Many were the nights she huddled beneath a blanket and tried to drown out their angry voices. "The strain of caring for Donny was too much for them. It's too much for most everyone. That's why so many people like Donny end up in asylums or begging on the street."

"Molly," he said, gently but firmly, as if to draw her thoughts out of the pocket of hurt she carried inside. "I'm a doctor. I know what I'm getting myself into."

"Do you? Do you really know? You see Donny a few hours a week. That's not the same as living with him day in and day out."

"Then let me learn firsthand what it's like to live with him."

"What?"

He laid his hands on her shoulders. "Let him come and stay with me. Give me a week to see what it's really like."

Stunned by this proposal, she had a hard time finding her voice. "That's . . . a ridiculous idea. You could never . . . your work as a doctor . . ."

"If I can't manage for a week, then I have no right to ask for anything more."

She shook her head and he dropped his arms to his sides.

"Unless," he said, "there's another reason

you won't let me help. The other night . . .
you said you would never forgive yourself."

"How can I?"

"So you're punishing yourself by pushing
me away."

"That's not true." She wasn't punishing
herself, was she? There he went again,
confusing her, making her doubt her own
motives. "It's all about Donny," she whispered. "It will always be about Donny."

That was only half of it; she wanted to
protect Caleb as much as Donny, protect
the fragile stirrings of love she felt for this
man.

She'd watched her parents' affection
shrivel up and die. She saw what it did to
her father, the nights he stumbled home and
collapsed in an alcoholic stupor. Saw what
it did to her mother, the bitterness and
withdrawal. Looking back at her parents,
she saw the future, saw what would happen
if she and Caleb were to marry. It nearly
broke her heart. She couldn't do that to
him. To the two of them. Wouldn't.

He stepped back, his expression hard as
stone. "I can tear down most of the barriers
you keep putting between us. But your
guilt . . . I don't know that I can fight that.
I don't know that any man can."

He spun around and walked away. She watched him go until blinded by tears.

CHAPTER 28

Molly kneeled in front of the wheelchair and pulled off Donny's shoe, her mind a thousand miles away. *"He'll always have a home with me. You both will."*

"Molly!"

She jumped. "Why are you yelling?" She started on his other shoe.

Donny gave her an accusatory look. "Because you're not listening to me."

"I *am* listening to you." She stood and rustled through a bureau drawer for his nightclothes. "You asked me . . ." Her mind drew a blank.

"Told you so," he said, frowning. He repeated the question. "Why are Hereford cattle more profitable than Longhorns?"

"Because they have shorter horns," she said, purposely giving him a wrong answer.

He made a face. "Come on, Molly. You gotta learn this stuff."

She flung his nightclothes on the bed and

sat, arms folded. "I don't want to know about cattle. I hate them. They're smelly and dumb, and I'd much rather work with horses." She dreaded riding the range and rounding up cattle, hated even the thought of branding them.

Donny frowned. "You better not let Miss Walker hear you say that." He inched his wheelchair closer to her. "When you take over the ranch I'll help you, Molly, I promise."

"When I take over?" He made it sound so simple. "And how do you propose to help me?"

"You're terrible with numbers, so I'll handle the books. I'll also negotiate with cattle buyers. All you'll have to do is tell the ranch hands what to do."

His enthusiasm made her smile. Never had she known him to sound so positive about the future and it did her heart good. "You have it all planned, don't you?"

He tapped his finger on his book. "Now will you settle down and learn this stuff?"

She stretched out on the bed and raised herself on her elbow. "Hereford cattle are more profitable because they mature earlier than Longhorns." Instead of satisfying him, her answer only seemed to encourage his questions and he continued to bombard her until her head felt ready to explode.

Caleb drove out to the old Madison place to check on a patient. Madison was a miner and sulfuric acid seeping from a silver mine had eaten away the flesh on his leg. After applying fresh bandages, Caleb headed for the Trotter place.

Jimmy and his family lived on a small farm a couple of miles north of town. He pulled in front of one of the few wood-framed houses in the area, scattering chickens in every direction, and turned off the motor. One of the Trotter girls walked out of the red barn carrying a bucket. She stopped in front of Bertha and stared at Caleb before hurrying to the house.

Jimmy's father threw down his hoe and sauntered over to where Caleb parked. A grizzled man in denim overalls, his sun-baked flesh was carved by wind and sand. He spit out a wad of chewing tobacco before placing a calloused hand on Bertha's frame and leaning over to look Caleb square in the face.

"The wife said Jimmy has some sort of cancer."

Caleb recoiled inwardly at the man's stale breath, a combination of tobacco and whiskey. "It's called leukemia and I'll do everything possible —"

"Jimmy's my only boy." Trotter pointed a finger at Caleb's nose. "Don't let anything happen to him, you hear!" He spun around and walked away.

Caleb watched until he vanished into the barn. Was that a plea from a worried father or a covert threat? It was hard to know. He jumped to the ground, grabbed his black case from the back of the car, and hastened to the house. Mrs. Trotter stood at the door waiting for him.

The front room was small and sparsely furnished with only a sagging leather divan and a cot stacked with folded clothes. Books were piled neatly in a corner and a hat rack stood guard by the door.

Jimmy looked less pale — a good sign. It indicated the medicine was working, but he still seemed lethargic and alarmingly thin.

Mrs. Trotter hovered nearby as Caleb examined him, wringing her hands. "He won't eat."

"Do you like ice cream?" Caleb asked.

Jimmy nodded.

"Miss Lily's has the best ice cream you ever tasted." Miss Lily ran the café located in the hotel. "Have your mother take you there and eat as much as you want." He glanced up at Mrs. Trotter. "The treat's on me."

Moments later Mrs. Trotter walked him to the door. "Thank you."

Caleb nodded. "I mean it about the ice cream. See if you can get some fat on those bones. The tonic should take care of nutrition."

She followed him outside. "Doctor . . ." She hesitated. "My husband . . . he's not taking this well. The day he found out about Jimmy's illness, he drove to town and got drunk. The marshal has brought him home twice since."

Caleb glanced at Trotter hoeing the ground with the same intent a man might use in digging a grave. "Would you like me to ask Reverend Bland to talk to him?"

Mrs. Trotter shook her head. "Harvey and the Lord haven't seen eye to eye for a good many years. Not since his pa was killed in that awful war. If that wasn't bad enough, his ma and two brothers died from malaria. I'm afraid he's given up on God altogether."

"That doesn't mean God has given up on him."

"But if he can't even pray —"

Caleb patted her on the arm. "Then it's up to us to pray for him."

She looked up at him with liquid eyes.

345

"Thank you, Doctor."

Caleb walked to his car with a troubled mind and a heavy heart. It wasn't just his conversation with Mrs. Trotter that had him worried. It was a nagging feeling that refused to go away.

Something didn't set right. Jimmy's lack of fever . . . was that it? Everyone reacted differently to disease, but everything he read listed fever as a symptom of leukemia. What if his diagnosis was wrong? What if it was something else?

He drove back to town so slowly that he stalled out twice. The second time he sat in the car, thinking. The wind had picked up and whirlwinds of sand cut across the desert floor and turned the sky gray. Magic held his face to the wind, fur ruffled and ears pinned back.

Caleb drummed his fingers upon the dash. What kind of a doctor was he? He couldn't do much for Jimmy and he certainly didn't know how to help the boy's parents. If Mr. Trotter's sudden drinking binges were any indication, Jimmy's illness had already taken a toll on the family.

"After my brother's accident, my parents . . . it broke them apart."

Molly insisted that Donny would come between the two of them. Now that he could

346

see firsthand how illness affected a family, he better understood her concerns.

Why did adversity bring some families closer and split others apart? It was a question very much on his mind as he drove the rest of the way to town.

Molly was surprised — shocked, really — when Caleb showed up that morning to drive her and Donny to church as if nothing had happened between them. It had been nearly two weeks since they last spoke.

He grinned and her heart did a flip-flop. "Caleb —"

He held up his hand. "Are you coming with me or not?"

It was the last place she wanted to go, but before she could reply, he brushed past her, hat in hand.

"Where's Donny?"

"In there," she said, pointing to the large room where she'd left Donny moments earlier.

Caleb greeted her brother with a smile. "I came to take you and your sister to church."

Donny didn't even bother to look up from his book. "I'm not going."

Caleb glanced at Molly as if to ask what happened.

"Donny, don't be rude." Embarrassed, she

spread her hands in apology. "I'm sorry. Donny has been in the worst possible mood lately and I have no idea why. I'm afraid you traveled all this way for nothing."

"I wouldn't say that." Caleb's gaze clung to hers and her pulse skittered. "I'm sure Donny won't mind staying home alone. We'll be back by noon."

She shook her head. "I —"

"You'll feel better, trust me," he coaxed.

No, she wouldn't. Church always made her feel like an outsider. She'd much rather worship God away from prying eyes. Still, escaping her brother's ill humor — if only for a couple of hours — was tempting.

"Just . . . give me a few minutes." Avoiding Donny's gaze, she left the room. She paused at the bottom of the stairs and wiped damp hands alongside her divided skirt. It was church that made her feel jittery — nothing more. But even the thought of all those people staring and whispering didn't spoil her eagerness at spending time with Caleb. With girlish anticipation she took the stairs two at a time.

She flung open the wardrobe in her room and pulled out the brightest, most attention-getting frock she owned. With a start she caught herself.

It would just be her and Caleb. No need

to worry about protecting Donny from prying eyes. Today she could be herself. She hung the dress back onto its wooden peg and chose the blue one. Giving it a critical eye, she reached for her sewing scissors and snipped off the froufrou. Without all the ruches the dress looked more sedate — or at least as sedate as the bright blue color allowed. Next she worked on the hat, pulling feathers off the upturned brim and leaving only a single bow on the crown.

After dressing, she reached for her face powder, but a quick glance in the mirror told her it was unnecessary. The prospect of spending time with Caleb had put a flush on her face and a sparkle in her eyes. No paint was necessary.

Church that Sunday was standing room only. Molly had never seen so many people in attendance. Caleb found a place for them to stand by a stained-glass window, next to Lula-Belle.

Molly greeted the older woman. "What's going on?"

Lula-Belle glowered, her springy curls shaking along with the feathers of her hat. "My sister is at it again. She got the saloons to close last night and the saloon keepers agreed to stay closed until after church.

Thanks to Bessie's meddling way, I can't even find a place to sit. When she gets something in her fool head, there's no stopping her."

Caleb leaned sideways to whisper in Molly's ear. "What you see are a bunch of sober men praying that the saloons will be open by the time church is over."

Molly giggled, which only made Lula-Belle frown more. Composing herself she said, "I can't believe the saloon owners agreed to Aunt Bessie's demands." Nothing like that would ever happen in Dobson Creek. Even after the fire, men lined up in front of makeshift saloons. The town was in ruins but whiskey remained king. "It was hard enough getting them to close on the eve of the wedding."

Lula-Belle tossed her head with a huff. "It didn't help that you two were in cahoots."

"I did give her a few pointers," Molly admitted.

Caleb nudged her with his elbow. "A few, eh?"

"More than a few," Lula-Belle said. "Thanks to you, my sister now looks like a loose woman with all that paint she wears."

"I think she looks quite lovely." Molly had grown quite fond of the woman. Aunt Bessie was one of the few people who treated Donny like a real person.

"You would," Lula-Belle muttered. She moved away, pushing past others standing by the wall, and took her place on the opposite side.

Molly watched her go. It was hard to believe she and Aunt Bessie were related. "She should be happy her sister is wearing commercial paint rather than homemade. I knew some girls in Dobson Creek who got sick from using paint made from zinc oxide, mercury, and lead."

Caleb frowned. "Mercury and lead are dangerous, but a combination can be lethal."

She knew that now. "One of the dance hall girls died. No one knew why. She just got anemic and complained about headaches."

Caleb's eyes sharpened. "How did you know she died from face paint?"

"I didn't. Not at first. Even the doctors didn't know what killed her. Then I read a newspaper article warning women about the dangers of homemade cosmetics. It described symptoms similar to what my friend had and I just assumed —"

"What kind of symptoms?" Caleb asked.

His brusque, abrupt question surprised her. "She got very pale and thin and —"

Caleb stopped her with a hand to her arm.

"I'll be back."

"Where are you going?" she asked, but already he'd left her side and was weaving his way to the door. She stared after him, not sure what she'd said wrong.

Caleb rushed from the church to his office. The town looked deserted. It seemed strange to see the hitching posts in front of the saloons empty.

Magic jumped up to greet him. "Down, boy."

One by one he pulled books off the shelves, flipping through the pages until he found the table of contents.

Could Jimmy have mercury poisoning? Mercury, or quicksilver as it was sometimes called, was the only known metal that liquefied at room temperatures. If that was the culprit, how could an eight-year-old become exposed? His father was a farmer, not a hatter or gold refiner, professions known to create a high level of mercury poisoning.

What about lead?

He thumbed through the tomes, running his finger down pages until he found what he sought.

One line jumped up at him: "Lead or its salts can often be taken into the system unawares." The article went on to explain the danger of lead pipes or reservoirs. Lead could also be ingested through paint, or preserved vegetables and fruits that came in contact with the soldered joints of tin cans.

The symptoms included headaches, anemia, and stomach complaints. Lead poisoning was known since Roman times. Some even thought it was the bottom of the mystery disease that affected so many inner-city children.

He left the book open on his desk and paced back and forth, hands behind his back. Could Jimmy have lead poisoning? He had all the symptoms. Still, how did an eight-year-old boy ingest lead? And why didn't the other family members show similar signs?

He shook his head. He was grasping at straws, looking for a ray of hope for Jimmy's parents.

Still, the boy's symptoms were more consistent with lead poisoning than leukemia.

What could Jimmy be doing differently than other family members? Something . . . it had to be something — but what? All he knew was that time was running out. God help him!

Chapter 29

Caleb returned just as Reverend Bland gave the closing prayer. Molly glanced at him before lowering her head. Even now his nearness made her heart beat faster, and she ached at the memory of being in his arms.

God, lead me from temptation. Make me strong so that I might do right by my brother. Help me be patient and less resentful. Please, God, help me.

After the benediction they left the church and a small boy rushed up to them.

"Hello, Doc Fairbanks."

Caleb tugged on the boy's cap with a broad smile. "Hi, Jimmy." He glanced at Molly. "Jimmy, I want you to meet my friend, Miss Hatfield."

Molly smiled at the child. "Pleased to meet you, Jimmy."

The boy grinned. He was a thin child with stick-like legs, his big blue eyes seeming almost too large for his gaunt face.

"Pleased to meet you too." He then wandered off to join a group of older boys.

Caleb's gaze followed Jimmy, his face grim.

"He's the one, isn't he?" she asked. "The patient that has you so worried."

Caleb turned to her. "Yes, he is."

"I'm glad you're his doctor. You'll do right by him. I know you will."

A middle-aged woman cornered Caleb with a laundry list of medical complaints. The woman rattled on nonstop and Molly marveled at Caleb's patience.

"And at night I get this pain right here." The woman pointed to her right hip. "And in the morning . . ."

Bored with the woman's complaints, Molly glanced around. Spotting the former slave Mr. Washington, she hurried to catch up with him. "Mr. Washington, may I speak with you?"

The black man worked his crutches around until he faced her. "What can I do for you, ma'am?"

"I wonder if you would be so kind as to write down the words to the hymn you sang in church a few weeks ago?"

Mr. Washington thought a moment. "You mean 'Swing Low, Sweet Chariot'?"

"Yes, that's the one. You sang it beautifully."

"Why, thank you, ma'am." His crutches tucked beneath both armpits, he pulled a pencil and notepad from his pocket and started writing. He explained each phrase as he wrote. "Swing low meant come and get us. Sweet chariot was code for the Underground Railroad. Jordan was the Mississippi River and the angels referred to the workers who helped us escape."

Molly was deeply moved. "It's such a haunting tune."

He grinned. "Are you a singer?"

"Yes," she said with a slight hesitation.

He glanced up but kept writing. "Reverend Bland asked me to organize a choir. We could use more singers. Would you care to join us?"

She stared at him. A saloon girl in the church choir? She could well imagine what the congregation would have to say about that. "Oh no. I'm not *that* kind of singer."

"What *kind* of singer are you?" he asked.

"I meant . . . I'm not trained," she said, so as not to embarrass him. Had he known her background, he would never have asked her. "I've never had singing lessons."

"And I never went to school but that don't mean I can't read and write." Mr. Washington's white teeth flashed against his ebony skin. "The Bible says to make a joyful noise unto the Lord. It don't say nothing about singing lessons." He tore a page from his notebook and handed it to her.

"Thank you." She folded the paper and tucked it into her handbag.

"I hope you reconsider," he said.

Before Molly could respond, quarreling voices cut through the low murmurs of churchgoers.

She turned just in time to see an older boy punch Jimmy in the arm. Jimmy retaliated with a spitball. The silver wad caught the sunlight as it whizzed through the air and hit an older man on the forehead.

The man grabbed Jimmy by the collar and cursed him out with a thorough tongue-lashing. He raised his cane and Molly bolted forward. Rushing in front of Jimmy, she protected him with her body.

"Don't you dare hit him," she stormed. "What is wrong with you?"

The man reared back in surprise and lowered his cane. He was a short man with no neck and a face full of pockmarks. "He spit at me!"

"It was an accident."

"Yeah, well, he's lucky I don't flog his ears."

"You're the one who's lucky, sir!" Her body shook with rage. "If you touch one hair on his head I'll —" She was just getting warmed up when Caleb grabbed her by the arm and pulled her away.

She swung around to face him. "Why did you do that?"

For answer, he gave his head a slight nod to the right and left. Molly glanced around to find more than a dozen people staring at her, including Reverend Bland. Apparently no one had witnessed the start of the fight, but judging by the shocked expressions, she alone shouldered the blame for the end. She was used to people — especially church people — judging her unfavorably, but she felt bad for involving Caleb.

After making certain Jimmy was safe, she allowed Caleb to steer her toward his horseless carriage and away from the disapproving glares.

"I'm sorry," she said, still shaking. "I didn't mean to embarrass you. Your reputation —"

He narrowed his eyes. "I don't care about my reputation — I'm concerned about you."

"And I'm concerned about the boy," she shot back. "He's just a child. It was an accident."

Caleb stood directly in front of her, his

stern face shaded by the brim of his hat.

"It *was* an accident," he said slowly. "Just like Donny's carriage tipping over was an accident."

She swallowed the gasp that rose to her mouth, the tightness in her chest making it hard to breathe. Of all the things he could have said, bringing up Donny's accident was the worst. She had trusted him and now he was throwing that trust back in her face.

"Why are you bringing that up now?"

"Because you were a child yourself when it happened," he said. "In fact, you were the same age as Jimmy is now."

"Jimmy is eight?" It didn't seem possible that she had ever been that young or that vulnerable. As Donny's sister she always felt older than her years. "I — I don't want to talk about it."

"I think we should."

She glared at him. "How can you compare Jimmy's little misdeed to what happened to Donny?" She turned to climb into Bertha, but Caleb stopped her, his hand encircling her arm.

"You were eight. A child. You needed protection, not blame."

Protection. The word nestled inside her, bringing a lump to her throat. No one had ever said such a thing to her. They stared at each other for several moments before he released her arm and stepped back.

He walked away to crank the car. She felt bad for arguing with him. He'd only tried to make her feel better, and it was obvious the sick boy weighed heavily on his mind. Moments later he took his place on the seat next to her. Hand on the steering column, he stared straight ahead.

She laid a hand on his arm. "You're a good man." The rumbling vehicle made her voice quiver — or was her trembling heart to blame? "And a good doctor."

He covered her hand with his own and held her gaze. "You're a fine woman, Molly Hatfield. A beautiful one. You're good and kind and probably the most selfless person I've ever met. I just wish you could look in the mirror and see what I see."

For a split second she caught a glimpse of the woman he described — and it shocked her. Shocked her so much that she pulled her hand away and closed her eyes.

She wanted to be that woman. She wanted to be good and kind and selfless, but she was none of those things. Sometimes she was angry and resentful. On one shameful occasion, she even wished her brother had never been born. Why couldn't Caleb look at her and see her for who she really was?

That would make it so much easier for both of them.

She opened her eyes to see Jimmy scramble into the back of his family's wagon with his sisters.

Caleb watched him too. "There's a chance he doesn't have leukemia."

Molly's mouth dropped. "Oh, Caleb, that's an answer to prayer." His dark expression made her frown. "If not leukemia, then what?"

He met her gaze. "What you said in church got me thinking. He may have lead poisoning."

"Lead . . ." Her spirits plunged. "But how?"

"That's what I'm trying to figure out."

She pressed her lips together. Their combined worry pushed away the tension between them, but not the physical awareness. His every move and gesture seemed significant in some way and she could hardly draw her gaze away from him. "Will he be all right?"

"It depends on how long it takes me to find the source of lead."

She let the statement hang for a moment before she spoke. "And if you don't find it?"

The question stretched between them like

a bridge neither wanted to cross.

"I have to find it," he said at last. He released the brake and Bertha rolled forward. "There's no other choice."

Eleanor Walker rode up to the ranch house, surprised to find her banker friend, Robert, waiting on the verandah. She tethered her horse to the hitching post and hurried to join him. As much as she cherished their friendship, she hated the way her heart leaped whenever she saw him. She was too old for such nonsense. Today, as always, she covered her feelings with a brusque, no-nonsense manner.

"Don't tell me it's the first of the month already," she said. Thanks to that unfortunate earthquake and fire of '87, which forced her to rebuild, she owed her soul to his bank.

Robert pulled off his bowler and ran a hand over his head, as if his silver hair would be so brash as to become mussed. "Not according to my calendar," he said with an amicable smile.

"So what brings you here in the heat of the day?" She opened the front door and called to Rosita. "Kindly bring my guest some lemonade."

She closed the door and sat in a rocker.

Robert sat opposite her, balancing his straw hat on his knee.

"I have good news for you, but I can't take any of the credit."

"I could use a little good news." She pulled off her gloves and tossed them into an empty chair. The morning had seen nothing but problems, ranging from a broken windmill to having to put an injured steer out of its misery.

Rosita appeared and set a tray with a pitcher of lemonade and two glasses on a small wicker table. "Thank you, Rosita."

The girl afforded the banker a quick smile before hurrying away. Eleanor poured Robert a glass of lemonade. "So what is this good news?"

"Mr. Hampshire has decided to put his idea of forming a cattle company on hold, perhaps even permanently."

Eleanor stopped pouring. "You can't be serious."

He leaned over to take the glass out of her hand and took a long sip before answering.

"I'm completely serious."

She set the pitcher down and leaned back in her chair. "What made him finally see the light?"

He grinned. "Apparently he traveled to Cactus Patch on Saturday night and didn't like what he saw. The saloons were closed and the town deserted. Just this morning he came into the bank and told me he'd changed his mind. He no longer had need for a loan."

"I don't believe it."

Robert raised his right hand. "It's true, every word. He said that a town unable to maintain its saloons is no place to do business."

"He's right," Eleanor said. The saloons provided most of the revenue to run the town. Without them, Cactus Patch would soon become a ghost town. "Why were they closed?"

"That's where it gets interesting," Robert said, obviously enjoying himself. "It seems that the womenfolk are on some sort of temperance kick."

Eleanor rolled her eyes. Arguments in favor of temperance dated all the way back to the Puritans. With much of government revenue derived from liquor and saloon taxes, Eleanor didn't see much hope of the temperance movement taking hold unless women got the right to vote. If the U.S. Brewers' Association had its way, that was never going to happen, despite the efforts of the Anti-Saloon League.

"It sounds like my troubles are over,"

Eleanor said. Or at least some of them.

"You can thank your new heiress."

Eleanor arched an eyebrow. "Molly? What has she got to do with it?"

"Apparently she and Bessie Adams were in cahoots. I understand that Molly came up with some sort of plan and it worked. You do know that Miss Hatfield was once a dance hall girl."

Eleanor gave a brusque nod. "I'm quite aware of Molly's former profession."

"This won't sit right with you, but I'm afraid you will forever be in Miss Hatfield's debt for ending your cattle problems, at least for the time being."

"Not entirely," she said. "There are still ranches I'm concerned about." The other ranchers soon figured out that gold fever was a ploy and just that morning she found her fence cut again.

"Yes, but you won't have to worry about a cattle company and the thousands of cattle Mr. Hampshire planned on stocking."

"Rest assured, Molly has my complete gratitude."

He set his glass on the tray with a chuckle, then rose and donned his hat. "I'm sorry to rush off like this, but I have to get back to town."

She hated to see him go, but she would

rather die than admit it. "So soon?"

"Sorry."

She stood, wrapped her arm around his, and walked him to his horse and buggy. "You're a good friend, Robert, and you'd make a great husband."

He grinned. "That's what I keep telling you, but you keep turning me down."

"You know what I think, Robert? I think you should be grateful that I'm an old fool."

"If you're an old fool, what does that make me?"

She smiled up at him. "A *dear* old fool."

That night Molly stared at herself in the mirror and, without her usual paint, hardly recognized the woman reflected back. Tonight her face was scrubbed clean and her wet hair hung down her back to her waist.

Nothing stood between her and the mirror except for voices of the past.

The loudest voice of all was her mother's. *"You wicked, wicked girl! Look what you've done to your brother. All because of you he'll never walk again — ever!"*

Other voices filled her head, childish voices of boys and girls who attended school with her. *"Molly, dolly, near killed her brother. If you don't watch out she'll kill her mother."*

But there was another voice too, a new

one. *"If only you could look in the mirror and see what I see."*

She recalled the feel of Caleb's mouth on hers, the approval in his eyes as he gazed at her, and a warm shiver rushed through her.

He once asked what she saw when she looked at a horse. Her answer was so different from his that at first she was shocked. But maybe people saw only what they wanted to see, were conditioned to see. For good or bad, Caleb saw things in her that no one else had ever seen.

He even saw her in the little boy Jimmy. *"He's eight. The same age you were at the time of Donny's accident."*

The same age she was when she gave up the dreams she had for herself. She swiped at the tear that trickled down her cheek. *He's too young, God. Eight is much too young to die.*

If she knew nothing else, she knew that much.

Donny sat up in bed still as a mouse, listening. Voices floated into his room from other parts of the house. Jose and his sister laughed, Rosita's soft giggle almost as timid as her walk. Bo, the cook, yelled about somebody messing up his kitchen. Miss Walker's firm, almost militant, footsteps pounded across the tile floor followed by the slamming of her office door.

Last night, while Miss Walker and the others slept, he'd wheeled his chair out of his room and into the parlor. For weeks he'd practiced easing himself out of bed and onto the floor like Doc Fairbanks had taught him. From there he'd belly-crawled to his chair and pulled himself up. He then wheeled himself from his room to the house's main room, spinning himself around until he got dizzy. In his mind he was running and he could almost feel the wind in his hair.

One night he crashed into a table, knocking the parlor lamp on the floor. The broken lamp puzzled Rosita and Jose, but no one suspected him.

He was more careful after that. It wouldn't do to let Molly know what he was capable of doing. He always dreamed of being independent, but that was before he knew that his sister had feelings for the doctor. Now fear of losing her consumed him.

Any guilt he might feel for standing between Molly and the doctor was quickly dismissed. Molly liked the ranch. Or at least she liked working with the horses and she was gradually learning about cattle. Donny made certain of that. Soon she'd get over her feelings for the doctor. He'd make certain of that too.

Meanwhile, he had to find ways of keeping them apart. Letting her go to church alone with the doctor had been a mistake and he wouldn't let it happen again. It would only be for a couple more weeks. Once Molly signed Miss Walker's papers forbidding her to marry, Donny could relax. Never again would he have to worry about a man stealing her away from him. Or putting him in an institution. He counted on it.

At long last the house settled down. Nonetheless, he waited until after nine before beginning the short but torturous journey from the bed to his chair.

Heaving himself into the seat, he waited a moment to catch his breath before pressing down on the wheels and rolling across the room. He opened the door and listened, surprised to hear low voices. He recognized Molly's voice at once, but who was the other? Dr. Fairbanks!

Donny froze. What was the doctor doing here so late? And why hadn't he heard Bertha? Sometimes the doctor parked a distance away so as not to disturb the animals or upset Miss Walker. Is that what he'd done tonight?

"Molly, you've got to tell Donny. He has the right to know."

Donny stiffened, waiting for Molly's reply, but either none came or Molly's voice was too soft for him to hear.

Donny strained his ears, but it was no use. Molly and the doctor had stepped outside. Hands shaking, Donny closed the door to his room.

Molly was getting married. That's what she didn't want to tell him. She and the doctor were getting married! Even now they were probably talking about putting him away in one of those horrid institutions.

Cold sweat broke out on his forehead. He could hardly breathe. His worst nightmare was about to come true.

CHAPTER 30

Molly threw up her hands. "Donny, you've got to help me. I can't move you without your help. I'd sooner dress a lamppost."

Donny stuck out his lower lip. "I don't want to sit in my chair."

"You can't stay in bed all day."

"Why not?" He made a face at her. "What difference does it make if I stay in bed or sit in my chair?"

Molly sighed. "It's not good for you to lie around." Weary of Donny's increasing bad moods, she sat on the edge of the bed. "Now what's wrong?"

"What's wrong with *you*?" His contorted face made him look older than his years. "You keep pushing me to do things I don't want to do."

She threw his clean shirt down and stood. "I never ask you to do anything that's not for your own good."

"It's not for my good, it's for yours!"

371

Hands at her waist, she glared at him. Already her temples ached. It was too early to argue, but she could hardly ignore him when he was this upset. "What's that supposed to mean?"

He stared at her with accusing eyes. "You just want to get rid of me so that you can marry the doctor."

Her mouth dropped open. "Whatever made you . . . Donny, I would never get rid of you and I'm not getting married. Why would you even think such a thing?"

"Quit lying to me. I heard you and the doc talking."

"You heard us?"

"The other night."

Molly's thoughts scattered. "I don't know what you mean. What did you hear?"

"I heard Doc Fairbanks say I had the right to know."

She pushed a strand of hair behind her ear. This was the moment she'd always dreaded, the moment she'd prayed would never come. "What you heard — it's not what you think."

"Then what is it?" His eyes narrowed. "What don't I know?"

She stared at him. Caleb was right. Donny was no longer a child and had the right to know the truth of his injury. "Something . . .

I should have told you long ago."

Donny's brows drew together. "Tell me now!"

"After you get in your chair." Perhaps by the time he was dressed, the right words would come to her. *Just don't let him hate me.*

"Promise?"

"Promise." Brodie had gone to Tombstone for supplies and she was in charge until his return. Today she could be a little late and no one would be the wiser.

Donny cooperated fully. Neither spoke, but he watched her face as if searching for clues. She helped him through his morning ablutions and for once he gave her no argument.

When he was fully dressed, he gripped the arms of the chair and leaned forward. "You said you would tell me."

"Let's go outside." It was hot and stuffy in the room and she desperately needed fresh air. She pushed him through the house and onto the shaded verandah.

In the distance, Orbit did his crazy circling. The colt kept stopping to look at the fence where she normally sat and sang to him each morning. She was wrong. Someone did notice she was late.

She drew her gaze away from Orbit to find

Donny watching her, his forehead shadowed with questions.

She lowered herself on a wicker chair and cleared her voice but the huskiness remained. "Caleb and I were talking about your accident. When you fell out of your carriage. That's what you heard." She blew out her breath. Not knowing where else to start, she started at the beginning. "The day of your accident Mama wasn't feeling well, so I took you for a walk."

She went to great lengths to describe the Christmas tree in the shop window. The porcelain doll, gray cloudy skies, and snow-muddied street were just as clear to her now as they had been on that long ago day. She'd never talked about Donny's accident except to Caleb. Maybe that's why it still hurt so much, why the memories had not diminished.

After her father died she recalled every detail of his last hours on earth with chilling accuracy. She repeated them over and over in her mind, as if careful attention to specifics would make his death seem more real. Particulars didn't help then and they didn't help now.

Donny sat perfectly still without uttering a sound.

"It was my fault. I . . . should never have

taken my eyes off you and for that I will never forgive myself."

"Is that the only reason you take care of me? Because it was your fault?"

The question cut through her but no more so than the accusations in his eyes. "I take care of you because you're my brother and I love you."

"More than you love the doctor?"

Her mouth dropped open. *Love?* "Donny . . . I . . ." She started to deny it but the words wouldn't come. Was he right? She knew she had feelings for Caleb but had simply brushed them off as a schoolgirl crush. Never had she allowed herself to call her feelings *love.*

Is that why the memory of his kisses still lingered? Why her heart skipped a beat the moment she heard Bertha's motor in the distance?

He glared at her. "You can't say it, can you? You can't say you love me more."

"I love *you,*" she said in a choked voice. "You're my brother. You mean the world to me."

"But you love the doctor more!"

"No!"

The vehemence of her voice made him lean back but suspicion remained on his face. "The only reason you take care of me

375

is because you feel guilty."

"I do feel guilty," she admitted. "I would give anything to change what happened, but that has nothing to do with my feelings for you. I hope we can live here forever." She'd worked hard — harder than she'd ever worked in her life — trying to prove to Miss Walker she had what it took to run a ranch. "You'd like that, right?"

"You don't want to live here. You want to get married and put me away."

"Donny, listen to me." She reached for his hands but he pulled back.

"Go away. Leave me alone. I hate you."

His words ripped through her. "You can't mean that."

"Go!"

It was no use trying to talk to him when he was like this. She turned and stumbled down the steps, her mind in a whirl. *You love the doctor more.* Was Donny right about her being in love with Caleb? Was that why he affected her so?

She shook the thought away. Even if it was true, nothing could be done about it. She wanted the ranch for Donny and the only way that was possible was to sign the agreement forbidding marriage.

I hate you.

Donny didn't mean it. Couldn't mean it.

He was upset. They both were. Later they would talk and everything would go back to the way it was. *God, please let it be so.*

Long after the argument with his sister, Donny sat on the verandah watching her work with horses. He felt bad for the things he said. He didn't hate her, he could never hate her. Nor could he blame her for his accident. He was just so afraid of losing her he hadn't been able to think straight.

Molly put a bay through its paces. Astride the horse she circled the corral much as Donny's thoughts circled in his head. She promised to sign those papers and that meant they could live on the ranch forever. Never again would he have to worry about losing Molly and facing the world alone.

Maybe when Molly took over as the full owner, she'd let him build an observatory on the property with a real telescope. He envisioned astronomers trekking to the Last Chance to view an eclipse, comet, or other heavenly spectacle. What discussions they would have. And how he would amaze them with his knowledge!

He was so engrossed in his thoughts it took him a while to realize something was wrong with Orbit. The black horse whinnied, teeth white against black lips. He stood on his hind legs, pawing the air with frantic hooves. He then dropped down on all fours, ran back and forth, and then rose again on his hind legs.

Donny narrowed his eyes against the glaring sun. It looked like Orbit was trying to escape. But why? And where was Molly? He swung his gaze from one end of the corral to the other. The horse that moments earlier had carried Molly now galloped around without a rider.

Alarmed, he craned his neck and quickly scanned the ground. Something blue caught his eye. Molly! She was lying on the ground and didn't move.

"Help," Donny cried. Sweat broke out on his forehead. Orbit wasn't trying to escape. Somehow he sensed that Molly was in trouble and was trying to get to her.

"Help, someone, help!" He yelled as loud as he could but no one was around to hear his frantic cries.

His chest squeezed tight and he could hardly breathe. He wiped his damp palms on his trousers and grabbed the chair wheels. Frantic, he forced his chair to the steps. Even in his panic, he knew he could never reach her. And even if he could reach her, he couldn't help. Not in a million years. No matter how much he wanted to or how much he tried, he couldn't help her. Never had he felt so helpless, so utterly, utterly helpless.

He whirled about, searching for something, anything. He pounded on the door with his fists. No one answered, which meant that Rosita was either upstairs or out back. He turned the knob and pushed the door open, yelling at the top of his lungs. Still no one.

The doorbell. It could be heard everywhere, even out back. He got as close as he could to the rope, but it was out of reach. Gasping, he stretched his body as much as he could, his arm rigid. His fingers touched the rope, making it swing back and forth. Bracing himself, he tried again and again.

With a mighty lunge he stretched high enough to get a handhold on the rope. He tugged it and chimes sounded inside the house.

Nothing.

He fought against panic and gave the rope another brisk pull. This time the door sprang all the way open and Rosita stepped outside.

"Get help!" he gasped. "My sister is hurt."

Rosita vanished inside, reappearing moments later with her brother.

"Molly!" Donny pointed to the corral, and

Jose leaped off the verandah and took off at a run.

Donny watched, helpless in his chair, and he did something he didn't normally do. He prayed. *God, don't punish me for the awful things I said to her. Please, please, please don't take my sister away. I'll do better, I will, I promise.*

CHAPTER 31

It was almost eleven p.m. when Caleb crossed the street to the hotel to check on Molly.

No one was at the desk as he strolled through the deserted lobby. He took the stairs two at a time and hurried to the infirmary at the end of the hall, floorboards creaking beneath his feet.

He opened the door. A kerosene lamp bathed the room in soft yellow light. Donny sat in his wheelchair snoring like a freight train.

The poor kid refused to leave his sister's side. By the looks of things, he hadn't even touched the bowl of stew and biscuits from Miss Lily's Café.

Molly still drifted in and out of consciousness, but the swelling on her head had gone down and that was a good sign. For a while, it looked like he was going to have to bore a hole in her skull to relieve the pressure on her brain, but trepanning was no longer necessary, thank God. Now all he could do was wait and pray.

He sat on the chair by her side, found her wrist, and checked her pulse. It was still below normal. He held her hand in both of his and wished he could smooth away the calluses on her palm, smooth away everything that brought her heartache or pain.

She looked pale but no less beautiful to him. Silky soft hair spread in disarray across the pillow. Thick, long lashes brushed against gently rounded cheeks. The curve of her pretty pink mouth brought back the memory of her kisses. He felt a tug in his heart. *God, make her well again. Bring her back to me.*

He often prayed by a patient's side, part of his job as a doctor. This time he asked for more than just healing; he asked God to bring her back to *him.*

Shaken by how close he'd been to losing her, he covered her hand with his own and sat perfectly still. From the moment Ruckus had driven her helter-skelter to town and helped him carry her to the hotel, he had acted and thought like a physician. He had examined her, monitored her breathing, dribbled water down her throat, measured the swelling of her head, and prayed.

But now he didn't talk to God as a doctor. Rather he prayed like a man in love.

He didn't know how long he sat by her side, but the stiffness of his body told him it had been a while. Low on fuel, the lamp sputtered and the light began to fade. Somewhere around midnight it went out altogether, casting the room in darkness.

At one a.m., a half-moon shone through the open window, bathing the room in blue light.

Rowdy laughter, shouts, and occasional gunshots rose from the street below. Caleb closed the window but it did little to mute the sounds.

It seemed that things had gotten worse, not better, since the saloons agreed to close on alternate Saturday nights. It was as if the town's roughnecks decided to party harder on the nights the saloons remained open.

Earlier he spotted Harvey Trotter stumbling from the Golden Eagle. Caleb was no closer to solving the mystery of Jimmy's illness, and his heart ached anew for the man's hurting family.

Someone fired a round of bullets and Donny stirred and called out in his sleep. "Fire! Fire!" The kid was having a nightmare.

Caleb stepped away from the window and

went to him. He shook him gently and Donny stiffened beneath his touch and his eyes flew open.

"There's no fire." Caleb nodded toward the window. "Just some rowdies."

Donny blinked and looked around as if trying to make sense of his surroundings. "Is my sister — ?"

"She'll be fine." Caleb picked up a chair, carried it to Donny's side, and sat.

Donny glanced at the bed. "She still won't wake up."

"She's not asleep, Donny. She's drifting in and out of unconsciousness. It's the brain's way of healing."

"How long will she be like this?" Donny asked.

"There's really no way of telling," Caleb said. He didn't want to worry Donny, but neither did he want to lie.

Donny sniffled and his tears looked like silver pearls in the dim, moonlit room. "I said some awful things to her. I told her I hated her and that's not true. I could never hate her."

Caleb handed him a clean handkerchief. "She knows that, Donny."

"How can you be sure?"

"I know your sister. We all say hurtful things from time to time, things we don't

384

mean. Fortunately, love is forgiving and your sister loves you very much."

Donny wiped his eyes and blew his nose. "I don't blame her for my accident. I don't."

"You know about that?" Caleb asked.

Donny nodded. "She told me it was her fault and that's when I said those awful things."

Caleb rubbed his throbbing brow. Molly must have been upset after the argument. Perhaps that accounted for her accident.

Donny's body shook with sobs. "I — I sh-should have told her not to w-work at the ranch. She was only doing it for me. She was tired and her hands were sore and she doesn't even like cattle . . . and . . . I should have told her I loved her."

Caleb groaned. *That makes two of us.* "You can still tell her that when she wakes up."

"P-Promise?" Donny pleaded.

"Promise." Caleb grimaced. He had no right to promise things he had no control over.

"I couldn't even get to her. I couldn't help her," Donny murmured. "I couldn't do anything. I'm as useless as a worm."

"That's not true, Donny. You got help for your sister."

"But what would have happened had I not

reached the doorbell? She could have been lying in the dirt for hours. What if Jose and Rosita were out back and didn't hear me ring? What if I'm here in this room all alone and something happens to her?"

"It's a waste of time to worry about what could have happened or might happen. You did what had to be done. That's all any of us can do." Donny looked so distressed Caleb felt sorry for him. "Come on, I'll take you to Aunt Bessie's house. She said you could stay with her while your sister is recuperating."

Donny shook his head. "I want to stay here with Molly."

Caleb started to argue but changed his mind. "All right. Just for tonight."

He found an empty room across the hall. Without bothering to remove the bedding, he grabbed the mattress and carried it back to Molly's room and placed it on the floor. He straightened the sheets and blanket and lifted Donny from his chair to the bed.

"There you go," Caleb said. "Get some sleep. I'll keep watch."

Donny settled for the night, Caleb sat by Molly's side, waiting for morning.

Eleanor sat on the buggy seat by Robert's side, staring at the horse pulling them. What a nuisance.

"Couldn't you have just given Molly my regards?" she asked, not for the first time. Did Robert always have to be such a gentleman? He insisted she travel to Cactus Patch and see for herself how Molly was doing. Eleanor hadn't been to town for some years, not since those busybody church women boycotted her beef following her divorce. From that time on she conducted her business in Tombstone.

"Miss Hatfield is under your employ."

Eleanor rolled her eyes. "Don't remind me." Nothing had worked out as planned, certainly nothing involving the ranch. If only her one and only child hadn't died. Thirty years — more than a quarter of a century — and still it hurt. Nothing that happened since — not the Indian trouble, not the divorce, not even the earthquake and fire that destroyed her ranch — had been as difficult as losing her only child.

She had no patience for sentimentality or weakness of character. For that reason she considered grief her greatest flaw.

"How long before Molly can return to the ranch?"

Robert took his eyes off the road just long enough to give her a puzzled glance. "A week or two."

"Hmm."

"I thought you said you didn't think she'd work out."

Eleanor sighed. "She'd work out just fine if she didn't have to worry about her brother. That's why I have a proposition for her."

"You mean other than insisting she not marry?"

"Marriage complicates things, especially for a woman." She knew from painful experience that no man was willing to play second fiddle to anything, let alone a ranch. "I'm going to propose that we hire a full-time caretaker for her brother."

Robert pursed his lips. "I do believe that's the wisest decision you've ever made," he said, his voice warm with approval. "Are you sure you're feeling all right? That doesn't sound like something you'd think up."

Eleanor kept her gaze focused ahead. "When you're my age, you have to" — she couldn't bring herself to use that dreadful word *compromise* — "meet people halfway."

He tossed her a dubious look. "If you're as poor at judging distances as you've been in the past, she'll be lucky if you meet her a tenth of the way." He clicked his tongue and the horse picked up speed.

388

The town had grown considerably since Eleanor was last there, though it was nowhere near as large as Tombstone. Robert pulled up in front of the hotel and set the brake.

"I need to pop into the bank, but I'll go up with you first if you wish," he said.

Eleanor waved away the offer. "Is that your way of saying you don't trust me to be on my good behavior?"

His mouth quirked. "I know how impatient you are around human frailty."

"You take care of the bank and I'll take care of . . . human frailty." She climbed out of the wagon and marched into the hotel. The sooner she got it over with, the sooner she could return to the ranch.

The desk clerk directed Eleanor to the infirmary upstairs. Eleanor gave the door a tap before entering. The room was dimly lit and a slight breeze wafted through the open window.

Molly's brother was asleep but his eyes flew open the minute she stepped into the room. "Miss Walker."

"Donald." She glanced at Molly and lowered her voice. "I came to see your sister."

"She keeps drifting in and out of sleep.

Doc Fairbanks says that's the way the brain heals."

"I guess that's good, then."

Donny nodded. "He said she has a concussion but he doesn't think there's anything more seriously wrong."

"Excellent." Now what? Eleanor knew what to do with a sick steer or injured horse, but a human? She hadn't even known what to do when her daughter was so ill all those years ago.

"Tell your sister that I came to see her and . . . and I'll talk to her when she's recovered." She turned and let herself out of the room. Robert said it was her duty to visit Molly and so her duty was done.

She'd barely made it to the stairwell when the boy called to her. "Miss Walker."

She turned and waited for him to work his wheelchair through the narrow doorway. He banged against the door frame, muttering beneath his breath. At last he succeeded in turning the chair sideways and easing himself into the hall. Working his wheels with his hands, he rolled within a few feet from where she stood.

"What is it?" she asked. "Speak up."

In the dim light of the hotel hall, his eyes looked like pools of green water. "I want to work for you."

She arched her eyebrows.

"Like I told you, I'm good with numbers."

"I believe I made it clear that my offer was contingent on your sister's ability to learn the ranching business." She turned toward the stairs.

"I like your ranch," he said, stopping her in her tracks. "I've read practically all your books and I know all about cattle."

She regarded him over her shoulder. "Do you, now?"

"I know that Hereford cattle were first brought to this country by Henry Clay. I also know that bulls can't see the color red so it's not true that it makes them angry." He quickly listed several other facts, some involving cattle heritage, weight, and habits. "Cattle also have amazing memories."

Resting a hand on the newel, she let him rattle on. Mercy, could she be any more accommodating? Visiting the injured. Stepping foot in a town she loathed. Feeling sorry for a young man who obviously didn't need her sympathy. Was all this insipid behavior a sign of old age?

"I also know that cows are the only mammals that pee backwards," he added.

Eleanor laughed; she couldn't help it. She was impressed not only with his knowledge but his obvious enthusiasm and interest.

She doubted that any of her cowhands knew as much about cattle or their history.

"And I have more ideas on how to make the ranch more profitable," he continued. "Do you want to hear them?"

No, she did not want to hear them. She wanted to go home. Still, there was something about the earnest face that touched a chord. He was a handsome lad, with the same green eyes as his sister. What a pity the boy couldn't walk. She could use someone like him.

"Perhaps another time," she said.

"So what do you say? Can I work for you?" he asked.

"We'll . . . discuss it after your sister has recovered," she said. Before he had another chance to plead his case, she started down the stairs. "Good day."

Outside, Robert stood by his buggy waiting for her. "Take me to the post office," she said. "Maybe there'll be a letter from someone interested in learning the ranch business."

A look of horror crossed Robert's face. "You didn't . . ." He glanced up at the hotel as if expecting to see someone jump from a second-story window.

"You'll be pleased to know that I didn't

even talk to Molly," she said. "She wasn't awake."

A combination of concern and relief suffused Robert's face before he frowned. "And you decided to dismiss the girl just like that?"

"Let's just say I'm keeping my options open."

"That's a switch," he said.

"Not as much as you might think," she said with a determined toss of her head. "Would you be kind enough to draft a bank note from my account to pay for Molly's medical expenses?"

His eyebrows shot up. "You're paying her medical bills?"

"Yes, and add extra to cover any other expenses she and her brother might incur during her recovery."

"Very well." Robert studied her from beneath the brim of his straw hat. "What happens if Molly doesn't return to the ranch and no one else steps forward? What then?"

She took a deep breath. "Then I suppose I'd have to take your advice and sell."

"I never thought to hear you say such a thing."

"What choice do I have?" she asked. "I may even have to break down and marry you."

He grinned and offered her his arm. "Now that's what I call meeting someone halfway," he said with a nod of approval.

"Only halfway?" She glanced at him as they started toward the post office. "And you accuse *me* of being a bad judge of distance."

CHAPTER 32

Molly opened her eyes. The sky looked strange: brown, odd — hairline cracks veering off in all directions. The "sky" was actually a dirty, cracked ceiling. She was in a strange room in a strange bed. Something made her turn her head, a shadow — a presence.

That's when she saw him, Caleb, kneeling by her bedside. Hands clasped, head lowered to the mattress in prayer, he looked like a man pleading for his life. Never had she seen anyone pray with such intensity.

Not wanting to intrude on his privacy, she turned her head toward the wall. The room grew dark. A wave of nausea washed over her and her moment of clarity was gone.

A distant voice cut through the fog. "You're awake."

She blinked. Gradually the ringing in her head subsided and her vision cleared.

With some effort his name fell from her

parched lips. "Caleb."

The moment she spoke, the lines of worry left his face. He leaned over and squeezed her hand. "Take it easy."

Her mind whirled in confusion. "What . . . what happened? Where am I?" And why was her mouth stuffed with cotton? "The fire —"

Caleb squeezed her hand tighter. "You're not in Dobson Creek. You're in Cactus Patch, Arizona, and you were thrown from a horse."

Visions flashed through her head. Fire, smoke. Then a horse. She held on to the last memory. She could almost feel the pounding of horse's hooves beneath her — then nothing.

"Can you say your name?" he asked.

Her mind turned over slowly. "Molly . . . Ann . . . Hatfield."

"Molly Ann," he said and smiled.

She tried to smile back but her mouth refused to cooperate. "Molly."

"Molly," he said in a quieter voice. He indicated the room with a slight toss of his head. "This is what we call the infirmary."

It took a moment for his words to sink in. She glanced around the room. "Donny!" Her brother . . . must get to him. She struggled to sit up but Caleb held her down, his hands lingering on her shoulders long after she'd grown still.

"Donny's fine," he said, releasing her. "He's staying at Aunt Bessie's house."

"You . . . you're taking care of him?"

"Actually, he's taking care of me. Aunt Bessie has taken a liking to him and that means she's spending less time worrying about me. Donny's helping her write letters to get support for prohibition."

She laid a hand on her forehead. That couldn't be right. Donny was interested in science, not . . . not prohibition.

Caleb grinned. "Donny is giving Aunt Bessie a thorough education in outer space and she, in turn, is teaching him about what she calls 'dens of iniquity.' "

She tried to smile but her face felt like it was about to crack. She could well imagine the conversations between the two. She tried to sit up but a sharp pain shot through her rib cage and she groaned.

"Careful. You're still bruised, but as far as I can tell, nothing is broken." He helped her sit up. Plumping her pillow, he arranged it behind her and she leaned back.

Something popped into her head. "Sandstorm. That's the name of the new bay. I remember putting him through his paces."

"Anything else you remember?"

She shook her head. Arranging the sheet, she realized she wore only her chemise. Someone had undressed her. Caleb? Blushing, she glanced at him pouring water from a pitcher, but nothing in his expression gave her pause.

"Here you go." He handed her a glass. His hand touched hers and he quickly drew away. His air of professionalism made it easier to maintain her distance. He was the doctor, she the patient. If only she didn't remember the night he was so much more . . .

She took a long sip before handing the glass back to him. "Thank you."

"I'll go downstairs to Miss Lily's and get you something to eat. Her soup will cure just about anything."

Her lips softened into a smile, but her mouth still felt parched. "How can I ever repay you for your kindness?"

"Seeing you smile is enough," he said. His gentle expression was anything but professional and a warm glow inched along the length of her, soothing her injuries like a healing salve.

She lowered her gaze and picked a ball of lint off the blanket. "How long have I been here?" It hurt to breathe but the huskiness in her voice had as much to do with emotion as pain. Donny was all right and for that she was grateful, but taking care of him was a demanding job. Caleb and Aunt Bessie were bound to grow weary.

"Since yesterday."

She touched her forehead. She could not believe it. She remembered being carried, remembered someone dabbing a cool sponge on her head, but after that, nothing.

"You have a concussion but the swelling has subsided."

"How long do I have to stay here?" She was anxious to check on her brother and return to the ranch.

"Another day or two. You'll be sore for a while. Do you think you can walk? The privy is down the hall."

She nodded and he helped her don a dressing gown. He held each sleeve until she slipped an arm into the silky lengths. He then tied the gown around her waist. Never had she known such tenderness or concern for her well-being.

"I borrowed this from Aunt Bessie," he explained.

She slid out of bed and the room started spinning. Caleb grabbed her. "Steady," he said, holding her until her head cleared.

She blinked. A riot of brightly colored blossoms spilled from baskets and vases, filling the air with sweet fragrance. She'd never seen so many flowers in one place. "What is all this?"

"I'm afraid the church members got a little carried away," he said.

"Church?" She stared all around her, stunned. "They . . . they did all this? For me?"

"Wait till you see what else they did," he said and groaned. "We have enough chicken pot pies to last six months."

She swallowed the lump in her throat but couldn't stop the tears.

He slipped his arm around her waist. "Are you all right?"

"Yes," she whispered. "I'm more than all right."

"That's what I like to hear." He walked her ever so slowly out of the infirmary. When they reached their destination at the end of the hall, he asked, "Do you think you can manage?"

Nodding, she shuffled into the tiny room and closed the door. She glanced into the mirror and shuddered. Her face was white and her hair tumbled down her back in unruly curls. Light-headed, she splashed cold water on her face and immediately felt better.

Moments later she stepped out of the

room and swooned.

"Whoa," he said, wrapping her in his arms. The short trip back to the infirmary exhausted her and she sank gratefully into bed.

"Better get some sleep."

He said more but her eyelids fluttered shut and the sound of his voice faded away. Was that his lips on her forehead? Did he kiss her or had she only imagined it?

When next she woke, he handed her a cup of chicken soup. "Drink up," he said. At the moment he was every inch the doctor. She must have been mistaken about the kiss, and a shiver of disappointment raced through her.

She took a sip. The soup tasted good and it went down with little effort. Caleb took the empty cup from her. "Just what the doctor ordered. If you're a good girl and follow my orders, I'll even get you some of Miss Lily's famous ice cream."

He set the cup on the table, stared out of the window for several moments, and then sat next to her bed. He looked so serious that she immediately clenched her stomach. She twisted her body around until she faced him.

"Caleb, what is it?" Were her injuries worse than he originally led her to believe?

401

His steady gaze never left her face. "Unless I'm diagnosing or prescribing something, I'm not very good at expressing myself."

She studied him, not sure what she heard in his voice. He sounded so unlike himself with none of his usual confidence. "Must be a doctor's curse."

He rewarded her with a brief smile. "You scared me," he said. "I thought I'd lost you."

She held her breath. This wasn't the doctor speaking. Nor were the eyes gazing at her doctor's eyes. "Caleb —"

He leaned forward. Elbows on his knees, he rubbed his palms together. "I told God that if He brought you back to me I'd never want for anything more."

She took a deep breath, letting her hand drop to the side. "Don't," she whispered.

"I know, I know. This isn't the time or place, but I thought I'd never get a chance to tell you how I feel. The truth is . . . I love you. I've loved you from the moment I first saw you wearing that ridiculous purple hat and pointing a shotgun at me."

She stared at him, unable to speak. *Love.* He said love.

"Tell me you feel the same." He lowered his voice but not the intensity.

Denial flew to her lips but went no further.

"I . . . I . . ." Raw hurt flashed on his face and she could no longer hold back. "I love you too."

A wide grin flashed across his face. "My dear, sweet Molly. I can't tell you how happy that makes me." He reached for her hand but she pulled away.

"This doesn't change anything," she whispered in a broken voice.

His jaw tightened. "Because of your brother."

"Because of what he will do to us. Because of what he did to my own parents, to our family. I'm sure Jimmy's parents must feel the strain of his illness. How could they not?"

"It's not the same thing. Donny's not ill and he's in no danger of dying."

"But he requires much care."

"Molly, you can't sacrifice your life for his."

"Nor can you, Caleb. The town needs you and you need a wife who puts your needs first." Despair almost cut off her breathing but she forced herself to continue. "I can't be that woman."

He started to say something but a knock sounded and his face darkened with annoyance. The door opened just far enough for Aunt Bessie to poke her head into the room.

403

"May we come in?"

Caleb leaped to his feet but his blue eyes bored into Molly. "Yes, come in. Molly's awake."

The door opened all the way and Aunt Bessie bustled into the room, followed by her slower-paced sister, Lula-Belle.

"We won't stay long," Aunt Bessie gushed. She stopped. "All these flowers. It looks like a funeral." Her glance volleyed between Molly and Caleb as if she sensed the tension between them.

"I asked these ladies to bring you fresh clothes," Caleb explained, his voice hollow.

Molly smiled at the two older women. "That was very thoughtful."

"We also brought you a little gift." Aunt Bessie laid a box on Molly's lap. The box was wrapped in brown paper and tied with a big red bow.

Molly fingered the satin ribbon. "Thank you, but you've done enough already. I can't tell you how much I appreciate you taking care of my brother."

"Nonsense. Tell her, Lula-Belle. Tell her how much I enjoy Donny."

Lula-Belle set a pile of freshly laundered clothes on the foot of Molly's bed, the feathers on her hat snapping in the air like flags at sea. "You can thank your lucky stars that he's only fourteen or she'd have him married off by now."

Molly's gaze settled on Caleb, whose dark eyes never left her face. His back ramrod straight, he looked distant.

It took enormous effort to shift her gaze back to Aunt Bessie. Never in her wildest dreams had she imagined Donny having any sort of normal life. Certainly not one that included marriage.

"He won't be fourteen forever," Aunt Bessie said, as if age were the only consideration. "I can't wait to tell him that you're awake. He's been so worried."

"How's he doing, really?" Molly asked.

"Unless I miss my guess, he's busy beating Sam at chess."

"I didn't even know he could play chess," Molly said. Between working and caring for him, she barely had enough time to teach him the necessary skills of reading and writing. Little time had been left for fun except for an occasional game of checkers.

Lula-Belle rolled her eyes. "You're lucky Bessie doesn't teach the boy to gamble."

"Oh, for goodness' sakes, Lula-Belle. Just because I won a bet doesn't mean I gambled."

Caleb raised his eyebrows. "You won a bet?"

Aunt Bessie got all flustered. "Not exactly. Some of the men in town were betting on how long" — she gave Molly a sheepish glance — "you would last as Miss Walker's heiress. Most didn't think you'd last more than — never mind that. I said you'd last more than two months and won even though I didn't put a single penny in the pot."

"It still sounds like gambling to me," Lula-Belle insisted with a stubborn look.

"Well, it's not!" Aunt Bessie gave a self-righteous nod. "It's not gambling if you plan to use the money for the Lord's work." She indicated the box on Molly's lap. "Open it."

Molly slid the ribbon off and tore away the paper. "Oh, bonbons!" she exclaimed.

Aunt Bessie beamed. "They're my favorite."

Molly took the lid off and pulled out a foil-covered chocolate.

Caleb watched with knitted brow. "I don't think you should be eating sweets yet." He looked and sounded every bit a doctor.

Aunt Bessie elbowed him. "I guess you haven't heard. Bonbons are not just your ordinary sweets. They're good for whatever ails you." She leaned over and helped herself to a chocolate treat.

Molly offered one to Caleb but he declined. Glad to have something to do besides avoid Caleb's gaze, she carefully peeled away the foil and tossed it toward the wastebasket and missed. Caleb stooped to pick it up.

She took a tiny bite of the luscious confectionary, letting the chocolate melt in her mouth. "Hmm," she said, smacking her lips. "I do believe they're my favorite too."

Aunt Bessie looked pleased and turned to Caleb. "Are you sure you don't want one?"

Caleb stood looking at the foil wrapper in his hand. "I've gotta go," he said in an abrupt voice. He grabbed his hat from atop the chest of drawers and literally ran out of the room.

Molly stared at the door. *Oh, Caleb. If only things could be different . . .*

Aunt Bessie gave a knowing nod. "A lovers' quarrel, eh?"

Molly felt her cheeks grow warm. She wasn't about to admit to Aunt Bessie or anyone else what she and Caleb had discussed. "No, it was . . . nothing like that."

"We should go." Lula-Belle stood and gave her sister a meaningful look. "We don't want to *tire* Miss Hatfield."

Aunt Bessie looked about to answer but thought better of it. "Very well. But we'll be back."

CHAPTER 33

Throttle wide open, Caleb raced along the bumpy dirt road toward the Trotter farm. *"I love you too."* He pushed the thought away only to have another take its place: *"I can't be that woman."*

Drat! He couldn't think about that. Not now. He had a patient, a very sick little boy who needed his full attention.

Wheels spinning, he turned onto the Trotter property and parked. As if to protest Caleb's heavy-footed driving, Bertha backfired and Magic barked in response.

In the distance Mrs. Trotter hung wash on the clothesline strung between the house and barn.

"Stay," he said, pointing at Magic. He jumped out of his car and sprinted across the yard.

Mrs. Trotter greeted him with a wary frown. "Dr. Fairbanks." Her hand froze on a half-hung pair of trousers. She looked tired and pale as the bedsheet flapping in the breeze.

"I didn't expect to see you." Her lips trembled. "I hope you aren't bringing more bad news."

"On the contrary. I believe I may have misdiagnosed Jimmy's illness."

She let go of the newly washed trousers and they hung precariously from a single clothespin before dropping to the ground. She didn't seem to notice. "I'm not sure what you mean."

"I don't think he has leukemia. I think he has lead poisoning."

She stared at him, her face suffused with confusion. "But how —"

"I have reason to believe there's lead in that foil ball he carries around with him. If that's true, it could be what's making him sick."

"The foil ball? The one made from bonbon wrappers?" She stared at him in disbelief. "But how is that possible? Wouldn't other people get sick from eating those sweets?"

"Most people discard the wrappers and they don't make spitballs out of them."

Miss Trotter made a face. "I've scolded him for that filthy habit but he persists." She placed her hand on her forehead as if to calm her thoughts. "You . . . you really think that's what's wrong with him?"

"We'll know for sure soon enough. I'd like to talk to him. Is he home?"

She nodded toward the house. "Inside." Leaving her basket of wash behind, she led the way, calling to Jimmy the moment they reached the front porch.

Caleb followed her into the house. Mrs. Trotter opened a door leading to another room in back. "Jimmy!"

Jimmy appeared rubbing his eyes. It was midafternoon but he was still dressed in his nightshirt. It was obvious he'd been sleeping.

"Hello, Jimmy," Caleb said.

Jimmy gave him a squinty-eyed look. "Hello, Dr. Fairbanks."

Caleb bent over, hands on his thighs. "I wonder if you would be kind enough to fetch me your foil ball."

Jimmy glanced at his mother as if to check her reaction before turning back to Caleb. "Why do you want it?"

"I'll explain when you bring it to me."

Jimmy left the room and Caleb straightened.

Mrs. Trotter wrung her hands together, lines of worry on her face. "May I offer you something, Dr. Fairbanks? Some lemonade?"

"No, thank you." Caleb was too wound up to eat or drink. What a day it had been. First Molly had opened her eyes and told him she loved him. Now this. *God, don't let me be wrong about what's causing Jimmy's problem.*

Jimmy reappeared and handed Caleb the foil ball. It was at least six inches round. "You must have eaten a lot of sweets to make a ball this size."

"I didn't eat them all," Jimmy said. "I collect foil from other kids."

Caleb examined the crushed foil. The ball smelled of chocolate. "Why? What do you plan to do with it?"

"I'm making a ball just like the ones on my trade cards," Jimmy replied with obvious pride.

"Trade cards?" Caleb looked to Mrs. Trotter for explanation.

"His uncle used to play for the Cincinnati Red Stockings and every Christmas he sends the children baseball trade cards." She shrugged. "I'm afraid he's filled Jimmy's head with all kinds of fanciful tales."

"The ball has to be at least nine inches round," Jimmy explained, his usual dull eyes almost as shiny as the foil sphere in Caleb's hands. "Otherwise it's not a baseball. Soon as it's big enough, I'm going to make me a baseball bat."

"I see." Caleb hated to spoil the boy's fun but it couldn't be helped. "The problem is, I believe there's something in the foil that's making you sick."

Jimmy gave the ball in Caleb's hand a dubious glance. "Is that what makes my stomach hurt?"

"I'm afraid so. That means you can't play with foil or make spitballs anymore."

"But if I don't have a ball, I can't play baseball." Jimmy's lip quivered and his eyes grew moist.

"I'll make a deal with you, Jimmy," Caleb said. "You promise to stay away from foil and I'll buy you the best baseball I can find."

Jimmy's face brightened. "Really?"

Caleb smiled. Jimmy's health problems were far from over, but with God's help, he would recover. "Really. Now go and wash your hands. And be sure to use lots of soap and water."

Jimmy turned to leave the room, but his mother stopped him and hugged him tight, tears rolling down her cheeks. He wriggled free and she called to her other children. Almost instantly five more freckled faces peered anxiously at their crying mother.

"Quick!" Mrs. Trotter said, motioning to her oldest girl. "Go get your pa. Tell him we have good news." She turned to her youngest. "Jimmy, wash your hands good now, you hear?"

Caleb stuffed the foil ball into his black bag for testing and pulled out a vial of Iodide of Potassium. "Give him a few drops every four hours." Jimmy's mother took the vial from him and slipped it into her apron pocket.

Harvey Trotter stomped into the house and tossed his straw hat onto the hat rack. "What's all the racket?"

Mrs. Trotter grasped her husband's sleeve. "Dr. Fairbanks thinks that Jimmy might not have leukemia after all."

Harvey turned to Caleb, his sunbaked face suffused with hope. "Is this true?"

Caleb nodded. "I believe he has lead poisoning." He quickly explained about the foil ball. "Lead poisoning is serious but I think we caught it before it damaged any vital organs."

Harvey beamed from ear to ear. He looked completely different from the tortured man Caleb had spotted entering a saloon the day before.

"Well, I'll be." He pumped Caleb's hand like the handle of a dry well. "We're mighty obliged to you, Doctor."

Mrs. Trotter clasped her hands to her

chest. "Praise the Lord."

Harvey looked at Jimmy, who had just returned to the room. He threw his arms around the boy. "Praise the Lord."

He then hugged his wife, and all six children huddled around their ma and pa.

Caleb drove away from the Trotter farm grinning. The blazing sun barely held its own against the warm glow radiating from inside him. "Whoopie!" One hand on the wheel, he pumped the other in the air. *Thank You, thank You, God!*

Jimmy's problems were far from over. If Caleb's latest diagnosis was correct — and he had every reason to believe that it was — the boy would still have to be monitored carefully. There could be lingering effects, but he had a good chance of living a full life.

Caleb needed this good news. Only God knew how much. He needed a reminder as to why he became a doctor in the first place. He'd lost three patients during the past week: one from a gunshot wound, another from a rattlesnake bite, and one an infant. It was the kind of week that brought a man to his knees and made him question his very reason for being.

"The town needs you and you need a wife

who puts your needs first."

Even the bumpy road couldn't distract him from the pain that accompanied thoughts of Molly. He recalled the night they stood in the moonlight surrounded by cattle. He shared his dreams for the future and she made him believe that even building a clinic was possible. If she was by his side.

"That woman can't be me."

He jammed his foot hard against the gas pedal and Bertha sped up. She bounced and spewed and rattled and roared, but not enough to shake away his troubled thoughts.

CHAPTER 34

Molly walked around the hotel room touching the bright bouquets and reading the messages attached to each one. So many kind words, so many said prayers. Such an outpouring of love.

The Bible said not to judge but that's exactly what she'd done. After being banned from her father's funeral, she wanted no part of church or its people. Would never have attended Cactus Patch Church had Caleb not insisted. And even then she'd attended with a closed heart instead of open arms. A few misguided deacons had kept her away physically on that long-ago day, but she never should have turned away spiritually.

God, forgive me. She wiped away her tears and continued reading the cards.

Many names she didn't recognize, but one she did. Or rather she recognized the stunted handwriting. Mr. Washington had written down the lyrics to a song he'd written for his newly organized choir.

The first stanza read, "Put God first and everything will be all right. Put God first and you'll never know another night. Put God first . . ."

She set the card down. *Simple for you to say, Mr. Washington.* For as long as she could remember, her first thought upon waking was Donny. He was her last thought at night.

Brodie said unlearning a horse was harder than training it. The same was true of people.

Caleb burst through the door, startling her. "You're up." Before she could say anything he added, "I have good news. I was right about Jimmy." He lifted the box of bonbons from the bedside table and shook it. "Has lead poisoning."

Confused, she stared at him. That didn't seem like good news to her. She already knew someone who died of lead poisoning. "Is he going to —"

He shook his head. "It'll take a while for him to recover and the lead may have lingering effects, but I believe we caught it in time."

"Oh, Caleb. How wonderful! His family must be so relieved." She clasped her hands

417

together. "But how does a child get lead poisoning?"

"It was these." He tossed the empty confection box into the wastebasket. "Jimmy saved the foil and even made spitballs out of it."

She touched a hand to her forehead. "That day in church, he spit a wad of foil at that old man."

He nodded. "Watching you peel away that foil made me think of it and I did some research. I sent a sample to a colleague in Boston for testing, but I'm willing to bet it'll come back positive for lead." He grinned. "Just think, had you not been thrown from a horse, I might never have figured out what caused Jimmy's illness."

Molly's mind whirled. "Aunt Bessie deserves the credit, not me." The dear lady's gift turned out to be more valuable than gold. Molly couldn't believe the way things worked out — amazing. God's work? She smiled at how easily God's name came to mind. Perhaps putting God first wouldn't be as hard as she thought.

"It seems like a day of discovery," she said, her voice soft.

"What?"

"I've been reading my get-well messages."

"Words of wisdom, no doubt." He held

418

her gaze. Unspoken words seemed to hang between them as if strung upon an invisible rope.

"Caleb, what you said . . ."

He shook his head. "I know that Donny is your main concern and I had no right to put you on the spot while you're recuperating. As a doctor I should have known better than to upset you. I apologize. It . . . it won't happen again." He pulled a watch out of his vest pocket. "I have a patient to see in" — he pressed the clasp and the cover sprang open — "exactly ten minutes." Closing the watch case, he slid it back into his pocket and turned to leave.

"Wait!" she called. He spun around to face her, his expression closed — a stranger's. "I — I —" He looked so withdrawn — professional, cold even. He looked nothing like the man who had declared his love for her.

The words she wanted to say died before reaching her lips. "I need a bath."

"I'll tell the clerk at the front desk." He hesitated. "Miss Walker covered the cost of this room with enough money left for expenses until you recover."

"Miss Walker did that? But why?"

"One of the advantages of being her heiress, no doubt," he said, his voice curt.

He walked out of the room, closing the

door behind him. She wondered if she only imagined him pausing outside the door before walking away.

Molly lay in bed and stared at the sunbeam pouring in the infirmary windows. She'd spent a long, sleepless night and greeted the morning with more than a little relief.

Caleb's words kept running through her head. *"I love you. I've loved you from the moment I first saw you wearing that ridiculous purple hat and pointing a shotgun at me."*

When had she first known she loved him? For some reason it felt as if she'd loved him all her life. She'd fought her feelings, denied them, pretended they didn't exist.

Put God first and everything will be all right.

Even her feelings for Caleb?

She closed her eyes and poured her heart out to the Lord. She'd been wrong about so many, many things. She judged all churches cold and judgmental like the one in Dobson Creek and she'd been wrong. She was also wrong — perhaps even arrogant — to think she knew what was best for Donny and that she could take care of him without help. But her worst mistake of all was putting God last and not asking Him to guide the way.

Falling in love with Caleb? Was that wrong too?

She jumped out of bed, hurriedly dressed, and battled her curls into a tidy bun. A loud chugging sound announced Caleb's arrival in town. She raced to the window and her heart leaped with joy. Bertha backfired and she laughed. Caleb glanced her way and she lifted her arm to wave, but he quickly dashed into his office, Magic at his heels. Had he seen her? She didn't think so.

She turned from the window and the room began to spin. Better get a bite to eat. She had no intention of falling on her face when she told Caleb her decision to follow her heart.

After eating her fill of flapjacks and nervously gulping down two cups of coffee in Miss Lily's Café, she felt better except for the butterflies in her stomach.

Outside the sun was hot and the sky bright. A horse and wagon was parked in front of Caleb's office and a wave of disappointment washed over her. Already he was with a patient. Never mind. She would sit in the waiting room until he was free — even if it took all day.

Just as she reached his office the door swung open and a woman stepped outside with a young boy Molly immediately recognized.

"Hello, Jimmy," Molly said. She then introduced herself to Jimmy's mother. "Dr. Fairbanks told me the good news."

Mrs. Trotter smiled. "I don't know how I'll ever be able to thank him." She gazed lovingly at her son. "You can go to Mr. Green's. I'll meet you there. And remember, no bonbons."

Jimmy gave a whoop and headed for the mercantile store.

"Dr. Fairbanks told Jimmy to order a baseball and he would pay for it," Mrs. Trotter explained.

"That's very kind of him," Molly said. Trust Caleb to know exactly what the boy needed. "I'm so happy for you and your family."

"We're very blessed. You have no idea how hard it is to care for a sick child. It affects the whole family, you know what I mean?"

"I believe I do," Molly said.

"And Dr. Fairbanks! I tell you that man is a wonder. Did you know that he was up all night at the Randall ranch delivering a baby? The poor man doesn't sleep. Thank God he doesn't have the responsibility of home and family."

Molly's heart sank. "I guess that would be

a problem."

Mrs. Trotter nodded. "Yes, indeed. Dr. Masterson always said a physician either cared for a wife and children or cared for his patients. He couldn't do both."

Jimmy called to his mom.

"I better let you go," Molly said.

"It was lovely meeting you." With a quick wave of her hand, Mrs. Trotter hurried along the boardwalk toward Green's Mercantile.

Molly turned to stare at Caleb's door and her spirits sank. *You have no idea how hard it is to care for a sick child.*

Donny wasn't sick but he needed a great deal of care, and she knew all too well what that could do to a family.

An older man with a cane brushed past her and opened the door to the doctor's office, a jangling of bells announcing his arrival. He waited for her to enter ahead of him but she shook her head, backed away, and turned. Without a backward glance she walked to the livery stables as fast as her still-woozy head would allow.

CHAPTER 35

Eleanor sat in the rocking chair on the verandah enjoying the warm night air when Brodie joined her.

"I heard she's back," he said. He leaned one shoulder against a post and rolled a cigarette.

Eleanor stopped rocking. She never thought to see Molly again. Certainly not at the ranch. It would seem that she underestimated the girl. "She's back."

He licked the paper. "The first thing she did was get back on Sandstorm. Not many people would do that after eating dust like she did."

The girl had spunk, all right. No question. "This is not a horse ranch. If she plans to stay she's going to have to learn about cattle."

Brodie stuck his cigarette in his mouth, swiped a match on the sole of his boot, and lit it. The smell of tobacco smoke wafted in the air. "What do you want me to do with Orbit?"

"Orbit?"

"The blind horse."

"Oh, that." The horse would never survive the wilderness, so releasing it was out of the question. Nor could they sell it. "Do you know anyone who might be willing to take him?" It was a long shot. What rancher would take on the expense of a horse that didn't earn its keep?

"Nope, no one."

Eleanor let out a sigh. "Let me think about it."

Brodie moved away from the steps and headed toward the bunkhouse. "Maybe we should just shoot it," he called over his shoulder.

But Eleanor's thoughts had already drifted away from the horse and settled back on Molly. All of a sudden the girl looked promising. Eleanor would never have guessed it, but it was true. Maybe, just maybe, she had found her heir.

Donny sat by the open window of his room, his body frozen in horror.

Shoot it! They're going to shoot Orbit!

He gripped the arms of his wheelchair, sweat dripping into his eyes. Brushing the back of his hand across his damp forehead, he tried to think.

His thoughts scrambled. Somehow he had to save Orbit, but how? It took him the best part of an hour, but he came up with a plan — a daring plan.

Molly had already retired for the night, but he waited until he heard Miss Walker climb the stairs to her room. He waited until the bunkhouse lights were out and the distant howling of wolves and moos of cattle were all that broke the silence of the night.

He grabbed the blanket off the bed and tucked it around his waist. He then flattened the feather pillow across his lap.

Ever so quietly he wheeled himself through the darkened house. A third-quarter moon slanted a white beam through the windows of the main room, allowing just enough light to see.

He opened the front door and wiggled his chair onto the verandah. He stopped to catch his breath. After closing the door he slowly approached the top of the steps. His heart thumped and sweat broke out on the back of his neck.

He arranged the pillow in front of his chest and face and almost decided not to go through with his plan. *"Maybe we should just shoot it."*

With grim determination he filled his lungs with air, reached for his wheels, and spun them forward.

The chair shot off the verandah. Missing the steps the chair hit the ground with a thud and tipped over. Donny was thrown facedown in the dirt. The pillow and blanket softened the blow, but even so he was dazed and out of breath.

Doc Fairbanks's voice sounded in his head. *"Breathe. Force those lungs open."*

He waited until his breathing was almost normal before reaching for the overturned wheelchair. Stretching full-length, he lifted the chair with one hand and tried pushing it upright. It took several tries before he succeeded.

Gritting his teeth, he propelled himself with his elbows and eased himself around until he faced his chair square on. He then worked his way forward on his belly. He grunted and groaned but kept plowing his elbows into the dirt, dragging his lifeless legs behind.

Grabbing hold of the footrest, he rested for a moment. Doc's voice sounded in his head, telling him where to put his arms, how to breathe. Inch by painful inch he made his way into the seat of his chair, turning his torso around until he sat square.

"Whoopie!" Startled by his own voice, he covered his mouth with his hand and froze, hoping no one had heard. He did it! He made it all the way outside and down the steps by himself. The rest should be easy.

Only it wasn't. It was difficult to wheel his chair over soft ground and several times his wheels sank into a rut, almost toppling him over.

By the time he reached the barn he was drenched with sweat, his shirt sticking to his back. He wiped his wet hands on his trousers before rolling inside. The barn smelled of heated horseflesh and hay. The moon shone through the hatch of the hayloft and he wheeled toward the beam of light.

"Orbit," he called softly, though it was doubtful that anyone could hear him inside the barn.

He rolled past each stall. Several horses stirred and one nickered. Orbit was in the end stall. His head hung over the gate bobbing up and down.

"It's me." He held out his hand and Orbit tickled his palm with his velvety soft nose. "I won't let them hurt you. I won't!" Donny swallowed the lump in his throat. If only there was another way. "Are you ready?"

He wasn't even sure *he* was ready. He slid his hand along the gate until he found the latch. It lifted easily. He rolled back, pulling the gate with him. The stall opened and Donny rolled away.

"Come on, boy." Orbit walked ever so slowly from the stall and Donny guided the horse out of the barn with his voice. "That's it. Keep going." He didn't stop until he'd rolled a good fifteen or twenty feet away from the barn. The horse stopped behind him. "Go. Go on."

Orbit cocked an ear but didn't move. His coat shone in the moonlight like one of Molly's shiny dresses. He swished his tail and lowered his head as if searching for Donny's hand.

"You can't stay here. It's not safe. You need to find your pack." Horses had a keen sense of smell and hearing, and he knew from careful watching that Orbit's were greater than most. He counted on them to guide the horse to safety. "Go!"

Still the horse stayed. Donny turned his chair around. "You don't give me any choice." He slapped Orbit's side and the colt bounded off.

No sooner had the horse's hooves faded away than a wolf howled in the distance. Shivering, Donny turned toward the ranch house and forced his wheelchair over the uneven ground. A couple of times he had to stop and work his way out of a rut, but he finally made it back to the verandah — and stopped.

He forgot about the steps. Going down was one thing, but going up was altogether something else. Spotting the pillow on the ground where he'd left it, he threw himself forward and landed on top of it. He hit his elbow hard and tears sprang to his eyes. "Ow."

Calm down, calm down, calm down. Gotta breathe. He went through the exercises Doc had taught him, forcing cool night air into his lungs. He then belly-crawled to the steps. He was out of breath and beginning to wheeze but he kept going. Hands on the bottom step, he tried pulling himself up, but without the use of his elbows he couldn't get enough traction. He tried again and again until at last he fell back on the ground, exhausted.

Molly awoke to banging on her bedroom door. Before she made it out of bed, the door sprang open and Miss Walker's voice floated across the dark room. "Molly, your brother needs you."

Molly's feet hit the floor before the words were barely out of Miss Walker's mouth. Grabbing her dressing gown, she shoved her arms into the sleeves as she ran. "What's wrong with him?"

"He may be hurt. He's outside."

"Outside?" Molly sprinted along the hall on bare feet, then raced down the stairs and out the front door. A couple of cowhands gathered in a circle.

Molly flew down the verandah steps and dropped by Donny's side. The sky was still dark but the light from Stretch's lantern bathed Donny in a yellow glow. Dry blood stained the elbows of his dust-covered shirt, but she could find no other injuries.

"What happened?" she cried.

"Now don't go gettin' all riled up," Ruckus said. "I don't see no broken bones. Far as I can tell he's got no serious injuries. Just some skinned knees and elbows is all."

She turned back to her brother. "What are you doing out here?" She brushed the hair away from his face. "How did you get outside?"

"I did just what Doc Fairbanks taught me to do. I got back in my chair by myself."

Donny grabbed her arm. "I had to let him go, Molly. I couldn't let them shoot him."

"The boy ain't been makin' much sense," Feedbag said. "I fear he's what you call delirious."

She studied her brother's face. He didn't

look delirious but he did look different — older somehow. "Who did you let go?"

"Orbit."

She pulled back. He was confused. "Orbit's in the barn. I put him there last night."

Donny shook his head. "No, he's not. I let him go."

She stared at him. "But . . . that means you made it all the way to the barn."

"I did. I had to. Brodie was going to shoot him."

Molly looked up at Brodie. "Is that true?"

Brodie gave a sheepish shrug. "He must have overheard me talking to Miss Walker. I was just joshing. Miss Walker would never let anyone harm a perfectly healthy animal even if he is blind as a bat."

"He might not be perfectly healthy for long," Stretch said. "A little blind horse ain't gonna survive very long out there."

Donny's eyes rounded in horror. "But . . . but . . . I thought he would find his way back to his pack."

Stretch shook his head. "He ain't got no pack. He was born and raised right here on the ranch. He don't know anythin' else."

"He'll be all right," Feedbag said. "Long as he don't fall in no canyon or meet up with no wolves —"

Donny gave a strangled cry and his fingers

dug into Molly's arm. "You gotta find him."

"I will, Donny, I promise, but first we've got to get you inside. Would someone please go and fetch Dr. Fairbanks?"

"Miss Walker already sent Wishbone into town," Ruckus said. "With the doc's new-fangled machine he should be here in an hour or so."

Donny's eyes filled with tears. "I don't need a doctor." His fingers dug deeper. "You gotta find Orbit. If anything happens to him . . ."

Molly squeezed his hand. "We'll find him. I promise." She stood and addressed Stretch. "Would you mind carrying my brother to his room?"

"What about Orbit?" Donny cried.

Brodie lifted his hat and raked his hair away from his face. "Since I'm the culprit that caused the trouble in the first place, I guess it's up to me to make things right. Soon as the sun comes up I'll look for the horse." He swung around and stalked to the barn.

Molly moved out of the way to let Stretch and Feedbag pick Donny up off the ground.

"But what if Brodie doesn't find him?" Donny called as the men carried him into the house. "What if it's too late?"

■ ■ ■ ■

An hour later Molly stood at the foot of Donny's bed watching Caleb wrap gauze around Donny's elbows and knees.

"Scissors," he said, holding out his hand. Molly quickly found a pair of scissors in his black case and handed them to him. Their fingers touched and she quickly pulled her hand away. It took longer to wrestle her gaze from his.

Caleb snipped the length of gauze and attached it with adhesive. "Looks like you gave your funny bone a wallop."

"I don't know what's funny about a funny bone," Donny muttered.

"Then you probably won't see anything humorous about the *humerus* bone either." Despite Caleb's best efforts he was unable to get Donny's mind off Orbit.

"How could I have been so stupid?" Donny moaned. "All I did is put Orbit in danger."

Molly's heart went out to him. "You didn't mean any harm, Donny. It was an accident. You thought you were doing what was best."

"Your sister's right," Caleb said. "We all make mistakes. I recently made a very bad one that could have caused a little boy to die. Sometimes God gives us second chances to set things right."

Molly nodded. "And sometimes third, fourth, and fifth chances." She looked directly at Donny. "We all make mistakes. My biggest mistake was treating you like an invalid when clearly you're not."

Donny gave her a beseeching look. "If you don't look for Orbit, you'll be making another mistake. Brodie won't find him, I know he won't."

Caleb tossed his supplies back into his leather bag. "Brodie's an expert in catching horses."

"Yes, but Orbit always goes on the far side of the corral whenever Brodie comes near."

"That's not true," Molly said. Was it? Come to think of it, she never did see Brodie and Orbit together.

Donny nodded, his eyes serious. "Molly, I'm right. I know I am. Orbit won't go to Brodie, but he'll come to you and he'll come to Magic."

Caleb glanced at her before turning back to Donny. "Your sister and I will go and look for him on one condition. You stay put until we get back. I'm almost out of bandages."

"I won't leave my room. I promise."
Donny waved them away. "Go! Hurry!"

CHAPTER 36

Magic sat on Molly's lap while Caleb drove. Nose in the air, the dog's pendent ears were pinned back by the wind.

"I think he knows that Orbit might be in trouble," she said, her voice loud enough to be heard over the rumbling motor.

Caleb nodded. "That dog knows more than what's good for him."

Something moved ahead and Molly craned her neck. "Wait, I saw something."

As if to concur, Magic barked. Caleb came to a rolling stop and a black cow and calf emerged from the brush onto the road in front of them.

Molly blew a strand of hair away from her face and sighed. They'd been looking for hours and nothing. She had no idea that the Last Chance covered such an enormous area. The ranch spread mostly north and south, with the east backing to free range. The south was bound by canyons, the north by hills. The property line to the east was fenced to keep out maverick horses and stray cattle. Unless someone had recently cut the fence again or the gate was open, Orbit couldn't have reached free range. That meant he was still somewhere on the ranch, but the rugged terrain to the south gave her little consolation.

They veered off the cattle trail and the auto bounced up and down and side to side.

Caleb stopped the car. A high granite wall rose directly ahead of them. "We can't go much farther," he said.

She glanced over her shoulder. "Maybe we should double back. We could have missed him."

He looked almost as frustrated as she felt. "We should have come on horseback. The motor is likely to scare him."

She shook her head. "No. He's used to the sound of the motor. Whenever you drive up he runs to the fence to wait for Magic. That's why —"

His gaze sharpened. "Why what, Molly?"

She moistened her lips. "Orbit would have heard the motor unless he was injured or —"

He reached for her hand. "Or out of earshot."

"He has very sensitive ears," she said.

Magic jumped up, paws on the dash, and barked.

Caleb groaned and released her hand. "All right, all right." He climbed out of the vehicle and reached for Magic. "There you go," he said, setting the dog down. Magic sniffed the ground, following some invisible trail around cacti and scrub brush.

"Probably a prairie dog or rabbit," Caleb said.

Molly shuddered. "I just hope it's not a rattler."

"Rattlers are too smart to be out in this heat." He mopped his forehead with a handkerchief. "You'll only find them out at night."

She climbed out of the car to stretch her legs. The sun was straight overhead and her stomach reminded her that she hadn't eaten all day.

Caleb handed her a canteen, and she drank her fill of lukewarm water before giving it back to him.

He tossed the canteen into the backseat. "Don't look so worried. We'll find Orbit."

She forced a smile. "I hope you're right."

"I am. Doctors are always right." He grinned. "Except when they're not." He glanced around. "I don't see Magic."

She shaded her eyes against the sun and

scanned the area. "Over there!"

He followed her finger and shook his head. Magic had his nose to the ground, his hind legs circling around. "Crazy dog."

She laughed. "Just like . . ." She drew in her breath. "Orbit was here!"

No sooner were the words out of her mouth than they both raced to Magic's side. Caleb dropped to his haunches and inspected the ground. "You're right." His finger traced a circle of hoofprints.

"Those tracks belong to Orbit," she said. She couldn't imagine any other horse sidestepping in a circle. She kneeled by Magic, petting him. "Where is he? Where's Orbit?"

Magic barked and started toward the canyon wall. He stopped and looked back as if to say, *Well, are you going to follow me or aren't you?*

Caleb rose. "Let's go!"

By the time Molly had gathered Magic in her arms and climbed back in the car, Caleb had already started the motor and was in the driver's seat.

The terrain was rough, forcing Caleb to drive at a snail's pace. Even so they bounced up and down like a rubber ball. They reached an outcrop of rocks.

"I don't see anything," Molly said. Magic sniffed the air and whimpered. "That way."

She pointed to the right.

Caleb drove until they reached open desert and stopped.

Magic bounded off Molly's lap and onto Caleb's. He strained to hang his head outside the auto, whimpering and barking.

"Go back," she said.

Caleb shook his head. "There was nothing there."

She brushed hair away from her face. "Try telling that to Magic."

Caleb handed the dog over to her. He then made a wide U-turn and headed back the same way they had come. Magic stiffened in her arms.

"Stop!"

Caleb slammed on the brakes. "What?"

"I think I saw a way through."

Caleb swung the car around in a circle.

"There!" Shadows falling across the rock had previously hidden the opening from view. Bertha barely made it between the twin mound-shaped buttes. Granite walls surrounded them, rising from the desert floor in jagged peaks.

Molly sat forward. "Over there!"

Caleb steered the car in the direction she pointed. It was Orbit, all right, standing on hind legs, front hooves frantically pawing the air.

Magic barked and tried to get out of the car, but Molly held tight. Something moved in the tall grass in front of the panicked horse. *Wolves.* No less than six of them were closing in on the helpless colt.

"Oh no!" Molly cried.

"Don't let go of Magic," Caleb shouted.

Magic had no intention of going anywhere. Instead he cowered on her lap, his body shaking.

One wolf leaped through the air. Orbit's hoof caught the wolf by the neck, throwing the animal against a rock. They were too far away to see if the wolf was dead or merely stunned. That left five wolves.

Molly pumped her fist. "Good for you, Orbit." The horse was blind but far from helpless. Neither, as it turned out, was her brother.

One wolf let out a menacing howl and a cold shiver shot down Molly's spine. If only she'd thought to bring her shotgun.

Caleb inched the car forward to within twenty feet of the animals and blew his horn. *Ah-ooh-ga.* The wolves glanced back, teeth bared, then continued to advance toward Orbit.

Molly handed Magic over to Caleb and jumped from the vehicle. She grabbed a rock and threw it at the nearest wolf. The wild canine stared at her, its amber gaze boring into her like a branding iron. She threw another rock and this time the wolf moved away, but another — probably the leader — slithered toward her. He looked thin and mangy but no less threatening.

"Get in!" Caleb shouted.

Molly tossed one last rock before heaving herself into the vehicle. Caleb slammed his foot against the gas pedal. Bertha lurched forward, trembled, and stalled.

Caleb pounded the dash with his fist. "Blast it!" The car shuddered and backfired, once, twice — three times! The loud booms echoed through the canyon like cannon fire and the wolves ran.

He burst out laughing. "Yahoo!"

Hand on her pounding chest, Molly gasped. "Th-Thank God for Bertha." She picked Magic up off the floor where he'd dived for cover and rubbed her nose in his fur. The poor dog was still shaking. "Your friend is okay."

Orbit whinnied and Magic leaped out of her arms, paws on the dash, and whined.

The colt lowered his front legs and stood motionless as if afraid to move. "Orbit, it's safe," she called. "Come on."

She scrambled out of the car and, after making certain no wolves lurked nearby, set

Magic on the ground. The dog sprinted forward with a joyful bark and raced through the dry grass to the colt's side. Orbit lowered his head and the two friends touched noses.

Caleb turned the flywheel and Bertha leaped to life. "Hurry, Molly. Those wolves aren't going to stay away for long."

"Come on, Magic." Molly clapped her hands. The dog raced back to the car. Orbit nodded his head several times, then cautiously walked toward them, stopping every couple of feet to sniff the air.

The moment Orbit reached them Molly thrust out her hand and the horse buried his nose in her palm. The poor horse was trembling, his coat covered in dust and sweat.

Molly ran her hand along Orbit's forehead, moving his forelock aside. "You're safe now, little fellow."

Caleb reached for the rope in back. "Let's get out of here."

"We won't need that," Molly said. "Orbit will follow us. Just don't drive too fast." A trickle of blood ran down Orbit's left hind leg. "Oh no, he's hurt."

"Looks like one of the wolves caught him with a claw," Caleb said. "I'll clean it up later. Come on. We gotta get out of here."

■ ■ ■ ■

Wasting no time, they left the hidden area behind. Caleb drove extra slow for Orbit's sake. Even so, they bounced over ruts and gullies.

Molly held on tight. She was still shaken from the ordeal, but no amount of jostling, heat, or hunger could dampen her spirits. What a day it had been. Donny making it all the way to the barn by himself. Orbit fighting off wolves.

Following her brother's accident, she'd vowed to protect and care for him always. What an impossible task she'd set for herself. No matter how determined, how watchful, how absolutely vigilant she was, it would never be enough. Only Donny could protect Donny. The rest was up to God.

Magic whimpered and barked and her thoughts scattered like seeds in the wind. "I think he needs to go," she said.

"Again?" He tossed a nod toward the windmill ahead. "I'll stop there so we can all get a drink."

Caleb pulled up alongside the high stilts. The towering blades cast a spot of welcome shade over them. Molly climbed out of the car and called Orbit. While the horse drank,

Caleb held Magic up to the trough. Magic lapped noisily, his ears dragging in the water.

After Orbit had his fill, he nuzzled his nose in her hand and nodded his head up and down as he did each morning to greet her. She laughed. "You want me to sing, eh?"

She cleared her throat. "Swing low, sweet chariot." *"Come down from above."* She sang softly at first, but her voice gradually grew louder, as did Mr. Washington's voice in her head. *What in my life needs God's help? What secret code is buried in my heart? What chains do I need Him to remove?* "Coming for to carry me home." *Help me to reach my true love.*

She finished the song and Caleb joined her. "That's the saddest song I've ever heard you sing."

She smiled. "Not sad, hopeful," she said. "It's a song filled with hope."

He took a step forward and cupped her elbow. "You're shaking. You're not still scared, are you?"

She stepped out of his reach but only to think more clearly. "I guess in a way I am. A little." She was about to make a big change in her life and that alone was scary.

"I realized I've been wrong about a lot of things. About the church. Donny." After a

446

short hesitation she added, "God."

He lifted a brow. "God?"

"I never really saw Him working in my life. Losing almost everything in the fire. Spotting Miss Walker's advertisement. Coming to Cactus Patch. Even my accident. I thought that it was all by happenstance. Now I realize God was working in my life all along, but I was just too blind to see it."

"We all tend to be blind at times," he said.

"Not you. You never saw Donny as crippled."

"Sometimes it's easier to see things more clearly when you're standing a distance away." He studied her. "Is that why you moved away from me just now? So you can see me more clearly?"

"I always saw you clearly," she said softly.

He tilted his head. "So where do we go from here?"

We. He said *we.* She exhaled. She ran her hands up and down her arms. She no longer trembled out of fear but rather anticipation, hope, and, more than anything, love.

"I don't know what the future holds. I leave that in God's hands. What I do know is that I love you with all my heart, and if you still want this stubborn woman . . ."

"Molly," he said, grabbing her by the arms. "Molly Hatfield . . . are . . . are you saying what I think you're saying?"

She nodded.

With a cry of joy he pulled her close. Laughing, she buried her head against his chest.

"Is that a yes?" she asked. "Does this mean you still want me?"

"Oh, Molly, how can you even ask me that? I want you, I love you, I need you . . . I . . ." Tightening his hold, he murmured the sweetest, most beautiful words in her ears, his warm breath showering down like gentle rain. "I know that Donny will always come first but . . ."

She lifted her head and touched a finger to his lips. "Not anymore. Thanks to you, Donny will do just fine. He doesn't need a nursemaid and he certainly doesn't need an overprotective sister."

Caleb gazed at her with such tenderness she was afraid to breathe. *Please, God, if this is just a dream, don't let me wake up. Ever!*

"You've made me the happiest man alive." He showered her with kisses, and the sweet tenderness of his lips made her tremble with pleasure. He kissed her again and again, each time his lips becoming more demanding, but then she had some demands of her own to make.

They might have stayed locked in each other's arms forever had Magic not barked and Orbit whinnied as if to say, *Hey, you two. Let's go home.*

CHAPTER 37

Eleanor sat at her desk staring at the contract clause forbidding her "heiress" to marry. Robert criticized her for including such a stipulation, but it was there for good reason. Marriage complicated matters. It diminished a woman's abilities, diverted her attention, and inevitably broke her heart. Married men could run a ranch; married women could not.

A knock sounded at the door. "Come in."

The door opened and Molly stuck in her head. "We found Orbit."

Eleanor barely bothered to look up. "It's about time. Now maybe we can get some work done."

"Do you have a moment?" Molly asked.

Eleanor sat back in her chair, pen in hand. "Come in."

Molly walked into the room and closed the door. Dressed in divided skirt, checkered shirt, and wide-brimmmed hat, Molly looked nothing like the girl Eleanor had first set eyes on all those weeks ago. It wasn't only the clothes that made the difference; she no longer seemed to carry the world on her shoulders, and the glow on her face had nothing to do with paint. Obviously ranch work agreed with her and this gave Eleanor a measure of satisfaction.

Molly moistened her lips. "I apologize for the disruption this morning and for taking the men away from their duties."

"See that it doesn't happen again." Eleanor folded her hands on the desk. "I guess this is as good a time as any to discuss your brother. I decided to hire him a nursemaid." Convinced that the girl would welcome the news, Eleanor was surprised to see Molly frown.

"Why . . . why would you do such a thing?"

Eleanor shrugged. "My banker friend told me that I have you to thank for chasing away that awful man Hampshire. It's the least I can do to show my appreciation."

"That's very kind of you but Donny doesn't need a nursemaid."

Eleanor discounted Molly's objection with a wave of a hand. "He might not, but you do. The ranch needs your full attention, and the only way that will happen is if someone else takes care of him."

Molly stepped away from the door and stood directly in front of the desk. "Donny made it all the way to the barn by himself."

Eleanor tossed her pen on the desk. "Am I supposed to applaud him for letting one of my horses free?"

"He only did it because he thought Orbit's life was in danger. He shouldn't have let him go, but it was still a great accomplishment." Hands planted on the edge of the desk, Molly leaned forward, her face earnest. "During the Dobson Creek fire he didn't even try to save himself and he could have died. I never thought to see the day when he could get in and out of his chair by himself."

"He still needs help," Eleanor said briskly. She glanced down at the contract in front of her. Molly's name was typed neatly at the top of the page. Was it too soon to have the girl sign it? Perhaps then Molly would more readily accept Eleanor's proposal.

Molly straightened. "I love your ranch. It gave Donny and me our first real home. I don't know how I can ever thank you. You are truly the kindest and most generous person I've ever met."

"Oh dear." Eleanor lifted her hand to her forehead. "I do believe those were the exact same words my husband said before he walked out."

Molly's face softened. *Good heavens, don't let that be pity.* Eleanor despised pity, especially when it was directed at her.

"I . . . I'm leaving the ranch," Molly said.

"Leav—" Eleanor quickly recovered. She glanced down at the contract on her desk. "I was about to suggest that. Since . . . you turned down my offer for a nursemaid, there are no other options."

"I'm sorry," Molly said, and she sounded like she really meant it. "I didn't mean to put you to so much trouble."

"No trouble. I've had to let a lot of people go in my time." Foolish girl. She had no idea what she was throwing away. "So what do you plan to do? Pursue your . . . *singing* career?" Eleanor couldn't imagine anyone choosing to work in a saloon over running a ranch but stranger things had happened. Kate Tenney marrying the blacksmith was a good example.

Molly hesitated. "No, it's not that. I'm in love with someone."

Eleanor hadn't expected this. "With whom?" she snapped. *It better not be one of my ranch hands!*

"Dr. Fairbanks. I plan to help him in his office. He needs a nurse assistant. It will make things a little easier for him. I'm not trained, but I'm a fast learner and there's nothing I wouldn't do for him. We love each other."

Eleanor felt like she'd been kicked by a mule. As if the doctor with his noisy rattle-trap hadn't caused enough trouble. "Love is like that horse you call Orbit," she said brusquely. "It's blind and won't get you anywhere."

"I believe love will take me wherever I want to go," Molly said.

Eleanor rubbed her temples. What was wrong with today's youth, believing such nonsense? In her day women married mostly for convenience — seldom for love. They married for security. The ranch offered all the security anyone could want, making such marriages unnecessary.

"I'm so very, very sorry, Miss Walker. I really wanted to do right by you. The money you loaned us . . . I'll repay every penny."

"The money wasn't for you," Eleanor said, her voice taut. "It was for Donald."

Molly's eyes widened. "Why would you give my brother money?"

Eleanor studied her a moment before answering. "Do you know that cows pee backwards?"

Molly frowned. "Pardon me?"

Eleanor gave a knowing nod. Molly's leaving the ranch really was for the best. The girl had no feel for cattle. Horses maybe, but not cattle, the lifeline of the ranch.

"Your brother knows a great many things. I suspect he also knows enough *not* to look a gift horse in the mouth. Now get out of here. I've got a ranch to run."

Molly looked about to say something but changed her mind. She quietly slipped out of the room, giving Eleanor one last questioning glance before closing the door.

Eleanor picked up the contract, glanced at it a moment, then ripped it up.

She stared at the empty space Molly left behind. *Drat!* She would miss the girl. As much as she hated to admit it, she'd even grown fond of Donald.

Love. What a thief. It sneaked up where it wasn't wanted and grabbed the best and brightest. Only the old and wise knew how to avoid Cupid's clever traps.

If Robert were here, he'd no doubt try to talk her into selling the ranch again.

Robert. What a dear, sweet man. He'd proposed numerous times but never once had he uttered the word *love.* A good thing. A *very* good thing. Because even an old hand like her couldn't protect her heart forever.

■ ■ ■ ■

Donny hadn't stopped grinning since Caleb broke the good news of Orbit's rescue. His smile grew even wider when Caleb pushed him out to the corral to see for himself.

"Why is he wearing a bandage?" Donny asked.

"One of the wolves swiped at him, but don't worry. It's nothing serious." Molly had groomed the horse while Caleb attended to the wound.

Donny stroked Orbit's sleek neck. "I heard you had quite an adventure."

Magic barked as if to concur, and Donny leaned over to scratch him behind a furry ear.

"What's going to happen to Orbit, Doc?"

"I don't know. I guess that's up to Miss Walker." Caleb straightened. "Right now I want to talk to you man to man."

"Does this have anything to do with the Flagstaff observatory?"

Caleb frowned. "Why would you think that?"

Donny folded his arms. "You promised to take me if I could get into my wheelchair by myself."

Caleb tapped his chin. "Hmm. I did,

didn't I?"

The sun in his face, Donny squinted up at him with one eye closed. The early stages of a moustache made him look older than his years. "Well?"

"We'll discuss that later. Right now I want to talk to you about something else." Caleb touched a finger to the brim and pushed back his hat.

Donny looked at him askew, curiosity written all over his face. "It sounds serious."

"It *is* serious." Caleb stepped aside so Donny wouldn't have to look into the sun. "I want you to know that as long as I live, you will never have to go into a sanitarium. You'll always have a home."

Donny stared up at him. "Why are you telling me this?"

"I want to marry your sister. And since you're the man of the house, I'm asking your permission."

Donny drew his brows together but said nothing.

Thinking Donny didn't understand the full nature of the proposal, Caleb added, "Marriage will make the three of us a family — all living under the same roof."

"You mean it will always be the three of us?" Donny asked.

"I can't guarantee the number. It might one day be four, or five, or six of us." Caleb waited for this to sink in. "Well?"

"I'm thinking," Donny said.

"Think faster. Your sister's coming."

"Okay, I give you my permission on one condition. You promise to take me to Flagstaff."

"I promise."

Donny nodded. "And you let me drive Bertha."

"That's two conditions."

"And you buy me a telescope and name the first boy after me."

"What?"

Donny wasn't finished. "And most importantly, you find a home for Orbit."

Caleb lifted his hat and scratched his head. "You drive a hard bargain."

Donny grinned. "What do you expect? She's my sister."

Caleb spotted Molly running toward them and he grinned. She lost her hat but kept running. Her shiny raven hair came unpinned but she kept running. Her face was flushed with heat but she kept running.

She didn't stop until she was locked securely in his arms.

EPILOGUE

Molly had just finished hanging the last pair of trousers on the clothesline when Caleb sneaked up behind her, grabbed her by the waist, and spun her around. They stood in the yard of their new home, a small but comfortable four-room adobe with a red tile roof and whitewashed fence. Designed to accommodate Donny's wheelchair, the house had extra-wide doorways and a ramp leading to the front porch.

"What do you say, Mrs. Fairbanks?" Caleb asked. "Are you ready for a delayed honeymoon?"

Her heart leaped with joy. "Do you mean it?"

He nodded. "My doctor friend from Boston arrived and agreed to take over my practice while I'm gone."

"Oh, Caleb, that's wonderful."

"If he likes it, he'll stay and help me with the clinic."

She flung her arms around his neck. "He'll love it here. I know he will."

Caleb grinned. "Do you think Donny can handle the clerical work for *two* doctors?"

"Try and stop him."

The last several months had been a whirlwind of activity. Between helping Caleb with his patients and supervising the building of their house, Molly hardly had time to breathe. Aunt Bessie had naturally insisted upon handling the wedding plans. Big satin bows had popped up everywhere, along with the usual disgruntled saloon keepers. Things got so out of hand that the marshal issued a one-year moratorium on weddings.

She smiled up at him. "You haven't told me where we're going."

"We're taking the train to Flagstaff." His gaze was warm with humor. "I understand you can look through the observatory telescope and see more stars than it's possible to count."

"Donny will be so pleased." Her voice was drowned out by Magic's bark and the clatter of wheels.

"I'm afraid we can't spend more than a couple of days away," Caleb said. "Soon as we get back we start building."

"I can't be away too long anyway. The choir is about to start rehearsals for Easter."

She laughed. She still couldn't believe she sang in the church choir.

She pulled out of Caleb's arms and waved as Orbit walked by, pulling Donny in a cart. Magic cheerfully led the way, steering the black colt safely down the road with little yipping sounds, though the bells on his collar made barking unnecessary.

It was Caleb's idea to purchase the colt for Donny's fifteenth birthday. Jimmy Trotter's father donated the cart in payment for Caleb's medical services.

"What about Magic and Orbit?" she asked.

Caleb's arms tightened around her waist. "Aunt Bessie agreed to take care of them while we're gone."

Molly smiled. Never had she known such happiness as she'd known these last few months. Brodie said lessons could be learned from horses. Orbit taught her that God had a plan for everything — even a little blind horse and a wheelchair-bound youth.

Maybe God even had a plan for the Last Chance Ranch. Miss Walker had another "heiress" and Brodie said she looked promising. Molly prayed it was true.

"Come on," Caleb whispered in her hair.

"Let's tell Donny to pack his things. We're going to Flagstaff."

MEET MAGIC

Caleb's dog is actually modeled after a darling Lhaso Apso owned by Reverend Diane Ryder, pastor of the Congregational Church of Chatsworth UCC. Rev. Ryder entered

Photo by Diane Ryder

her pet in my "Your Dog in My Book" contest and Magic won both the contest and my heart.

Named after a street in Phoenix, Arizona, where he was born, Magic lived with a special-needs family and helped people unable to speak. Magic "wrote" that "every time I chased my tail or sat in a lap I would make my special friends smile."

Magic loves to eat and play with squeaky toys. Since no commercial pet toys seemed to exist in the 1800s, in my story Magic had to be content chasing after a squeaky wheelchair. Sounds like the perfect dog for Dr. Caleb Fairbanks, wouldn't you say?

Magic has a long and noble heritage. Lhaso Apsos originated in Tibet and are one of the oldest recognized breeds in the world. Trained as watchdogs, these hardy canines guarded Tibetan royalty and Buddhist monasteries. They were highly prized and never sold. The only way a person could acquire a Lhaso Apso was through a gift.

Lhaso Apsos didn't reach American shores until the 1930s, which rules out finding one in the Old West. But with a name like Magic, anything is possible . . .

Dear Readers,

There's nothing I like better than visiting old friends, and that includes the literary kind. I especially enjoyed getting reacquainted with Caleb Fairbanks. Some of you may remember him as Lucy's sixteen-year-old brother in *A Vision of Lucy*. I will forever be indebted to the reader who suggested Caleb as the hero in a future book. So here he is, all grown up and as much fun as ever.

Caleb is the perfect hero for the 1890s. What an exciting time. The telephone, originally thought to be a frivolous toy, began to change the way people communicated. Thomas Edison's "smokeless light" took longer to take hold mainly because of costs and fear. President Harrison and his wife were reportedly so afraid of being shocked by the newly installed electric light switches in the White House that they continued to use gas lights.

Perhaps the biggest change came with the horseless carriage. Clanging steel could be heard in barns and sheds across the land as men young and old raced to create the perfect vehicle. Like Caleb, one determined mechanic did indeed build his auto on the second floor for want of another place. Even

Henry Ford had to postpone test-driving his first Model T in 1896 because it was too big to fit through the door.

In 1895, the *Chicago Times-Herald* held the first horseless carriage race to prove that the newfangled machines could outdo the traditional horse and buggy. Ninety people originally entered the race, but because of bad weather and motor problems only twelve showed up. Frank Duryea won after driving the entire fifty-two-mile course, thus changing history forever.

The late nineteenth century also saw many changes in the medical field. In 1892, the American Psychological Association was formed, but perhaps the most important change was the development of the field of biology. The knowledge that infection was caused by germs led to rubber gloves being used for the first time in surgery.

Lead poisoning was a problem, especially in inner cities. Sadly it remains a problem to this day. According to a 2012 article in the *Los Angeles Times,* a troubling amount of lead can still be found in toys, paint, and, yes, even candy.

I hope you enjoyed Molly and Caleb's story. You can read Kate and Luke's story in *Dawn Comes Early.* What's next for the Last Chance Ranch? Mysterious doings

bring a Pinkerton Detective to the ranch —
and you won't believe who it is.

Until next time,
Margaret

DISCUSSION QUESTIONS

Set your affection on things above,
not on things on earth.
Colossians 3:2 KJV

1. Donny was so dependent on Molly, he didn't even try to save himself from the fire. Miss Walker depended on the ranch to fulfill her family's legacy. Many men in town, including Jimmy's father and Reverend Bland, depended on alcohol to drown out pain and sorrow. In what ways does dependence on God differ from dependence on earthly things?

2. Molly couldn't see much past her guilt. Donny saw himself only as crippled. Other characters were blinded by worry, fear, or grief. Think of a problem in your life. In what ways is it blinding you or distorting your vision of God?

3. What character did you most identify with and why?

4. In John 9:2, Jesus talks about a blind man and how the works of God might be displayed in him. In what way did God make His presence known through Donny's affliction?

5. Caleb doubted his abilities as a doctor. In some ways this was a good thing because it made him seek answers. Doubts force us to study and examine beliefs. In what way has God worked through your doubts to help you grow professionally, personally, or spiritually?

6. Caleb's horseless carriage is a metaphor for change. Change never comes easy and can sometimes rattle us. To accept change is to grow. Which characters best represent the positive side of change? The negative? Can you think of a time when something in your life changed for the better?

7. Brodie said there were lessons to be learned from horses. What lessons did Molly learn from the little blind horse, Orbit? How did these lessons apply to her brother? To her own life?

8. Eleanor's search for an heiress is really a cry for family. That's the one thing she doesn't have. Yet she ruthlessly holds on to the ranch that keeps her from the thing she most wants. Molly longed for love and marriage, but she let guilt and commit-

ment to her brother stand in the way of her heart's desire. Name the emotional or physical blocks in your own life that keep you from reaching a goal or cherished dream.

9. Lead poisoning has been called a silent killer. What were some of the silent killers of faith that plagued Molly? Donny? Caleb? Eleanor?

10. Donny's accident "crippled" his ma and pa, even Molly. An illness, job loss, or death can affect the entire family. Name a time when your family overcame difficult times. How did God lead the way?

11. Molly's bad experience with church following her father's death made her wary of all churches and churchgoers. Has there ever been a time when something said or done at church made you wary?

12. Molly was a gifted singer but it never occurred to her she could use her singing talent for the glory of God. In what ways do you use your unique gifts and talents for God's work?

13. Mr. Washington wrote, "Put God first and everyone and everything will be all right. Put God first and you'll never know another night." Has there ever been a time in your life when God fell by the wayside? What does it mean to put God first?

14. Molly learned to look back at her childhood through the eyes of God. How did this change her perception of the past? Who or what in your life would benefit if regarded through the eyes of God?
15. Finally, what was the main message you carried away from the story?

ACKNOWLEDGMENTS

My cup runneth over with far too many blessings to list here, so I will name but a few: I'm especially grateful to Chelley Kitzmiller and Have a Heart Humane Society for sponsoring the "Your Dog in My Book" contest. A big thank-you goes to the winner, Reverend Diane Ryder, for letting me use her darling dog in my book. My only hope is that I did Magic justice.

Also thanks to Andrew James Winch who kindly answered my questions about lumbar spine injuries. Any errors are solely mine.

My heart is filled with gratitude for my amazing agent Natasha Kern and her constant support, encouragement, and wisdom.

I'm eternally grateful to my editor Natalie Hanemann who shared my vision for this series and whose insightful comments and guidance help make any story stronger, and this one even more so. Also special thanks to Rachelle Gardner whose eye for details has saved this author's hide more times than I care to enumerate.

A great big thank-you to all the readers who entered the "Daily Reasons to Smile" contest. I'm especially grateful to Katie Bond for spearheading the contest and babysitting the potted cacti that made up some of the prizes. Thanks also to Gaylene Murphy, Kim Miller, and Nancy Berland.

As always I thank God for instilling in me a love of words and the opportunity to do what I most love to do — make up characters and create stories. I appreciate the love and support of my family, especially my husband, George, who has taken on the unenviable task of being this writer's assistant.

Thank you to all my readers for your kind letters — and especially to the readers who suggested that Lucy's brother, Caleb, from *A Vision of Lucy* needed his own book. Keep those ideas coming! You can find me on Facebook, Twitter, or my website.

Until next time,
Margaret

ABOUT THE AUTHOR

New York Times best-selling author **Margaret Brownley** has penned more than twenty-five historical and contemporary novels. Her books have won numerous awards, including Reader's Choice. She has published the Rocky Creek series, and *A Lady Like Sarah* was a Romance Writers of America RITA finalist. Happily married to her real-life hero, Margaret and her husband have three grown children and live in Southern California.

Visit MargaretBrownley.com
for more information.

The employees of Thorndike Press hope you have enjoyed this Large Print book. All our Thorndike, Wheeler, and Kennebec Large Print titles are designed for easy reading, and all our books are made to last. Other Thorndike Press Large Print books are available at your library, through selected bookstores, or directly from us.

For information about titles, please call:
(800) 223-1244

or visit our Web site at:
http://gale.cengage.com/thorndike

To share your comments, please write:
Publisher
Thorndike Press
10 Water St., Suite 310
Waterville, ME 04901